**The tig** ~~...~~ **d for a mom** ~~...~~

This wasn't possible. He couldn't love her, not like that. That was folly. Confusion, brought on by the nostalgia of the season, which meant so much to them, and of a long journey. Actually, thinking on it, he did love her, and not like that.

Right.

No use denying it—he loved Mena.

She was his friend, his confidant, his partner, his...

Home.

Damn.

Had he not declared himself, stepping foot on that wharf not an hour ago, that London had and never would be home? Yet since he'd stepped foot into the house, even before, simply thinking on it, he'd used the word *home* freely. And this house *was* home. Merely because of the fact that Mena was here. And she...

*She is my home. The shore I return to, ceaselessly.*

"No, no, no, no," Freddie muttered, eyes burning as he began to pace the room. Not possible. Not right. Not acceptable, not any of it. "No, no, no, no..."

## Author Note

Considering Freddie and Mena's tale lived with me for a long time before I began writing it, oddly enough, it was one of the most difficult to finish, becoming far more personal than expected. A severe case of life imitating art, shall we say.

Admittedly, I also got lost in research. Though hugely enriching, somewhere along the way I forgot that I write historical fiction and that readers can be asked to suspend their disbelief. So there will be times when I will ask you to, and hope that in the spirit of it all you can.

I would like to thank those who helped with my research, particularly Professor Frank Trentmann, who reminded me there isn't always one definite answer, but that "the most interesting question is how...characters at different times answered."

For there have always been people asking questions, fighting inequality and exploitation in all its forms. When looking at the past, we must interrogate it, challenge it, but we must always remember to interrogate and challenge our present too, and what we build for the future.

Though many may know, I should note for anyone missing decorated trees and carolers that much of what we consider to be Western Christmas tradition was born during the Victorian age. Naturally, much came from older traditions or was borrowed from other cultures. Of course, Mr. Dickens also has his part to play, and as may become apparent, I do have a particular penchant for a good Christmas ghost story.

All that to say, there are many ways of "keeping Christmas"—and I hope that however you keep the season, whatever name you have for it—it is full of joy.

# LOTTE R. JAMES

---

## The Gentleman of Holly Street

HARLEQUIN
HISTORICAL

Recycling programs
for this product may
not exist in your area.

ISBN-13: 978-1-335-72358-1

The Gentleman of Holly Street

Copyright © 2022 by Victorine Brown-Cattelain

For questions and comments about the quality of this book,
please contact us at CustomerService@Harlequin.com.

Harlequin Enterprises ULC
22 Adelaide St. West, 41st Floor
Toronto, Ontario M5H 4E3, Canada
www.Harlequin.com

**Printed in U.S.A.**

**Lotte R. James** trained as an actor and theater director, but spent most of her life working day jobs crunching numbers whilst dreaming up stories of love and adventure. She's thrilled to finally be writing those stories, and when she's not scribbling on tiny pieces of paper, she can usually be found wandering the countryside for inspiration, or nestling with coffee and a book.

### Books by Lotte R. James

### Harlequin Historical

#### *Gentlemen of Mystery*

*The Housekeeper of Thornhallow Hall*
*The Marquess of Yew Park House*
*The Gentleman of Holly Street*

Look out for more books from Lotte R. James coming soon.

Visit the Author Profile page
at Harlequin.com.

To those who press the latch three times.

To all my friends and family, far and wide.

To you, reader—
may the season bring you light and joy.

And always, to my mother, Brigitte,
with whom I keep the very best Christmases.

## Chapter One

*London, December 23rd, 1823*

Tiny, glittering specks of snow swirled around him, drifting down from the heavens like slivers of moonlight come to blanket the earth in cleansing, quiet beauty. It wasn't late, only just past four, if the bells of St. Paul's were to be believed, yet already it was pitch black. The moon was hidden behind thick clouds tonight, so the only illumination came from the few gas lamps, and light spilling from the nearby shops and homes.

Despite the amount of people still on the streets—shopping, working, simply existing—it was oddly quiet. Snow always had that power, to silence the world. Not ominously, but almost in reverence, as if everyone and everything made a concerted decision to pause, and appreciate the magical wonder. Still, there was hushed excitement in the air, in the few voices and laughter that reached his ears. The excitement and promise of the season. Of time spent with family, or friends; full of hope, joy, and good cheer.

Fiddling with the heavy set of keys in his pocket, Freddie stared up at the building before him, and vaguely wondered if that feeling would be at all similar to the one currently residing in his own breast.

For he felt excitement at the promise of what awaited him in the four-storeyed, squashed-looking house, patched into a whole with brick and stone as if an afterthought following the erection of its neighbours. And after ten years on the seas, travelling to every corner of the globe, he had to admit, the idea of establishing roots of some kind, spending a few years on land, it held a sort of fascination he could classify as excitement.

Freddie felt hope at what the future held; at what the house before him *could* hold. There was no family, there were no friends, to share it all with, but this house before him, it would bear the name of the man who'd been the closest thing to family he'd ever truly had. What he built here would celebrate that man, and all Freddie had learned at his side. This house would bear witness to it all, and perhaps, that would be enough.

*It will have to be.*

*And hopefully, this place, this endeavour, will help redeem my sins.*

Yes, here, he would build something good. Something worthwhile. He would fulfil his vow to live a good life; to honour the second chance bestowed upon him for some unknown reason.

*Starting tonight.*

Fuelled by renewed purpose, Freddie adjusted the bag on his shoulder, picked up his trunk, extracted the set of keys, and strode to the front door, gently tucked away beside the boarded-up bow windows. Without hesitation, he opened it, age and disuse making it a little stiff, then strode in.

A cloud of dust, and damp, musty air, met him, and deciding it best not to add snow to the list, he quickly shut the door behind him. Dropping the trunk with a thud that echoed in the empty place, he plopped his pack on top of it, then felt around inside for the packet of candles and flint stowed away for this very purpose.

It took a few tries, his hands were a little more frozen than he'd thought despite the thick leather gloves, but finally a flame burst to life, and he shielded it quickly, before the whistling gusts sneaking through the door could extinguish it. Stepping over little piles of, well, he wasn't quite sure he wished to know actually, he made his way to the front parlour, and let his hand fall away from before the flame.

*Perfect.*

The squat, square, low-ceilinged room would be perfect, as he'd known it would be. Here, he could set up the shop, full of tasteful wares, sourced from across the world. He could already see the delicate glass from the Venetian artisan on that wall there, to best catch the light of the morning; and there, on the table, he could have the music boxes from the Turkish family he'd stayed with last year. And there, bolts of silk, cotton, wool, and linen, all sourced from various makers across the globe. All of it would surely enthral even the most demanding clientele, if he could convince them to come; the sales sustaining him whilst he saved and built the rest of his company. His family had taught him how to evade the law; Mr Walton and years at sea among the best tradesmen had taught him how to wield it, how to build all he dreamed according to the principles he'd sworn to live by.

Wandering around, he noted the stray pieces of newspaper and glass that had tumbled from the windows, the cobwebs, and traces of vermin. Bits of rope, and wood, even a hat stand. There was a stout old oak counter that needed only some freshening up to be good as new once again, this having been a haberdasher after all. It was part of what had made this place perfect.

Along with the rooms upstairs, which would become his living quarters, his office, and storage rooms. The previous owners had had a similar layout to what he envisioned, though it would need much to make it serviceable, well, *liveable*, really, and in time, he could even modernise it. The place had good bones—and a good spirit. Empty, certes, but full of potential. Even the shadows held promise. It was that feeling of having *arrived*, which had cemented his mind on this house.

Moving along to the back parlour, much like the front one, save with less newspapers and neither counter nor hat stand, then downstairs to the kitchen, Freddie chuckled to himself as he remembered how the solicitor had nearly fallen out of his chair when he'd had announced he intended to move in as soon as this house was officially his. But Freddie had a roof, a blanket, *and yes, a useable fireplace*. He didn't need anything more; in fact, he'd survived with less.

*Much, much less.*

Perhaps, once it was all done, he would get a lodger; maybe someone to work the shop when he was properly set up. For now, he would settle. Tomorrow, he would begin cleaning; the furniture he'd ordered would arrive, and then, his work could truly begin. He'd never shied away from hard work, and knowing what he was working towards would make it all the sweeter.

*You'll see, Mr Walton. I'll make you proud.*

Within the hour, Freddie had made himself at home in the kitchen. He'd cleaned, fixed up a tidy little corner to sleep in, even got a hearty fire started, having braved the cold again to fetch both coal for the night, and water. He'd already bought bread, cheese, and ale before coming, so now he was all set to enjoy his new home for the evening.

Though, just as he was about to tuck into his little feast, he realised he would need to brave the cold one last time, having not had the forbearance to think of a chamber pot or bucket. So to the outdoor privy he would go, though perhaps whilst he was outside he could root around the pile of rubbish that had kindly been left in his miniscule, but serviceable private courtyard, and be lucky enough to find a bucket or such among the disused, broken furniture, wares, and general detritus. He added *get rid of that rubbish* to his list of chores, slipped on his coat, and made his way up the stairs and to the back door.

As he opened it, a sound caught his attention. Something between rustling and knocking. Frowning, he turned and glanced to his right, spotting the dark, shadowed heap that was the rubbish pile he'd just been pondering, and dismissed the sound as that of the vermin likely living therein.

At least, until he made to step out into the courtyard, and noticed the pile of freshly disturbed snow, and footprints.

*Not a rat, then.*

'Hello,' he called into the night, his hackles raising. He bent down slowly, and retrieved a handy broken table leg, should he need to avail himself of it as a weapon. Not that he truly needed one to be...*efficient*; however, it did serve to intimidate, and generally avoid fights. Violence was a thing of his past. *No more.* 'I know you're out here,' he added, slowly stepping into the courtyard so he could face the rubbish heap head-on. 'Come out now, or I shall call the watch, and on your head be it.'

More shuffling.

Wood shifting, and clothes rustling.

The heap moved as if alive as someone emerged, and Freddie took a step back, into the moonlight, so he could see whoever it was. He thanked the heavens for dispensing with the clouds, if only for a moment, though the fog of each breath seemed to hang before his eyes, clouding his vision nonetheless. He raised his arm, mimicking best as possible a fearsomely discouraging pose.

Freddie wasn't quite sure what he'd been expecting; however, it certainly wasn't the sight which met his eyes.

A girl, woman, perhaps, he couldn't quite tell, crawled from her hiding place, into the light. Her hair was shorn short, matted, and unwashed, for God only knew how long. Her clothes were threadbare and torn, more like suggestions of what they'd once been, a simple linen dress, wool cloak, and short boots. No hat, no scarf, no gloves.

Slowly, she rose, tall, yes, as tall as he, but nothing more than skin and bones. She hugged herself tight, tense, and ready to bolt at a moment's notice, and that's when he caught her eyes, round, wide with fear, green or brown, he thought, though he couldn't quite be certain in this light. Remarkably, that bothered him. As did the sight of her hollowed cheeks, and cracked lips, which he noticed, as she rolled them together, shivering with both cold and nerves.

*Damn.*

'Sorry, sir,' she muttered placatingly. 'Didn't mean no 'arm I didn't. Thought 'twas empty.'

'It was,' he answered stupidly. 'I am the new owner.'

'I'll go, sir,' she said, carefully edging towards the passage at the side of the house that led to the street. *Ah yes,* he thought, adding to his list of chores. *Repair the broken gate and fence.* 'Meant no 'arm.'

'Go where?' he asked gruffly, stopping her in her tracks.

She didn't answer, and that was her answer.

She would go find another alley, another doorway, another place which wouldn't be safe, to sleep, and likely die considering the current conditions. Some part of him wanted to let her go. Some part knew that taking her in would make him responsible for her. Which he neither wanted nor needed. He certainly hadn't asked for such responsibility.

*And did Mr Walton ever ask for you?*

An image of the scared, starved, lost little boy he'd been rose to the forefront of his mind. The boy Mr Walton had found in a ditch, somewhat like this.

Mr Walton hadn't turned away.

Mr Walton had seen it as Providence, and though Freddie no longer believed in such things, he knew that he couldn't turn away either.

That would be both an insult to his own firmly held beliefs—and to the memory of the very man he sought with every breath to honour.

'What's your name?' he asked on a sigh, dropping his would-be weapon.

The girl jumped at the sound, stopping her retreat, then blinking at him dumbly for a moment, as if of all the questions or reactions she'd expected, that was not one of them.

'Philomena.'

*Philomena. Odd name.*

'I'm Freddie. Freddie Walton,' he told her. 'Now, you have two choices, Philomena. You can disappear into the night, and likely die from the cold or something else by morning. Or you can spend the night inside,' he said, gesturing towards the door. 'There's nothing in there but food, a fire, and water to wash yourself. For what it's worth, I won't harm you. On my honour, I will not hurt you.'

Philomena studied him closely for a long moment, searching, he knew, for any sign that he might prove to be more of a threat than the winter, and indeed, of the city itself. Her choices, her thoughts, swirled in her eyes.

'Why?' she breathed finally, the question nearly written, it seemed, in the mist of her breath.

'I can't not.'

He was tempted, for the first time, to tell her of his past. To say, *because someone once did the same for me.* Only, he couldn't. They were strangers and would remain so until they parted ways tomorrow morning.

Philomena nodded.

'Get on inside, then,' he said. 'I…will be in shortly. Warm yourself, then we'll both wash up before supper.'

With one last look, she scurried inside.

Freddie did as he'd come to, even managing to find a bucket that would be of good enough use for the night. Already, his mind was full of peculiar thoughts, such as perhaps he should fetch more water, so she could wash a bit more thoroughly, and lend her some clothes for the night, and how much coin he could spare in the morning to get her on her way.

For even if this arrangement only was for one night, he could make sure she had some measure of comfort.

Though, even then, Freddie somehow knew deep in his heart that the arrangement would last longer than one night.

# Chapter Two

*December 6th, 1831*

'You can do this,' Mena whispered to herself, cinching the bonnet's bow tightly beneath her chin. She eyed the door in the flickering of the single candle set beside it, and reminded herself that it wasn't nearly as large, dark, and imposing as it seemed. Viewing it in that manner was… It was a remnant of the past, is what it was. When she couldn't even set foot beyond the threshold.

*And the past is past. Today, you must only think of the future.*

'You can do this. A lovely, brisk morning walk is just the ticket.'

*Quite so.*

Only, it was a walk, that little bit further than the normal boundaries of Mena's world.

*And? It is not the first time for that. Each day, you must grow your circle.*

*Even if you wish to still be warm and safe with Hawk.*

*Quite so.*

Really, it was only that. Today was the sort of day an extra hour in the soft bed, Hawk snuggled beside her, his coarse fur tickling her nose, would be absolutely delightful.

*But you have important business to attend to.*

*Quite so.*

Breathing deeply, slowly releasing each breath, Mena tapped her fingers against the rough, but tightly woven wool of her coat. Her heart slowed, and she nodded to herself.

'Right out the door,' she whispered. 'Left. Straight, then right. Nothing to it.'

Nodding again, repeating the directions in her mind, she pulled on her gloves and closed the distance between herself and the door before she lost her nerve.

*It's only this meeting and Freddie's return that has you out of sorts.*

*This is a walk like any other.*

*Right, left, straight, right.*

Blowing out the candle, licking her fingers, and ensuring it was fully extinguished, she unlocked and opened the door, and stepped out, the brisk cold biting at her nose; the sounds of the awakening city assailing her all at once. Forcing another deep breath in and out, she closed the door, locked it, and pressed the latch three times before turning back to the street.

*Right, left, straight, right.*

*Right.*

The bells across the city echoed as they rang the hour of six, the different tonalities and melodies pleasantly discordant. Mena focused on the sound for a moment as she began her journey, steady-paced and sure-footed.

That was one of the tricks. Not to be too hasty, and to focus on each and every step. Smiling at some familiar faces—merchants, shopkeepers, stall-keepers, and workers —she let the business and routine of it wash gently over her, imagining it all as lapping little waves, rather than some giant tidal wave of unstoppable force. She made a concerted effort to notice particular details, and added them to the mental painting she made in her head. That helped too; knowing and noting what surrounded her, making little watercolour paintings in her mind. It made the world...

Palatable. Manageable. Less threatening and overwhelming.

And in the early mornings like this—still dark, but lined at the edges by the light of the city itself, coloured and tinged with the soft, buttery glow of the streetlamps—she felt almost part of it. As if it called out to her, gently saying: *welcome.*

Smiling to herself, she paused to let a harried hack pass before crossing the busy thoroughfare, not fully awake, but never fully asleep either, checking both directions twice.

*Left. Straight on until the cathedral.*

*See? Nothing to it.*

As the industry increased around her, Mena reminded herself again why she was going beyond her usual boundaries. It wasn't about her. It wasn't *for* her. It was for others. That is what this expedition was. A quest, for others.

*Just so.*

One more investor, and not just any *one*, but a man of the press. Not only did Mr Greer have, if he were to be believed, such capital to offer, as would not only secure her project for an additional year on its own, but he could potentially publicise the whole venture. The bones were in place, well, actually more than that, but if word spread of what she'd built...more perhaps would follow in time. She wasn't a revolutionary, nor did she think she could change the entire world; only perchance she could change a small part of it. Then others could change it a little more. No one could change the entire world by themselves, no matter how much money or power they wielded. However, if you helped one person, they in turn might one day have the opportunity to help another. That was what Freddie had taught her, all those years ago.

St. Paul's came into view, and she glanced up at the enormous edifice, commanding, majestic, and reassuring. A symbol in itself, with all its simple, but strong lines, of rebirth. Of renewal. At least to her. Her heart swelled at the sight; or perhaps it was the thought that flitted into her head again as she passed one of the city's most significant markers.

*Freddie is coming home tonight.*

Another reason she was having this meeting *today*. Sneaking out, and getting all that still needed to be once he was home would be significantly more challenging. She'd been lucky in a sense this year; he'd been away quite a few times, this last time for nearly four months, which had given her the opportunity to get her plans in motion without having to be constantly looking over her shoulder. Because he couldn't learn of her plans until… Well, until she was ready. Until it was all ready. Ready enough. It wasn't so much a secret, as a surprise.

*Quite so.*

*A Christmas surprise.*

Even if, when she pondered it truthfully, it felt more like a secret.

*Only because of all this sneaking.*

*And because of your own, dishonourable little heart.*

*Quite so.*

Forcing herself to focus on the journey, rather than

useless meanderings of the mind which had been overly explored as it was, she picked up her pace as she came onto Ludgate. It was as busy as elsewhere, though the streets were slightly narrower, forcing the traffic to congregate more than before. Mena forced herself to take in deep breaths, even as she weaved around bankers, and innkeepers, shopkeepers, and visitors, barristers, and even men of the Yard and runners as she drew closer to the Fleet.

*Deep breaths. In. Out.*

*In. Out.*

*Just a little further.*

Keeping her pace steady, Mena continued on, instructing her mind to think on her long-prepared speech, and not the deafening noise, nor the dizzying blurry of sights. Sweat formed at the back of her neck, and in her palms; still, on she went, gently murmuring words, as she tried to hone in on specific details she passed.

*A pile of horse manure.*

*A bunch of holly in that woman's bonnet.*

*The horses' hooves and jingling of their harnesses.*

It all worked, though she was out of breath and took a moment when she finally stood before the offices of the *Londoner's Chronicle*.

*In. Out.*

*In.*

*Out.*

The building was, as many others were here, simple, tall, built in the style of some forty years ago. A glossy black sign with bold white letters set above the door and windows of the ground floor proclaimed this to be her destination. People dressed in sombre business attire, all black wool suits and unadorned gowns, came and went, some entering, others not, whilst nearby carts tended by men, and sometimes boys, loaded or waited for the city's papers.

*You've a right to be here too. You've business.*

*Good business. And no matter what happens in there, you know it is.*

*Quite so.*

A young man, looking very much like some manner of clerk, raised a brow questioningly as he passed her, his destination her own.

'Need any help, miss?'

'I've an appointment with Mr Greer,' Mena said with a slight smile, applauding herself for the steadiness of her voice.

'This way, then,' he said with a polite smile, offering out his arm.

Mena took it, and together they entered the offices of the *Londoner's Chronicle*.

*See?*

*Nothing to it at all.*

Inhaling deeply of the frigid air that, now, most definitely announced snow, though most would argue it smelt only of the river, and putridness of the city, Mena took a moment to survey her enterprise from across the road. Below the rising sun, whose rays were turning the edges of the sky to the most delightful *mélange* of greys and lavenders, there it stood, Nichols House. No different than yesterday, save for the fact it had one new benefactor.

*Mr Greer.*

There had been no time after her meeting concluded to bask in, or even truly realise, her success, not if she wished to visit here before opening the Holly Street shop. But during the walk back, a bit more harried, and hurried, due to the increasing bustle, she had relived her conversation with Mr Greer over and over, until finally, she had managed to capture, and absorb, the truth of her success. To *feel* it.

Whilst she'd explained all about Nichols House, Mr Greer had been quiet, an intent listener. Though at times it hadn't felt like that—rather her mind had, as was its habit, envisaged the worst explanations for his silence: *not interested, bored, believes me to be mad*—she'd made it through, reassuring herself that Henderson, one of Freddie's associates, and one of the first investors himself in Nichols House, had brought them together for a reason.

When she'd finished, Mr Greer had actually apologised for having underestimated her—right before he agreed to invest. He'd even tentatively agreed to send one of his writers once the house was *officially* open mid-January. It had all gone, well, rather swimmingly. Sure, there had been that rather awkward moment when she'd had to ask him to keep it a secret from Freddie— but then too, Mr Greer had demonstrated keen understanding.

*'We all need to see what we can achieve on our own, sometimes, Miss Nichols,'* he'd said.

That was the truth of it—even if it wasn't the *whole* truth.

The pernicious little demon of guilt came crawling into her heart for a moment, because was she really doing this on her own? This meeting, like so many others, well, she would never have got it if she hadn't been *associated* with Freddie. Though she knew those who agreed to help her did it for more than that association, the truth was, without having been at Freddie's side all these years, making those connections, she wouldn't have had such access to people who could help her realise her dreams. It was a strange mix of privilege, and independence. And one which some days left her feeling a bit guiltier for all the secrecy.

Somehow, it also made her feel…more *sullied* than any of the whispers that circulated about hers and Freddie's *association*. Oh, she'd heard all the gossip before, and none of it mattered. To her, in any case. It seemed to matter a great deal to others, particularly those in some circles, but as yet she hadn't truly been judged, or rather, *excluded*, because of what people *thought* her ties to Freddie were. The proof was the fact that so many had agreed to help her—including Mr Greer. So no, she didn't care much about the gossip, but all this *sneaking*, well, it was becoming harder and harder to bear.

*But you shall not dwell upon it right this moment.*

No. Because standing before the project she'd just convinced another powerful man to support, Mena told herself she must allow herself a tiny moment, to simply feel…*pleased.*

To feel her success, her joy, and her excitement.

When she'd first embarked on this journey, alone, she'd hoped, but never dared believe, she could achieve even half of what she had. And now… Everything was coming together. What she'd built rivalled her own dreams for it. Pride swelled within her at the sight of Nichols House, and the bustling hive about it, though technically they weren't officially open.

*Technically being the operative word…*

Though the concept of the place—a house, a home, a hospital, a school, a haven, *all those things*, merely Nichols House on paper—had been born years ago, it hadn't truly begun to take form until last year. Freddie had gone away—*to help Lady Mary and her family*—for some part of the summer, and something inside Mena had, if not broken, then clicked into place. She'd known the time had come. To face reality, knocking, *banging*, on the door as it was, and to make her dreams become reality, before she was left alone, with nothing but a pocketful of money, grand ideas, and a pleasant *goodbye*. It had been four years since Lady Mary had come into Freddie's life, and each year brought them closer together, as Freddie continued to rise far above the life he and Mena had shared for so long. As he continued to rise, far above Mena's reach—as he was always meant to. So last year, she'd finally stopped denying reality, set the wheels in motion, so to speak, and now…

*Now I stand before my dream.*

Which was exhilarating, and utterly unreal. Just as the enthusiasm for her project had been. Not only among investors and donors, supporters, and helpers, but among those she'd always wished to help. Those like her.

The ink had barely dried on the warehouse papers, and somehow, those in need had already known to come. It had spurred Mena on, and though she couldn't offer all she intended to, she'd made it so she could offer some food, then after a month or so, a roof. Some who came had offered services in exchange—not that they needed to—but Mena had graciously accepted. Many had trades or talents which could be put to use, and so the endeavour which had begun as hers, and hers alone, had in fact been built up by all those who would benefit from it.

Now, weeks before the official opening, they were already operating with a fully functioning kitchen, two floors of beds, and the building itself was nearly done up as it was meant to. Though, to anyone who knew nothing of it, it would look much like any other plain stone, five-storeyed warehouse in these parts. Imposing frontage, large windows, mostly covered now with newspapers, it had suffered some disuse from its years of emptiness, though now with the life teeming from within, it was recovering. As those within would be. Mena had leased it for a desperately low price, the lordly owner apparently keen for *any* money, and from what she'd heard having a charity such as hers within could only improve his reputation.

*A profitable deal benefits both partners equally, compensating for lacks in their enterprises.*

One of many lessons she'd learned at Freddie's side. Along with the one which had given her the idea for this place: *just because no one has done it does not mean it is impossible, only that it will be a likely hugely sought-after novelty.* The thought of Freddie both bolstered her, and made her heart twinge with that pernicious demon of guilt. It didn't help that this place was barely fifteen minutes' walk from his own wharf and warehouse, which meant that every passing day increased the possibility of discovery once he returned.

*Soon*, she promised herself for the millionth time. Soon, she *would* tell him.

Rather than rehash the same argument in her own head *yet again*, Mena strode towards the building. Workmen moved in and out with various building materials, while passers-by sometimes offered a glance, and others came to see if they could find help. They'd needed to install a desk in the front hall, manned by those who had already sought shelter here, to speak to the latter, orient them, explain the rules or mealtimes, or add them to a further list, depending on the assistance they sought. Those who came for a night, or a meal, were easier to accommodate just now; those who sought more permanent aid sometimes needed to wait as the place wasn't quite finished, and what few places there were had already filled up.

That was the one negative aspect of Mena's project, its popularity. And the fact that there were no restrictions imposed on those who wished to come, no demands for *repentance* or adherence to a particular set of morality, made it even more so. The only rules which were to be followed were a respect for one's self and others, no criminal behaviour, and no *fraternising* within the house unless in a private enclave and within an established relationship. But then, the last two all fell under the category of *respect*, in Mena's opinion.

Those rules, or rather, as some viewed it, the lack thereof, were integral. It had caused some problems, and made attracting donors and investors sometimes difficult, but then, the people who only wished to help if others swore to follow *their* beliefs, or the path they set, well, that was not true charity. No matter good intentions, to Mena, assistance should always be given without strings. Refusing to aid those who did not abide by one's own beliefs, was...

*Antiquated.*

Mena nodded and smiled to the guards who kept watch for thieves and troublemakers, then to the young man currently at the desk, Pawel, who had been here since the beginning with his young wife and child, but did not tarry. She was here to check on the progress of everything, and besides, Pawel was busy, directing this workman or that, this new arrival or that. She smiled to herself as she made her way around the ground floor, which was well on its way to becoming what it would finally be.

The building had been redone to both cut cost—in

keeping as much as they could of the bones, plain stone and wood floors and walls, serviceable stone stairwells in the front and back, and smaller, wooden ones at each side—and to maximise space, specifically in dividing the old merchandise open floors. There would be decorations, and warmth, added in time, with furnishings on the living floors, and perhaps some artworks from the children elsewhere, but for now, it was about getting it open, and functionable. Much of the furniture, bought and donated, had come, so they had beds wherever there were meant to be, desks, shelving, all the fittings for kitchen, and laundry, and some equipment that was already being used to sew and dye, preserve, or even woodwork, both for this place, and to sell.

The ground floor would be the welcoming and enrolment offices, along with the day meal hall, the permanent dining hall, and rooms for those who couldn't use stairs. Above, Mena listed, weaving past long trestle tables and benches to head upstairs, would be the infirmary, schoolrooms, and learning rooms. Not only for children, but for those who, like her, hadn't ever been given a proper education, as well as rooms dedicated for learning trades taught by those who already knew them. This floor too was already well on its way to being ready. Distantly she could hear voices repeating the alphabet, and the smell of chalk was thick on the air.

The fourth and fifth floors would be—*were*—the living quarters. The fourth, for those who would only be here temporarily, and the fifth, for those remaining longer. There were a small amount of tiny private rooms, for families, and the rest were dormitories. As for the third floor…

Mena grinned as she stepped onto it. The third floor would be the library, the operating offices, her own office, and eventually, the room which would become her living quarters.

*Once I finally get the courage to tell Freddie everything.*

*Once I finally find the courage to leave him.*

Shaking the grim thoughts away, opening the door to what would be the *headquarters* as such of this grand enterprise, the least finished of the whole building so far—only a few chairs along with bare tables piled with papers, and ledgers—Mena allowed herself a moment of tranquillity. She let the sounds of work, and laughter, fill her up, as she wandered to the window, dusty, but with a good view of the yard below, which, despite the weather, was full of industry and play. This place... It invigorated her. Made her feel, if not at home, full of purpose. As if she'd finally found her own path, after all this time. Done what she had been created for by whatever power may have created her. It was soothing, and yet, overwhelming.

For though this was *her* dream, those here, every soul who had come and gone, believed in her, had contributed to this. It wasn't only her dream; it had become something more, and she wasn't quite certain how to feel about that. Glad, bolstered, certainly, but also...

*A little at sea.*

Footsteps drew her attention, and she turned to find the woman responsible for the accounts striding in, muttering at a bunch of papers in her hand. Josephine was a veritable master of numbers, as if their language was part of her flesh, and not one to be trifled with. She was about Mena's age, perhaps slightly older, with sharp, patrician, yet striking features, and the temper of someone who had suffered too many fools on her quest to be accepted, or at the very least, tolerated, for herself.

Mena had had some dissent over hiring the woman; until those dissenting had been treated to a lengthy presentation by Josephine herself about how they were codgery old simpletons who didn't understand the first thing about basic arithmetic and should thus refrain from attempting to understand concepts far beyond their own abilities.

A risky approach, yet an effective one.

'How goes it, Josephine?' Mena asked, and the woman stopped, stared at her for a moment, as if calculating the reason for Mena's presence, then nodded, having reached an apparently satisfyingly logical solution. 'Anything I should know?'

'Numbers are good,' Josephine said flatly, heading for one of the tables which at the moment constituted her desk. 'Even with your extravagant Christmas celebration.'

'Yes, well, that is all coming from my personal funds. Naturally you know that.' She grinned, narrowing her eyes at the woman.

Indeed, though they wouldn't be *officially* open, so many already dwelled here, and deserved a proper Yuletide celebration.

It was extravagant, *unnecessary*, many would argue, but to Mena, peace, joy, and celebration, were neither. They were food for the soul, and if she had to spend her last penny to give people that, she would.

Not that she was down to her last penny, even with all she'd already invested into Nichols House; eight years of working for Freddie, who paid her *more* than fairly, barely spending any of it, added up.

'So why you continue to chastise me, I wonder.'

'I find it amusing to watch you explain to me ceaselessly the importance of normality, festivity, and to-getherness.'

'How have I not noticed this before? Here I was, believing you to be merely miserly, and instead I discover you do it to amuse yourself? Hm. I'm not quite sure how I feel about knowing you derive amusement from torturing me.'

'It isn't my fault you take me at face value. No one ever seems to believe I could be in jest.'

'How often are you in jest?'

'Point zero one percentile.'

'That might explain it. Let me reassure you, however; I will be sure to remember you can jest in future.'

Josephine grinned down at her papers, then nodded, and Mena laughed, knowing their conversation was over.

Not that there was actually anything they needed to discuss, not even Mr Greer's investment. The solicitors would handle all the details, and Josephine would deal directly with them when needed. In fact, the only reason Mena had come here… Had been to *be* here. To remind herself what it was all for. And perhaps, in some measure, to reassure herself of one thing before he returned tonight.

*Freddie will be proud.*

*Just as soon as you get the nerve to tell him.*

*Quite so.*

The bell in the yard rang quarter to eight. With a yelp, and a muttered goodbye to Josephine, Mena took herself swiftly back to Holly Street, lest she be late.

*For all today still has yet to bring.*

# Chapter Three

The lighter hadn't even properly moored yet, and already Freddie was jumping off. As soon as his feet touched the stone of the wharf, a weight lifted from his shoulders, and he let out the breath he'd been holding seemingly since they'd first sighted England again. Nearly four months he'd been gone, and once, it might've felt like nothing, but every year, each voyage, each parcel of time spent...not here, seemed to lengthen into eternity.

Once, the promise of a distant, unknown horizon had been all he craved. Then, each voyage, each new expedition, each encounter with new people in faraway lands, had left him hungering for more. He'd once thought it would always be so. London may be where he'd established his business, but it was not, and never could be, home. Only now, it was almost as if his cravings had, not ceased, but lessened. He didn't miss London, and he didn't tire of seeing the world, but he did miss—

*Just getting old, you are.*

Yes. He was. And that's all there was to this dulling of his cravings. This was his thirty-seventh year on earth as far as he knew. No longer was he a young man, able to withstand what it took to keep his little federation running. These jaunts around the globe... Someday soon he would have to stop; even if his boots on the ground, his handshakes, had been what set him apart. Gave him that edge, the personal touch, and helped his business grow into what it was. Not many realised just how old he was; he was lucky, he supposed, to project a youthfulness that often was an advantage—when people thought to underestimate him.

Readjusting the pack on his shoulder, running his thumb over the wooden *Klabautermann* one last time before stowing it away in his pocket, where it would remain until his next voyage, Freddie gripped the parcel in his other hand tightly, and glanced around the wharf, alive with stevedores and customs men, clerks and lightermen, all busy unloading and sorting the new haul of goods from a continent half a world away. He should go in, make sure it was all done, head up to his office on the top floor of the warehouse, and get some work done. Four months he'd been gone, tending to affairs across the Atlantic, all because some men just couldn't be satisfied with steady business and good profits; no, they had to—

*Stop.*

*It is resolved. Done.*

Yes. It was. Now, he was back, and the rest of his business needed tending to.

Only, as the workers continued to swirl around him, like the sea around an island, as if he weren't even there, Freddie realised, that really, his business didn't need him to tend to it. At least, right this minute.

*Perhaps not at all.*

A strange little laugh escaped him, and he wondered if this is what it felt like, to *succeed*. To move up so high that you didn't truly *need* to work anymore, like all those lords who went so far as to view any occupation distasteful and went through life like useless flotsam and jetsam. Freddie would never be able to endure such an existence, yet still. He'd built his company. He'd secured all the pieces, fitted them together, cultivated it all like some strange gardener. It all grew, functioned, *lived on* in some way, without him. He was the captain, or rather no, the figurehead now. If he died tomorrow, it could all survive. It was what he'd wanted, to create an endurable legacy that profited sustainably, constantly evolving, and so he had.

Of course, he still had a purpose, *work* to do. He steered the way to new ventures and secured new deals. He would say he ensured everyone in his employment was paid, but actually, no, that was the clerks. And the banks, and his overseers. He set the tone, kept his venture going according to his own creed, and that was essential. If he died tomorrow, and someone new took over, they might not follow in his footsteps, regardless of the directives he'd put into place for his succession. In that way, he himself was essential, but he wasn't…

*Needed.*

It was a strange feeling, realising your own superfluousness in a sense, particularly when it came to a company which you'd built, and bore your own name. Well, not technically his name, but the name it should. The name…which represented it best. The name for which it stood. Which he'd taken, which he'd lived for, which he'd, hopefully, honoured with his life.

All those years ago, he'd made building this company, this venture, his purpose. It had demanded all the focus, all the energy, he had. And somehow, it had grown beyond him. In a sense, his success had freed him to…

*Do what?*

'Mind yerself, sir,' one of the stevedores shouted as the men prepared to haul crates out with the winches.

Freddie waved, and, shaking his head at himself, took himself well out of the way of those actually working.

Those actually serving a purpose.

In fact, he took himself off the wharf entirely, and was not even spared a second glance, though some he passed tapped their caps or nodded. As he crossed the gates securing his enterprise, joined the bustle of the streets, and began to make his way home, Freddie felt glad, actually, that he didn't have any more work to do this evening. Well, at least nothing pressing that would delay him any longer. And, shaking off the earlier melancholy thoughts, he reassured himself that the loss of old responsibilities only meant he would have time for new ones. He had money and influence now. He could find new ways to yield it. Perhaps politics.

*Perhaps not.*

Though it was tempting, to think he could make change that way, it didn't quite fit.

*What does?*

Right this moment, Freddie couldn't think of anything. Likely because of the toll of his journey. Though every step that brought him closer to Holly Street seemed to belie that summation that he was *tired*. Because with every step, he felt...*lighter*. Excited, happy, really. To be home. To be *going* home.

A smile even lifted the corners of his lips as he weaved around dockers and merchants, shoppers, and visitors. As he dodged coaches and carriages and fishmongers and women of the night. The brisk, somewhat foul air was a tonic, a balm, reminding him that he was home.

*Right on time.*

*As promised.*

A light dusting of snow began to fall, tiny little flakes that would likely not survive the night, but then, more would follow soon enough. A shiver ran through him, turning his mood and making his gut clench, and he ignored the prickles at the back of his neck, though he did glance over his shoulder.

*Merely the cold*, he reassured himself, spotting absolutely nothing out of the ordinary as he tightened his scarf. And he didn't mind the cold, nor the snow for that matter; it was certainly better than London in the summer, and, well, it never ceased to remind him of his first night at Holly Street.

*Of Mena.*

Yes, very soon now, he would be home. And then, everything would be right again. Everything would come together, somehow, and he would be able to see, and plan for his future, with clarity, good sense, and verve.

*Back where it all began...*

*The perfect place to begin again.*

The delectable smell of stew, mingled with that of crisped sugar, apples, and spices, met Freddie when he stepped into the kitchen, mindful to leave his muddied boots at the door. No matter how hard it snowed, how severe the frost, there never ceased to be mud. And other things he rarely cared to think on.

*All things better left a fair distance from the rest of the house.*

The kitchen itself was empty, save for the bubbling concoction, and traces of Mena's artistry, though she would deny it came close to anything such. To him, however, it was. Dropping his pack, he peeled off his gloves, slid off his coat, scarf, and hat, hanging them on the hooks by the door, and pondered why precisely that was.

*Because it is the art of simplicity.*

As was everything Mena did. There was nothing complex about the way she prepared a chicken, or organised the shop. It was efficient, and constrained, as she herself was, but it also had... *Care* put into it. Which made all the difference.

Cheekily, Freddie lifted the pot's lid, stirred the stew, and tasted it.

*Home.*

Grinning, he was about to run his finger around the bowl which had held the apple concoction, when he heard a creak above. Snatching his finger back, he turned instead to the stairs, and quietly as he could, carefully avoiding the noisy third one up, he made his way up to the back parlour.

His grin became a wide smile, and everything quietened at once when he spotted her, her back to him, balanced on a stool as she hung greenery above the door to the shop. The rest of the room had already got a similar treatment, boughs of holly and pine, and wreaths of evergreens and mistletoe covering the otherwise unprepossessing parlour. As always, they livened, and warmed up, the cool blue of the wall furnishings, brought out the leaves in the fabric of the chairs, and complemented the burgundy velvet of the settee. The festive adornments even seemed to make the gilding on the rare picture frames, all maps, and sights from across the world, glisten. A blazing fire completed the welcoming and soothing atmosphere of it all, and Freddie's mind flashed briefly back to his first night here.

How empty, and full of potential, it had seemed then.

It had not seemed empty since, and yes, its potential had been fulfilled. But over the years, this room, *every* room, had been filled with much more. With…

*Life, I suppose.*

*And warmth, and that same special care of Mena's.*

Who was humming now. He quirked his head, trying to recognise the melody.

*Ah yes, of course.*

'"*The holly and the ivy,*"' he sang when the tune came around again. '"*Now are both well grown…*"'

'Freddie!' Mena exclaimed, whirling around, nearly toppling off the stool.

He made for her, but she righted herself against the door frame, and good thing too, for he was struck dumb for a moment when the force of her broad smile hit him.

'You're home,' she breathed, eyes bright, their sweet, gentle blue like that of eryngo today.

The navy wool gown she wore was new, but it complemented her eyes, as well as her hair, which had grown a little, reaching her shoulders rather than her chin now. Well, she'd *let* it grow. Since she'd arrived here, she'd always kept it short. Her hair, her choice; and he hadn't ever questioned her on it, though now, oddly, he felt as if he should know. He knew the rest of her so well, the quirks of her brows, the way she tapped her fingers on her skirts when she was nervous, and even the pattern of the freckles across her nose; it felt as if he was failing, somehow, by not knowing about her hair.

*And so much more.*

Shaking the ridiculous notions from his head, he closed the distance between them, and offered out his hand.

'I did promise I would return today,' he said, as she slid her hand in his, and came carefully down from her perch.

It struck him then, how very much indeed he'd missed her.

Perhaps it was how natural her hand felt in his—not that he took it often, or generally touched her; naturally, that wasn't something he did, unless, like tonight, he was helping her down, or up, or some such—perhaps it was that rightness which set his mind down that path. But then, of course he missed her. That was no great revelation. He'd thought it earlier, hadn't he? And why shouldn't he miss her? She was his best friend. They'd lived together, built this place, his company, together. Seen each other through so much. She was his constant. She was warmth, and kindness, and great fun, and beautiful—

*Wait, what?*

'I know you promised, Freddie,' she smiled softly, and he forced himself to drop her hand, not that he moved any further away. 'Only, I also know sometimes the tides do not cooperate. There are problems to be solved, and new markets to discover.'

'I promised,' he said seriously, though with a measure of incomprehension.

He felt his brows drop a little, as he realised, that explained it all.

He'd promised he would be home by December the sixth—he'd promised *Mena* he would be home by the sixth—and therefore, no tide, no problem, no accident, would prevent him from keeping that promise. He'd have *swum* the damn Atlantic if he'd had to, to fulfil that promise.

Clearing his throat, Freddie tried to return to the room.

What was wrong with him tonight? First, he was wondering about *futures*, and *purposes*, and *usefulness*, and now he was calling Mena *beautiful* and speaking of promises made to her as if they were the most important law he'd ever abide by?

*Except that she is, and they are.*

'Are you well, Freddie?' Mena asked, her eyes searching his. A frown furrowed her own brow, and he wanted to reach out and smooth it away.

*What the Devil is wrong with me?*

'Perfectly well,' he assured her. 'Long journey. Still a bit turned around, I suppose.' She nodded, though unconvinced. 'For you,' he added, nearly thrusting the parcel he'd been latched onto since the Channel at her.

'Thank you,' she smiled, taking it, and rounding him to go settle on the armchair closest to the fire.

Freddie took the opportunity to sort through his apparently addled and muddled brain, following slowly to settle across from her, studying her as she opened the parcel.

Objectively, she *was* beautiful. He'd known that for a while, or more aptly, *allowed himself to notice*. Her hair, the colour of dark mahogany, was neither fine, nor thick, straight, and like curtains of silk, except for the little hairs around her forehead which had a tendency to curl and refuse to be tamed no matter what. Her eryngo-coloured almond-shaped eyes were very pleasant indeed, changing to the light blue of a summer's day or the misty twilight depending on her moods. She was tall, and long-limbed, though one wouldn't know it for the way she contorted herself to fit into small spaces, like the chair, as she did now, and over the years, as her health had improved, so her skin had taken on a healthy glow, though she remained naturally lithe. Her features were fine, and sharp, though not as sharp as they'd first been, and her nose was long and straight, not the preference of the current *mode*, but then, it suited her, and he'd never truly understood why there should be *modes* at all when it came to people's appearance. To finish it all, she had a wide mouth, wider, naturally, when she smiled, and her teeth were good, though he supposed if he was being objective in his study, she did have a slight overbite; only personally he found that charming, as he did the odd dimple on the bottom left side of her chin that made an appearance when she grimaced.

So yes, objectively, she was beautiful.

And it wasn't that he'd never noticed before, they had lived together for eight years, but he'd never... Been touched by it?

*That would be a lie.*

Indeed. However, that again, was natural, considering their living arrangements. He'd dismissed whatever thoughts or inklings that came upon him over the years as fleeting—mere illusions born of closeness—which they had been, since he'd moved on from them.

So what was different tonight? His fatigue? Combined with the flush in her cheeks from her work, and the heat of the fire? Perhaps his relief, at being home again. With his friend. Who he had missed.

*Sorely.*

Something tightened in his breast, and he massaged it gently with his fist, twisting in his seat.

*Must've pulled something on the journey.*

'These are wonderful, Freddie, thank you,' Mena said, rooting through the pine box he'd had to purchase to put all his finds for her in. He forced a smile, though luckily she didn't look up to check, too fascinated by the treasures.

*What the Devil is wrong with me?*

'What is this one?' she asked, holding up a glass vial where a tan-and-black-spotted, fearsome-looking insect with pincers for a snout now resided.

*'Scarabaeus tityus,'* he told her. 'Hercules beetle. Found it legs up near a pile of rotten timber, and thought you might like it.'

Mena grinned, nodding excitedly, before returning to the box.

'Freddie...' she breathed, dropping the contents of a pouch into her hand.

And that sound...

*What. Is. Wrong. With. Me?*

'Do you like it?'

'Like it? It's wondrous,' she said, shaking her head, her eyes devouring the pink-and-black stone in her hand, which he'd had wrapped in gold and set on a chain whilst in Boston. 'I've never seen anything quite like it.'

'Rhodonite,' he said.

Mena began to try and fasten it herself, but she couldn't quite work the clasp, so Freddie rose, and went to help her.

Gently sweeping her hair to the side—*it is like silk*— he took the ends and clasped them together. His fingertips slid across her skin as he did, and there was that tightness again.

'The goldsmith said something about the Greeks using it as protection.'

'It's beautiful, Freddie,' Mena whispered, twirling the stone in her fingers, as his feet refused to obey his own commands, and move away. Only, stood here, he could feel her warmth, and smell her scent, strange as that sounded. That particular mix of cedar, and spice, and the sea, and freedom, and home all at once.

*What is happening?*

'You shouldn't have. You spoil me.'

'I—'

'My tart!' Mena exclaimed, jumping up.

She slid the box onto his chair, and bolted down-stairs, and only then did Freddie catch the whiff of burnt caramel.

He chuckled to himself, then glanced down at the box.

*Treasures indeed.*

*Spoiling indeed.*

Apart from the necklace, there was nothing of true value in that box. Insects in vials, pamphlets, one small novel, and rocks he'd found at various places she would interrogate him about later. A diary of sketches and musings—his travel diary so to speak. Essentially, the same he would bring her back from every journey, though sometimes there would be a new scientific tool, or a piece of lace or some such. Yet to her, it was all treasure. He loved that about her. The way she saw wonder in everything, the way she cherished every tiny thing, as if it were gold and diamonds, not sticks and leaves and shells.

It was perhaps the thing he loved most about her.

*Difficult to say. I love so much about her.*

And then it hit him, like some great bolt of lightning, some rock tumbled from a great height onto his head, some bucket of ice thrown at his face.

*I love her.*

The tightness in his chest returned, and for a moment, he couldn't breathe. This wasn't possible. He couldn't *love* her, not like that. That was folly. Confusion, brought on by the nostalgia of the season, which meant so much to them, and of a long journey. Actually, thinking on it, he did love her, and not *like that*.

Right.

No use denying it, he loved Mena.

She was his friend, his confidante, his partner, his…

*Home.*

*Damn.*

Had he not declared himself, stepping foot on that wharf not an hour ago, that London had, and never would be, home? Yet since he'd stepped foot into the house, even before, simply thinking on it, he'd used the word *home* freely. And this house, *was* home. Merely because of the fact that Mena was here. And she…

*She is my home. The shore I return to, ceaselessly.*

'No, no, no, no,' Freddie muttered, eyes burning as he began to pace the room. Not possible. Not right. Not acceptable, not any of it. 'No, no, no, no…'

He tried to think on all the worst parts of her, how she was annoyingly stubborn, and messy in the kitchen, though tyrannical when it came to where and how and when he put away *his* things, and how she was so very matron-like when he was ill and she tended to him, though she wouldn't let him near her when she was the one poorly, and…and…

It was no use.

Even all that, he loved about her. It made her, *her*.

*It can't be.*

And yet, it was.

The immutable, undeniable truth.

He was *in* love with Mena.

*Not good. How could you let this happen? How—?*

'Freddie! Supper!' she called from below.

'Coming!'

*Pull yourself together.*

Rubbing his hand over his face, he willed himself to push it all away again.

He couldn't face this right now, couldn't think on it, or sort it out. He simply had to push it away.

*For now, and for ever.*

Because loving Mena…

Was not an option.

# Chapter Four

Something wasn't right with Freddie. It wasn't that he was quiet—he was always quiet. He never said anything unless he thought it might be of more value than silence. He never spoke more words than necessary, and never said anything he didn't mean. It was one of the many things she loved and admired about him. Only tonight…

*Tonight he is different.*

And she couldn't put her finger on it. She tried, pondering it whilst she took purposeful spoonsful of the thick mutton stew—his favourite—and toyed with the extraordinary rock around her neck.

*Well, that's two things, right there.*

First, Freddie had barely touched his meal; he'd been moving his spoon back and forth for as long as it had been before him. Just as he'd barely touched Hawk when the little devil had returned from his outdoor escapades.

Normally, and this despite the fact that Freddie had been reluctant to welcome the *bag of fleas* into the house, whenever he saw Hawk, he was crouching, petting the dog until the creature was lolling in ecstasy. Or they were both rolling around together, playing. Yet tonight, when she'd opened the door to let him in, Hawk had gone straight for Freddie, barking, and wagging what remained of his tail excitedly, whilst Freddie patted him on the head. Even the dog had stared at him in confusion, and still did, sat at his feet, expectant not for scraps, but for acknowledgement.

*Very strange.*

And then there was this whole necklace business. Not that she didn't appreciate it; it was the finest, most beautiful thing she'd ever owned. And she loved it, not because it was fine, or precious, but rather it was precious for she knew he had got it, and had it done up in intricate gold filigree, because he knew she would like the unusualness of it. Diamonds, rubies, sapphires…were nothing to her compared to this, and she should know, having seen a fair few pass through the shop. Only, it was a deviation from the norm.

Over the years they'd lived and worked together, there had been a certain set of rules. It had taken time to establish them, some spoken, but most unspoken; and those rules had preserved the tranquillity, steadiness, and security of their relationship. Simply put, their friendship had boundaries. As it should; as all relationships did.

In close quarters, working alongside each other as they had for so long, it required trust, and intimacy. But also…safety. From crossing invisible lines. Their life together had been a strange sort of balancing act between intimacy and cold co-operation, and with the gift of the necklace Freddie had upset said balance, and sent them tumbling into the foreign emptiness below.

*Or perhaps he is simply tired from the voyage, and you are making something out of many nothings.*

Possible. It wasn't the first time Freddie had given her a thoughtful gift. *Anything* he gave her was thoughtful. Something else she loved about him. It didn't matter if it was a scrap of paper decorated with the quick lines of a distant horizon, or a dead insect, insignificant things of no value to others, there was *thoughtfulness* behind them, which made them priceless to her. As for the food, and Hawk… Well, yes. Tiredness explained both.

Though looking at him now, he did seem…shocked? Stunned? She was sure he hadn't been so before, when she'd first seen him standing there, returned to her.

*Not to me.*

*Quite so.*

Regardless. He had seemed himself, if a bit worn by the journey, but then he was getting older, they both were, and the seas were not so easy this time of year. Except… This mood of his, it seemed altogether something new. And she knew all Freddie's moods; what every twitch of the eyebrow or crinkling of the eyes meant.

*Yet this state of his I do not know…*

Discreetly, Mena allowed herself to examine him again, more meticulously than she normally did, for that way lay danger; she was not so fool as to not recognise that. If there was one sure way to completely destroy what she and Freddie had, it would be to be caught mooning at him. It would be for him to realise what she'd so carefully kept locked away for, oh, about six years now. The very inconvenient fact that she was in love with him. Perhaps, if she had fallen in love with him earlier, when they'd both been *somewhat* equals, it might've been different. Well, if she'd *realised* her love earlier. Before he'd already begun his astronomical rise. Before the difference in their stations became an insurmountable chasm.

*A titan of industry—and a simple country girl who can barely stand to be out in the world. Laughable, really.*

Even if there hadn't been that inequality, Mena knew her love would not be accepted, even wanted. Freddie had made it inescapably clear that anything beyond that cold co-operation and essential intimacy would shatter the bonds of their agreement. It hadn't hurt so much when she'd thought his only love would ever be his business, but now that she knew better…

*Enough of that.*

Clearing her mind, Mena returned to her original problem. Where was she? Oh, yes. A closer examination of the subject at hand. An examination in the interest of…*science*. Entirely possible, for six years of living with this love in her breast had taught her how to keep it to herself. And it had evolved, from a startling, seemingly glaringly obvious thing, to a simple fact of life, that changed absolutely nothing.

*Exactly right.*

*Back to your examination.*

First of all, his form. It was the same as it had always been—well, more *matured* than when they'd first met. Tall, topping her own *gigantic* height as people often teased her, by a mere couple inches. There was visible strength, and a…*developed* musculature, but it was not imposing. Freddie was solid, from the thick, corded forearms, to the defined arms and legs, to the broad shoulders, yet not some titanic brute. He'd never been one of those men who had thin, trim waists, rather he was solid everywhere, even his hands, though those held a gentleness and grace which would seem at odds with the rest of him if the person doing the examination didn't know him. His clothes were always well-tailored, yet even so, it continuously seemed as if they strained, just that little bit, whenever he moved. Then again, perhaps that was also due to the *way* he moved, almost like a boy sometimes, who had no idea how *significant* his body was. Or someone who knew, and was extremely mindful of their bulk and strength—somewhat as she'd always been with her height. There was a hesitancy to his movements sometimes, and—

*Enough. Focus, Mena, you dullard.*

Right. Mena spooned some potatoes into her mouth, then returned to her purpose.

One should begin by noting, so that it was out of the way, that Freddie was incredibly handsome. There. He had a heart-shaped face, sharp, sloping jaw ending in a well-defined and dimpled chin usually covered as it was now in some days' old scruff, that had become with the years, as had his thick coffee-coloured locks, peppered with grey. His cheekbones weren't sharp, except that they were, when he smiled, or one examined his profile. He had a straight, but blunt, and rather large, nose, which fit his face, and his dark, straight eyebrows would look severe, if he didn't tend to express himself so much with them. There was the remnant of a hole from the earring he used to sport in his left ear; the roguish look it gave him had been abandoned in favour of the gentleman he'd become. His mouth was generous, but almost as if drawn into a perfect shape one might see on a Greek statue, and he had little dimples that were often concealed in his scruff, and which paired rather symmetrically with the smile lines that ran from cheek to chin. Those lines had deepened over the years—she'd watched them grow with every smile. As for his eyes… Those truly were the window to his soul.

*Which is shuttered away…*

*Focus.*

Hooded, slightly downturned, with, at the corners, fans of little lines that too had grown with every smile,

they were extraordinary; really, there was no other word.
Striking, perhaps. Mena supposed they would be considered hazel, but they varied across the spectrum of colour
depending on his mood, from a sea-like grey-green, to a
pale green, to a bright, startling blue. And the most in-
definable thing about them, was the kindness they held.
The softness—though even that couldn't quite describe
them. It was his eyes which had told her from that first
second that she was *safe* with him. That she could trust
his word; that he wouldn't harm her, and that—

*Wandering again.*

Indeed. Back to his eyes. Tonight, they were in the
pale green spectrum, which occurred when he was pensive, and generally mulling over distasteful prospects.
Had his business in America not gone well? Had something happened on the voyage? But then why had this
change occurred between when she'd left him in the
parlour, and when he'd descended for dinner?

*You could just ask him.*

Quite. It wasn't as if she was getting any answers
with her examinations.

*Not that you're likely to get any answers from him.*

If this was something beyond business, if this was
something personal… Mena would have better luck in-
terrogating the king.

*Doesn't mean you can't try…*

'Freddie,' Mena began carefully, dragging Freddie
reluctantly back to the room, away from the remorseless
wanderings of the mind he'd lost himself in. He stared
down at his untouched meal, at his spoon, seemingly
frozen in it, then glanced over at hers to find it half-
empty. She ate slowly, deliberately, so he must've been

gone for a while. He hadn't meant to, only that realisation upstairs…

*Was incredibly unsettling to say the least.*

'How was the voyage?'

Clearing his throat, Freddie straightened, and took a healthy bite of his now tepid mutton stew.

Though even tepid, it remained perfection. Simple, hearty fare that stuck to your bones, warmed your insides, and reminded you of happy things.

*My favourite.*

But then, Mena knew that, didn't she? Knew just how he liked it, with that extra heat from the chilis she had taken to using after learning of them from someone at market. Because that was something else she did, beyond special things like making his favourite meal for his return. She tried, *everything*. If she learned there was a new way to plant carrots, she would try it. If she learned of a new philosophy doing the rounds on the Continent, she found a way to learn more of it—and everything that had led to it. It wasn't only that she possessed a natural curiosity, it was there was dedication poured into the learning process. She didn't simply accept facts, or set ways of thinking. She tested them, interrogated them, and made her own conclusions.

If less than half of the people he met went through life similarly, the world would indeed be a very different place. He smiled to himself, then glanced over at her, to find her staring at him expectantly.

*Dolt. She asked you a question.*

'Um, yes, it was fine,' he managed to say. 'The return was a bit tricky, but we managed. The new timber suppliers I found are beyond expectations, and so it was fortunate after all. Our old associate has been thoroughly dealt with.'

'You didn't hurt him too badly, did you?' Mena said with a knowing grin.

'Of course not,' he reassured her, though he needn't have, as she knew well he never used his fists to settle disputes. Though in cases such as this, it was admittedly tempting. The man he'd thought honourable, and aligned with his own ideals, had turned out to be nothing more than a cruel master to his employees, and an unrepentant villain who thought the earth's resources to be infinite. 'However, he shall never trade so much as a stick ever again.' Mena smiled, a soft, proud smile that made his heart swell. Hurriedly, he returned to his food. He needed to get this…these feelings under control. 'How was everything here?'

'Perfectly well. I have a new woman working here now, as Alicia returned to Lincoln to take care of her mother. Her name is Susie; you'll meet her tomorrow if you're about before the shop opens.' Freddie nodded, though he doubted he would be, he'd be down at the warehouse before dawn, but he appreciated Mena keeping him informed of any decisions she made, including him in them, even if this shop was hers now. Had been for a long time.

*In spirit, and…*

'Otherwise, much is as it always is. Oh, actually, Mr Simpson from three doors down passed away in early November. Their son and daughter-in-law have taken over the shop.'

'What did we send them?'

'A basket of pies and some fruit.'

'Thank you.'

'Of course.'

*'Of course,'* she said.

As if anything at all about this conversation, about

the events, were following a natural course. They weren't. Or rather, they were, for the both of them, but it wasn't natural. He shouldn't be asking what they *together* had sent to grieving neighbours. They shouldn't be a *we*, a pair who were seen as such, and sent baskets of pies and fruits with a card that likely bore his name next to hers. And everything shouldn't be *much as it always was*.

This…this was precisely the problem with him feeling as he did.

This was precisely why he couldn't be in love with Mena.

Because she could never be his. Their years together…

Had been exceptional, and trying, and astounding, and full of trials, and triumphs. They were, undoubtedly, the best years of his life, because of the gift he'd been given. The gift of sharing it, with another. Yet, all their years together had been about building *his* enterprise. Realising *his* dreams. Yes, he'd taught her how to read, and write, and do her sums. Beyond that… She'd educated herself. She'd become herself, all on her own.

And instead of setting her free, sending her off to live her own dreams, build her own life, what had he done? Kept her here. Not by force, not by demand, but by the sheer act of not saying, *the time has come for us to part.* He knew she felt she owed him a debt, for taking her in, and giving her work, and the bare bones of an education. Even though he'd never wanted her to feel thus, he knew it was inevitable, for had he ever been able to exorcise those same feelings from his own heart despite all Mr Walton said? Mr Walton had done for him, as he himself had done for Mena. And despite Mr Walton saying just as plainly, *'You owe me nothing, dear boy,'* he'd never been able to stop feeling as if he did.

So why hadn't he ever said anything to Mena? Why had he merely assumed, or rather, convinced himself she stayed of her own free will? At least once she'd got past those first tricky couple years and was able to go out on her own. Why hadn't he told her to take the money she made working for him, which he knew she rarely spent any of, and go? Why hadn't he told her when he'd given her even more means to be free? Because…

*Because I couldn't.*

Because he was a selfish coward. It felt good, no, it felt *exceptional*, and peaceful, and extraordinary, coming home to her. It felt natural, and *right*, and he loved it so much he couldn't put an end to it. He was addicted to her presence, to her being in his life, and…

It had gone on for far too long.

How many years already had she wasted, standing steadily beside him, never asking for anything for herself? How many prospects might she have had? To marry, have children, open a shop of her own, or join a travelling players' troupe for all he cared? Whatever she wanted, she could have. The worst of it was he didn't even know what she might've wanted. In all these years, not once had he asked, what she wanted from her life. How despicable was that?

*Some friend you are.*

Well, no more. This…realisation was, as the French were wont to say, the drop that made the glass spill over. So he loved her. Was *in* love with her. That meant letting her, *pushing her*, to be whatever she wished, wherever she wished, with whomever she wished.

*Which should never be me.*

No. It shouldn't ever be him. For…he didn't deserve her. He didn't deserve…*that*, love, from anyone. A life of love, or marriage, of passion or even companionship, as others had—had never been, and would never be, for him. His vow, his purpose, his business, were his life. Because beyond this whole idiocy of the past eight years, ignoring Mena's wants and desires and dreams, there was the matter of his past. Of who he truly was, what he'd been, and could never escape. Those things which had leapt to the forefront of his mind when he'd realised his feelings for her just now.

So no. Loving Mena was not an option. He was done being a selfish lily-livered dastard. It would tear him to shreds, he knew, letting her go. It would perhaps be the hardest thing he ever did, for even the thought made him feel as if sulphurous burning claws were tearing into his flesh. Yet he would do it.

*And soon, for if not—*

'Freddie?' Mena said loudly, and he rocked slightly in his chair, her voice a resounding slap bringing him yet again back to the kitchen, and her. He blinked a few times, clearing his eyes from the unwelcome visions forming therein, and forced a smile. 'Are you certain you're well?' she asked, concern darkening her gaze again.

'Making plans now that I've returned,' he said, unwilling to lie, and unwilling to say yet again that he was *tired*. She would know he was lying—they both knew each other well enough now to read each other, even if it felt that after all this time, perhaps they didn't know each other at all.

*And whose fault is that, Sir I-Won't-Talk-About-the-Past? Or anything at all of import?*

'Apologies for getting distracted and neglecting this delicious meal of yours.'

He made a good show of returning to his meal, even helping himself to a fresh slice of spelt bread.

'You don't have to apologise, Freddie,' she shrugged. 'Only you seem a bit… Well, it doesn't matter,' she concluded, though he could tell it mattered quite a lot, and she was merely humouring him. 'Actually, my question relates to your thoughts. Making plans, I mean,' she specified, almost… *Awkwardly?* As if she were trying not to show whatever was coming was important to her—as she had when she'd brought the mongrel currently warming his feet home from who knew where, and declared *she wouldn't be so very disappointed if he did not agree to let the beast stay.* 'Will you be here for Christmas?' she asked finally, staring down at her empty bowl.

'Of course,' he said without thought. 'Where else should I be?'

'I thought perhaps you might go with your friends again, to the North. You've not seen them since summer.'

*Ah.*

A valid question, he supposed. The friends she spoke of, the Marquess and Marchioness of Clairborne, the marquess's sister, Lady Mary, along with the Earl and Countess of Thornhallow, were perhaps the best friends he had—other than Mena, and one or two of his fellow shipping men. Over the years since he'd first met Mary, he'd become part of their circle, their family, largely thanks to the lady, who knew he could benefit from such associations, and over time, he'd been witness to many private things.

Then three years ago, on Mary's *and* Mena's urging, he'd joined the Spencer family at Clairborne House for Yuletide—in fact, it was the year he'd first met William Reid of Thornhallow, and the housekeeper who would be his wife. He couldn't deny he considered them close friends—though rather reluctantly. Like everyone, he kept them at arm's length. Though now he was returned, he should gather some news. He would check the pile of post which would be waiting for him, as always, on his desk, later.

Back to the point.

Which was that no, he would not be anywhere but at Holly Street for Yuletide.

*Particularly not if it is to be our last one together.*

'No, Mena,' he told her softly, ensuring he caught her eye before giving her a smile. 'We shall have Christmas together, you and I.' All hesitancy and tension disappeared instantly from her, and she smiled broadly. 'And those are plans, I believe, we should discuss.'

'Yes, we should,' she agreed, though something was…*off*. She rose, clearing their dishes, replacing them with dessert plates, and her rather dark apple tart. 'In the next few days,' she offered, serving them, with some difficulty as the knife refused to leave the burnt caramel. 'As you say, you had a long journey, and we should speak properly when you are rested.'

'As you wish.'

Something wasn't quite right with that excuse, but Freddie let it lie.

Because he realised she was right. They needed to speak, *properly*, soon.

So he resolved that, after this Christmas, he would say all he had to, and let her go.

*It is for the best.*

# Chapter Five

*December 29th, 1823*

The tantalising scents of roast meat and carrots met Mena's nose as she carefully made her way downstairs. She wasn't entirely sure how long she'd been abed; only vague memories of sounds, of sensations like the trickle of cool water or warm broth down her throat, remained. It must've been days, going by the shaky languor in every muscle, and the odd, rested feeling in her bones, the daze of her mind.

What she knew for certain was that she'd grossly overstayed her welcome.

When Mr Walton had taken her in, the offer was clear. One night, and then she would be on her way. It had been more than generous, and even if she'd slept the night through with her trusty knife clenched in her fingers, just in case, she'd slept the night through. She'd had food, and even clean, warm clothes, a blanket, and a fire. She'd felt safe, for a whole night, and in the morning, she'd been ready to go.

Only, he hadn't let her. Not in a bad way. Quite the contrary. He'd fetched and cooked a hearty breakfast.

Then, he'd given her a parcel of new clothes, well, new to her and more than serviceable. After a delivery of furniture, a doctor had come by to see to her, and after that, a full bath of warm water, all for her, had been waiting. With each gesture, he'd mumbled things like *'Couldn't have that'* or *'Might as well,'* as if his kindness was reluctant, not inherent, though she knew it was. It was in his eyes.

It was what had told her that she *would* be safe. Some might think because he was handsome, and well put together, that he would be safe, but Mena had met the very worst of men who were such. No, his eyes had told her the truth.

*He is kind.*

Except she'd abused that kindness. The second night, he'd grumbled, *'Christmas, can't have you wandering the streets,'* and told her to stay until St Stephen's. And what had she done? Gone and slept well through it. When she'd woken, and realised, she'd, as hastily as possible, risen, washed, and dressed in her new clothes—not that she had a choice as he'd burned her old ones. Now, no matter how tempting those scents, she would say *thank you*, and take her leave as she should've long ago.

Even if it was the last thing she wished to do.

'Good morning,' Mr Walton said when he saw her, smiling in a way that made her silly heart flip about like a floundering fish. 'Or good evening. Whichever you prefer.'

'Good evening, Mr Walton,' she smiled back, careful to say each syllable best she could.

'Freddie, please,' he ordered, bending to remove that juicy, fragrant roast from the fire. 'Why are you wearing your coat?'

'I've overstayed me—*my*—welcome. 'Pologise for that. Won't bother you no—*any*—longer.'

'You can't go. I mean—blast. You can't leave now, it's night and I've made dinner, and it would be foolish. Unless you truly wish to go?'

He looked up at her hesitantly, as if he were as scared of her leaving as she was to.

Mena shook her head, and he relaxed.

'Good, sit, please.'

'I can 'elp—'

'Nonsense,' he said, waving her off. 'Just take off your coat, and we shall eat. I hope it will be all right; I wasn't sure you'd be ready for a full meal,' he rambled on as she did as instructed. 'Thought it would keep though, and I hoped you'd be up soon enough. The doctor said you needed rest, and lots of hearty food when you returned to us.'

He cleared his throat, and frowned, as if confused by his own words.

Shaking it off, he cut the meat, served them both healthy portions, along with some ale, then he sat down at the head of the table to her right.

They both tucked in quietly, Mena taking her time, slowly cutting and chewing each piece lest she make herself ill. Besides, she wanted to savour it; do it justice, not shovel it into her waiting belly. That never ended well, and food lasted longer when eaten slowly. Something she'd learned quickly. They ate in silence, a comfortable, gentle silence. When Freddie was finished, he pushed his plate away slightly, and steepled his hands.

Mena could feel his stare, and so she looked over, a question in her eyes.

'Philomena, I've been thinking.' At once, her heart

pounded, panic rising, as her meal sloshed in her belly. 'I think you should stay, here.'

*What?*

'What?'

'Is there something or someone waiting for you?' Freddie asked, raising a brow, and Mena flushed, dropping her eyes. 'I didn't think so. And I can't… Thrust you back out into the streets. So you should stay. If you want to stay. Would you like to stay?'

Hope soared in her breast, and she stared up at him.

He seemed to mean it—again, almost as concerned with how she would answer as she was.

'I would,' she admitted.

'Good,' he smiled, nodding. 'We'll speak in the morning, I have some work to finish,' he said, rising and clearing his plate. 'Take your time, I'm just anxious to get on. But you should know, Mena. *Philomena.* My offer is not without…strings,' he added seriously, stopping at the door. 'I think we can come to an arrangement that benefits us both. If you stay, you will have to pay your way.'

'I understand,' she said quietly.

Satisfied, he strode out, bounding up the stairs.

The hope in Mena's breast hadn't died, only, it had dimmed. For she understood, and she might've known that no matter what, he was still a man, and no different to any other that had offered her a bed, or a meal. She might've known there was no such thing as charity without selfishness, and his offer didn't bother her so much as her own temporary delusion, which she would blame on exhaustion.

After all, it wouldn't be the first time she would enter into such an agreement. Hopefully, it would be more… permanent. Maybe, she would be safe, for a little longer, the winter through, and he was handsome enough.

The kindness in his eyes was still there, and perhaps that meant this experience could be…good. She'd never balked at doing what she had to to survive, and just because she'd thought for a moment—

*Well, never mind.*

Though, she wouldn't wait until tomorrow to seal their deal. She would go to him tonight and prove that she could be good. That she could pay her way and earn her keep.

*Best not to wait.*

Exhausted, Freddie rubbed his eyes with the back of his hand, aware of the grime on his fingers. He should feel satisfied, having worked well into the night, scrubbing, and clearing out the old to make room for the new. Hard work usually did that—gave him a pleasant sense of having made good use of the day, good use of his life. But tonight, he just felt… Weary.

With a sigh, he rolled his shoulders, picked up the candle, nearly to its end anyway, and called it a night, even if he knew there would be no sleep in his immediate future. If he was honest with himself, which, he typically tried to be, he knew where his weariness came from. Not the work, not the house.

*Her. Philomena.*

And the trouble his own mouth had got him into. His own sense of responsibility. His own need, really, if he was, again, honest with himself. The deal they'd struck earlier—he hadn't wanted to make it. He hadn't ever pictured having someone *helping him,* being part of this endeavour. This was his goal—no one else's. But then, faced with the prospect of her leaving, of being alone, when he could have *someone…* It chafed.

Why, now that was an excellent question, and one he

could certainly spend hours contemplating, not that it would change anything, since the deal was struck, and he was a man of his word, and—

'What the everlasting Hell are you doing?' Freddie exclaimed when he opened the door to his room and saw what awaited him there.

Philomena, dressed in nothing but a thin blanket.

She jumped slightly, but to her credit recovered quickly, standing strong, and undeterred, in whatever she was doing.

Freddie strode over to the washstand, and poured some water into the basin, hoping that she would just go away, leave through the door he'd purposely left open. He wasn't sure what she was thinking, but actually, he was glad of this. Tomorrow, it would give him an excuse to be rid of her—he couldn't have this, he didn't need a woman latching onto him—

The tiny rustle and thump tore him away from his grim thoughts and vigorous ministrations.

*Dammit.*

She hadn't left.

Instead, she'd let the blanket fall, and Freddie drew in a deep breath.

'I know I ain't much, sir,' she said quietly. 'But t'others made due. I won't disappoint, promise.'

*What?*

'What?'

Freddie frowned.

He studied her for a long moment, careful to keep his eyes on hers as he tried to make sense of her words. Even though he tried not to look, it wasn't as if he couldn't see. She was right in a way—she wasn't much, but only because she'd been bloody starved, and ill. She was beautiful, only a fool wouldn't notice, especially in the warm candlelight, but harrowed by life, and unwell. What was she thinking? Trying to seduce him when she'd only been able to rise out of bed this evening, after three days of being barely conscious, of him having to pour water and broth down her throat?

It wasn't even as if she seemed *truly interested*. She was unyielding, yes, strong, and determined, but she was *pushing* herself to be strong, to do this, and there was no heat, no interest, in her eyes. Just…

*Resignation.*

And then her words hit him.

*The others.*

He cursed for a good long while, shoving his fingers through his hair. What an idiot he'd been. He'd never thought she'd take his words thus. But then again, until just now, he'd never thought of what else she might've faced before she'd arrived on his doorstep.

It made him want to go punch his way across the country, but instead he drew in another calming breath, and slowly strode to her.

'Philomena…' he said as gently as he could, crouching down to retrieve the blanket. He slid it over her shoulders and held it tight across her chest when she refused to take hold. Tears gathered in her eyes, and she cast them down. 'Please don't cry,' he breathed, sweeping his thumb across her cheek.

'I don't want to go,' she whispered, looking up at him, desperation in her eyes now. 'I can be good, I promise,' she added, taking a step closer.

'Mena, please,' he said, his hand on her cheek a little firmer. 'I am not rejecting you because of what you look like. I am not going to throw you out because you are not to my taste.' He didn't add that in *very* different circumstances, he wouldn't hesitate to seduce *her*. 'I am sorry I was unclear; I should've told you precisely what I meant, but I knew you were tired, and I had so much work… I never imagined…' He shook his head and relaxed slightly, seeing that his words *'I won't throw you out'* had penetrated her haze of desperation. He swept away a rogue tear and stepped back when he felt her take hold of the blanket. 'I see I'd best explain, so if you would… Put something on, I will meet you downstairs in the front parlour.'

Mena nodded slowly and slipped away.

Freddie finished washing himself, then grabbed a new candle and went downstairs. It wasn't long before Mena joined him, standing uneasily at the doorway, as he leisurely paced the room.

'I intend to open a shop,' he said after a moment, letting his imagination once again fill the room, so he could see it as it would be, hoping that through his eyes, she could see it too. 'Filled with luxurious wonders from around the world. A place of exquisite rarities, crafted by independent, and free, tradesmen. I mean for it to be a success, and I hope to build a shipping business from it. I have spent years developing contacts across the globe, and I have a ship currently on its way from America. In time, I intend for there to be a hundred. Or perhaps, only twenty,' he chuckled. He glanced at Mena, just visible in the gloom, the rays of light from his candle catching the glint of her wide eyes, and now relaxed shoulders. 'Only time will tell, I suppose. When I said, rather stupidly, that if you stayed, I would have you pay your way, I meant only that I would ask you to help me. Build this place.'

Mena stepped forward cautiously, not afraid of him, but perhaps wary of all he offered.

'Not sure I can 'elp,' she said quietly, glancing at the

walls as if she truly *could* see all he'd imagined there. 'Don't know numbers, and can't read.'

Ah, so it was her usefulness or rather lack thereof she was wary of.

'That is remedied easily enough,' he shrugged. 'We have time. There is much to do before the shop is near ready, and the ship on its way only has bulk cargo. There will be a few more voyages before it returns with stock to get us started.'

'Y'd teach me? Writin' and numbers?'

'Yes.'

*As Mr Walton taught me.*

She stood before him, watching him closely for a long moment, before turning her gaze to the floor, a slight frown appearing. When she met his eyes again, the frown was still there, along with a question.

The same she'd posed before.

'Why? Why would you do tha' for me?'

'It's not for you I would be doing it,' he lied. 'I had planned on hiring. You... *Our* paths crossed, and perhaps there is a reason for that. It will be hard work, Mena. Once this place is in order, not only would I ask you to take on the shop, but also this household. I shall be gone often, but when I am here, I would ask you take care of all that for me. And I imagine I shall have to entertain, so there is that to consider. It is a lot, I ask.'

'Ain't afraid o' 'ard work.'

'Very well, then,' he smiled, offering out his hand. 'We have a deal?'

Smiling slowly, she took his hand, and shook it, with the same strength and determination he realised then was as deeply woven into the fabric of her being as it was in his.

'About earlier...' he began once they'd released each

other. Her cheeks coloured, and she looked ready to bolt, shame in her eyes. But this was precisely what he didn't want. 'There is nothing to be ashamed of,' he said firmly, and surprise flickered in the now dark blue depths. 'Your life, your body, are your own. The only shame belongs to anyone who leveraged a roof, or a meal, for anything.' She swallowed hard, and nodded.

*Bastards.*

'Though I now do the same... Regardless. Your choices are your own, and I will never judge you for them, you should know that. I have no right to judge anyone, with the sins I bear on my soul.' He clenched his jaw for a moment, pushing his past back down to the deepest recesses of his heart, where it belonged. He could see Mena's questions; but he couldn't allow her to voice them. Because if she did...

*I would answer.*

'But I also need you to know that you owe me nothing. You owe no one, anything. I never want you to feel as if you are trapped. By me, this place, anyone. You are under my protection, so I would hope that you would trust me should anything trouble you. At least in time, when we have come to know each other better.'

'Thank you,' she said softly, carefully enunciating her words, as if to prove something.

To herself, or him, he knew not.

He nodded, and she smiled softly, before turning to leave.

'Goodnight, Mena.'

'Goodnight, sir.'

Freddie remained, standing in the middle of the empty room, for a long time, his exhaustion gone, somehow feeling more settled despite the oddness of the night's events.

Though he'd made the deal hours earlier, now, it felt as if so much more had come to pass. As if much more than a deal had been struck. As if strange new bonds had been formed. As if, the final piece had been set; to seal his fate into being a *good* one, with some measure of happiness.

*Or perhaps exhaustion is becoming delirium now.*

Shaking his head, an amused smile on his lips, Freddie finally dragged himself back up to bed.

It didn't take him long at all to tumble into slumber, still smiling.

## Chapter Six

'Good morning, Susie,' Mena said brightly as she found the young woman waiting, as always, at the bottom of the stairs, well before she was due to start. The first day Susie had come to work, she'd waited outside for nearly three quarters of an hour—though thankfully it had been the end of summer then, and good weather. Susie smiled, her apple-like cheeks rosy with the cold, as perfect as a doll's.

She was a very fetching young woman, with the perfect, springy chestnut curls that people the world over sought to replicate with hot irons, and which Mena herself was not immune to jealousy over; a petite but strong figure, and gentle amber eyes. They'd first met at market about a year ago, when Susie had left her native Belgium because of the revolution. Susie had worked around the docks, in the kilns, in the inns, even selling eels, and over time they'd become friends as Mena constantly encountered her. And Mena didn't have very many of those. Freddie was her very best friend, and she was friendly with neighbours, some of the people who had helped her tend the shop, and locals. But true friends, who understood each other without needing to say much, well, those she hadn't really ever had at all.

Except for her brother and sister, but those days were long gone.

*That life is long ended.*

With Susie, it was an easy, uncomplicated rapport. And much like Mena, Susie had plans—dreams of something more than what others might declare her *'lot in life.'* After much needling, this summer, Mena had convinced her to come work in the shop, and that only after pleading that she absolutely needed the help so she could focus on her *other* endeavour. Susie had been instrumental with that too—the woman was a natural born negotiator, and wheedled many a bookcase, lot of linens, or repair from reluctant donors. She'd even been overseeing the project when Mena couldn't leave the shop.

Mena had no doubt that without Susie's help, she might never have been so close as she was now to fulfilling her dream.

'Good morning, Mena,' Susie said, slipping by, rubbing her wool-covered hands, as Mena closed and locked the door. 'How are you this morning?'

'Very good, thank you, and you?'

'Good, thank you.'

They glanced at each other, then started laughing.

Together, they made their way through the shop down to the kitchen, where Susie left her things, and where they now took tea together before starting the day.

'I think we sound very proper now,' Susie commented as she divested herself of her layers, extracting a jar from her pocket as she did. 'Though you always do,' she added, wrinkling her nose.

'I didn't always, and it's still a struggle some days,' Mena admitted.

She'd spent years training the country out of her words, learning to speak as a proper lady, so she could tend this shop, without shaming Freddie. And especially, so that no one, ever, could dismiss her simply on account of her *lack of breeding*. At least not at first hearing her speak.

Susie, on the other hand, had been trying to rid herself of the traces of her native French and Flemish, not because she was ashamed, but because she quickly realised that the British were the masters of judging based on language. So whenever they were together, they did their best to speak as those of, if not quite the *haut ton*, then those of the upper echelons of proper society.

*Look at us country girls, dreaming beyond our stations...*

'Is that what I think it is?' Mena asked as she set tea on the table, then served them, staring excitedly at Susie's jar.

'My marmalade?' Susie said both innocently, and smugly. 'Why, yes. Yes, it is.'

'Goddess—'

'Tut,' she interjected, tapping Mena's hand. ''Tis not for you. 'Tis for that master of yours. I had hoped to finally meet him.'

Grimacing and sticking out her tongue, Mena moved away from the jar dramatically. It wasn't her fault. The prized concoction of lime, lemon, orange, and spices was the best she'd ever tasted. And she didn't even like marmalade as a general rule.

With a sigh, she sat down, and stirred some milk into her tea.

'I had hoped so too,' she admitted.

It had been four days since Freddie had come home, and each day, he was up before she was, and out of the house before she was dressed. In the evenings, he returned well after supper, and if she hadn't known better, she might've thought he was avoiding her.

*If I didn't know better I'd think I was happy being ignored.*

If she was honest, she was glad he'd taken that decision out of her hands. Despite the chance she'd had the other night to come clean, tell him everything of her plans, she hadn't been able to. She'd used the excuse that he *did* seem tired, *off-kilter*, but in truth, it had been her own cowardice, her own fear of ruining what they had when he'd only just got back, that had kept the words firmly behind her teeth. She'd promised herself she would do it—speak to him of Christmas, and her plans—*all of them*—when they had both settled back into their routine, except there hadn't been a chance.

*Liar.*

So there had been chances, those times in the evening when he retired to his study before bed, when she might've knocked on the door, and been truthful with him. Yet every time she wandered by, stared at the light streaming from below the door, raised her hand to knock, something stopped her. She told herself she didn't want to bother him, but the cold hard truth was that, as always, she was *too bloody scared*. Even if she knew that, soon, she would need muster, if not courage, then at least some mindless nerve, and speak to him.

Only she couldn't help feeling that then everything would change—and not for the better.

*I could lose him.*

*Even if he isn't mine to lose.*

'You haven't told him yet,' Susie said, her mouth set in a disapproving pout, the wretched little mind-reader.

'I will,' she promised, with gaiety, and what she thought would pass as conviction. 'He's been busy.'

'Time waits for none of us, and you can't wait until Christmas to spring it on him.'

'I know, I do. I suppose I thought it would be easier,' Mena shrugged.

'No, you didn't.'

'No,' Mena chuckled. 'I didn't... But since we are on the subject, I'll be heading over there once the shop is open. I've not managed to go since he's come back.'

'Afraid of getting caught?' Mena stuck her tongue out again and Susie made as if to grab it. 'All was looking good yesterday, those who came in ill are starting to look better, and we have that delivery of books today.'

'Yes, of course.'

They'd been lucky, a circulating library near the Strand had gone out of business, and they'd managed to convince the owners to sell the lot for a very, *very*, fair price. They had everything from law manuals to lurid novels; all of which would be the perfect addition to their own fledgling library.

'Oh, the Cornish women on the fifth floor should be done with the curtains soon.'

'Perfect,' Mena smiled. 'I've that solicitor for the trust coming in next week; I should like to have it as close to finished as possible, so there is no doubt of our competence.'

'Ah yes, the very severe Mr Thurston,' Susie said, making a gently mocking, severe face to imitate the man who would, it was true, never be in fear of being called *jovial*. Still, he was excellent at his job, and one of the fairest, most objective men she'd ever met. Hence why he'd been chosen. In setting up the trust which would take care of the project, Mena had been *encouraged* to have a very particular set of by-laws and deadlines set in stone, to both measure the progress of the charity, and give something tangible back to the investors, so there was no doubt as to the uses of their money. 'We cannot disappoint him.'

'We won't,' Mena proclaimed. In her heart, she knew they wouldn't. 'Enough of work, how are you? How are the new rooms working out?'

'Good. Mrs Wilferry is a very interesting lady,' Susie said diplomatically. Mena knew of her reputation as a fierce but good-natured lodging house owner. 'She's promised to teach me how to make her fish pie.'

'How lucky you are. I hear that is a closely guarded secret.'

Susie preened a little, and they laughed.

They spoke a while longer, until their tea was finished, and it was time for the shop to open. Mena collected her things, and unlocked the door, leaving Susie in charge, whilst she headed off towards her new venture.

Promising herself, yet again, that she would tell Freddie.

*Soon.*

'That there's the last one, miss,' Tom, the retired stevedore who had led the charge of hauling up the crates, upon crates, of books that had been delivered, said as he dropped the last one before the mountains of others, tugging his forelock. Mena hadn't realised how much the small circulating library had possessed; she was quite sure her eyes had bugged out upon seeing the train of carts hauling them to the doors. And now, it looked as if a fortress had been erected inside the building.

Or rather, several fortresses, as they'd had to erect some minor castles in the adjoining offices, much to Josephine's dismay.

Luckily, Mena had an army to help her get them all on the shelves—some older children keen to make use of their recently acquired reading skills, and a group of younger ones who were currently sat at the windows, practicing their writing and art whilst making signs for the different sections.

'Thank goodness,' Mena smiled, nodding to the old stevedore. 'I don't think one more would've fit. Thank you, Tom. I'm not sure what we would've done without you, and please thank the others.'

'Aye, miss.'

With a nod, Tom left, and Mena turned to her army of little workers.

'Very well, then,' she proclaimed, hands on her hips, and they all stood a tiny bit straighter. 'Let's see how much we can accomplish in the next few hours. I shall begin unboxing, and then you bring them to the shelves they belong in. I've put some temporary cards on all of them until our artists finish their work. If you have questions, come find me. Many should be straightforward—but some of the novels I imagine will be tricky. Ready?'

'Yes!' they all shouted in unison, grinning widely.

'Huzzah!' Mena responded, smiling as she turned to the tower closest to the door.

Picking up the crowbar Tom had left, Mena wasted no time in opening one of the crates.

At once the smell of the books hit her, and she sighed contentedly. Setting aside the top, and moving the crate so the children could begin their task, she opened another, and whilst they were occupied, she took a moment to let the smell, the look and feel of them, seep into her. Running her finger along the spines, the excited chatter of the children behind her, she felt...*happy*.

So many had vaunted the power of books, but Mena, she felt it, to the very core of who she was. She was where she was today thanks to books. They had given her the most precious thing—an education—and a future. They had given her hope, taken her on adventures, and taught her who she was.

After she'd arrived on Freddie's doorstep, she'd been unable to leave the house for a long time. The world outside, the world she'd faced, had become too much. She'd discovered that in a rather inconvenient manner—when she'd tried to go fetch some dinner perhaps a fortnight after her arrival, and panicked. Unable to move, to breathe, even to see, she'd been stuck, crouching behind a poor grocer's stall for who knew how long, before she'd been able to breathe the words *Freddie Walton* and *Holly Street*. Someone had fetched him, and he'd carried her home.

After that, there had been no excursions, not for some months, and then, slowly, step by step, with Freddie beside her, she'd managed to make it out the door again. Still, every day it was a struggle, and any time she went somewhere unfamiliar, it was a trial. It had taken years for her to understand how she'd gone from someone who lived as she had, faced what she had, to someone who couldn't turn a doorknob. And then, she'd understood, with the help of books, and quiet contemplation, that when Freddie had taken her in, she'd found a safe harbour. And when faced with leaving that, her mind and body had balked.

It had cost her much over the years, but she lived with that side of herself in peace now. Thanks again, to the books. Ones Freddie brought her; ones she found. Through the pages, she had lived countless lifetimes, seen as many different horizons as Freddie. She'd often followed his progress around the world with books; reading of the places he visited, and going there with him, in spirit at least. The characters and authors were her friends, her companions on dark and lonely nights. So yes, she *felt* the power of books.

And they were a gift she was honoured to be able to give to others.

*Well, you won't be giving it to anyone unless you get a move on.*

*Quite so.*

Brushing aside the bittersweet meanderings, she got to it, *properly.*

On they went for hours, unboxing their haul, the children asking for help on where to put things, or coming to show her their work, until the sound of running feet caught Mena's ear.

A young girl, Fortuna, stood panting at the door, a glint of anger in her eyes.

*'El padre está aquí.'* The priest is here.

Cursing silently, her blood boiling, Mena nodded, and wasted not one moment heading downstairs.

Within moments, she was at the front door, where a crowd had gathered as they watched the literal scene the man was creating on their doorstep, though he was careful to remain on the public road.

*El padre* in question was the fervent, fire and brimstone devotee leader of the nearby Church of St Catherine, who thought it his Christian duty to oppose Mena's work. They'd had a few confrontations before, one of Mena's least favourite things. Fight, disputes, of any kind, made her nerves nearly unbearable. Half the time, her mind would shut down, and she'd stand there too stunned to say anything at all, and the other half, she lost any sense of decorum, or even fair play.

Every incident with the priest had been of the latter sort, though as the encounters multiplied, she'd got better at not falling into the trap and behaving as he thought her—some *crazed servant of Lucifer*—and they'd had peace for a time as he went to shout his gospel elsewhere.

'And there she is, Satan's mistress,' the tightly buttoned-up middle-aged man shouted, waving the Bible above his head as he spotted Mena making her way through the crowd. As she did, she discreetly ushered away those who normally stood guard, knowing their intervention would only inflame matters. 'Keeper of this den of sinners, promising hope without God and the Light of the Redeemer.'

Determined to keep her wits about her, Mena took a deep breath, and shoved her shaking hands onto her hips as she faced him.

'If you have business,' she said to the gathered masses, 'I suggest you tend to it. If you wish to hear this man's sermons, you may head to St Catherine's this evening for the hour of six. If you wish simply for a spectacle, move along. And if you are here for aid, step inside and speak to Pawel.'

There was grumbling, and some whistling and applause, as the crowd thinned.

Father Bartholomew's eyes sought them out as they moved, desperation growing.

Those who kept watch moved back as she'd ordered, stood at their normal posts, and she nodded gratefully.

*This man is mine to deal with.*

'Do not set foot in that place of no morals,' he warned those who remained, as Mena approached him carefully. So much she'd faced to get here; she wouldn't let some small-minded ninny make her cower. 'You shall never achieve salvation!'

'I thought salvation available to any who prayed and sought redemption from the Lord,' Mena countered, her voice blessedly even despite the storm raging inside her breast. 'Or did I misunderstand that lesson?'

'You would not understand any lesson, Jezebel!'

'Ah, hadn't heard that one in a while, Father.'

'Others may think you an angel, but I see you for the devil-kissed witch you are, promising worldly comforts to those in need so you may seduce them with your immoral life.'

'How novel your insults, Father,' she smiled mockingly, standing before him now. She looked at him, *truly*, and saw someone as lost as she'd been once. The realisation prompted a change in tactics. 'If you took but a moment to set aside your preconceptions, you might find we both wish to help others. Though I may not espouse your beliefs, others do. I prevent no one from worshipping whatever they believe, and you might welcome more to your flock should you open your heart. We could help each other, should you choose to look past your prejudices. Christmas is nearly upon us, and is that not a time for us to gather, together, in love, and peace?'

For the briefest moment, Mena thought she might've got through to him.

Until his lip curled back in disgust, and he spat at her.

She couldn't move, couldn't breathe, not even to wipe it off where it had fallen upon her dress.

Tears burned her eyes, but she drew upon all the strength within her and stood tall.

'Burn in Hell, Salome,' the priest snarled, before taking himself, and his viciousness, away from her, and her refuge.

Only when he'd disappeared from the street did she manage to move, slowly extracting her handkerchief, wiping away the few tears which escaped, and that which he'd left upon her. She stood there a while longer, letting the wind whip around her, freezing her, but not as thoroughly as the *good father* had. She wished his words didn't affect her so, that his insults didn't cut so deeply. Not moments ago, she'd been *happy*. So excited; at peace. And now... Now, she felt *dirtied*. Angry, disgusted, and sad, yes.

It wasn't the first time she'd been called such names, nor would it be the last. Every time she found some good in this world, there was someone to snatch it away. Usually, she was able to cast insults off like pieces of dust. She knew who she was in her heart. She knew what she was doing here was good. She knew that some needed to tear others down to feel stronger. Only, today, somehow, she couldn't quite simply brush it all away.

Because today her demon of guilt wouldn't relinquish his hold on her heart. Despite all *she* preached—charity without strings—the truth was, she had selfish motives too. Father Bartholomew was right—she was no angel. Nichols House had been built for others; but also for herself.

*So you are mortal. Do not dimmish the good. 'Tis only tiredness making you weary.*

*The blossoming of new beginnings. The season.*

Indeed. This time of year was always… Full of bittersweet nostalgia and remembrance along with the joy.

*'Tis nothing at all.*

When vicious, sharp snowflakes began to fall, tumbling in cutting swirls, Mena finally went back inside, and did what she'd come here to.

*Build something incredible.*

## Chapter Seven

Over a week since his return, and Freddie still hadn't *properly* spoken with Mena. He hadn't even seen her, and it was tearing him apart. He missed her worse than when he was gone. Being faraway, knowing she was home in Holly Street, was a different breed of longing. It was an anchor, a port to return to. Even before this *love* business, he'd felt that pull. That invisible connection neither time nor space could sever. *This* longing… This was a pernicious, sharp, rusted thing that twisted his gut and heart.

It was having her, within reach, and denying himself her company. The pain, the regret he felt now, were his own doing, and he knew he was taking the coward's way out. The problem was, he couldn't trust himself to be in her presence. It was too easy. Too familiar, and he knew he would be tempted to let it all just go back to the way it was. Which would be wrong, on so many counts.

Standing at the windows of his office, overlooking the wharf and the river, murky, crowded sea of sails and masts that it was, Freddie felt a stranger in his own life. Countless times over the years, he'd stood here, survey-ing his creation, watching it morph from a run-down set of buildings to the very epitome of modernism, the beating heart of his enterprise. He'd built it, if not in his own image, in the image of what he believed man could be. In the image of the man who'd taught him all the good he knew.

It was a place of fairness, and safety, of new ideas, and efficiency.

The newest inventions and systems dominated the wharf that had existed since before the city exploded and grew. His men were paid fairly, actually in his employ, not simply pulled in from the nearby inns for a day's labour, and though they worked hard, they were not *overworked*. He wasn't the first to do so, others downriver had, before he'd even come here; but he hoped adding his own example might inspire even more in the future.

Once, looking down at the efficient hive below, he'd felt a swelling of pride. Just as he had when he'd finally opened the shop. Or when he'd modernised the Holly Street house, mostly, yes, for Mena's comfort. But now, he felt betrayed, somewhat, by his heart. Because of his heart, because of what it had done—*fall in love*—he felt more at sea than he ever had in the most volatile, horizon-less seas.

For a time, he'd felt a sense of belonging. With Mena, in Holly Street; here, among his men, or the other owners such as he; even with Spencer, Mary, or Reid. He'd felt he'd found a place, where he could, if not rest, *be*. He'd found friends, and a purpose, but now... He felt at a loss of what to do. There were things he *needed* to do, and things he *should* do, only he couldn't quite bring himself to do them. Because doing them would mean *changing* everything. And right now, he was just...*tired*. Unsure he had the strength to do all he must.

It didn't help that, every day, the gnawing pit in his

stomach, *telling* him that time was running out, that
prickling at the back of his neck as if he were being
constantly watched, were growing worse.

He *should* be making plans to grow his business further; only he couldn't seem to even think on ways to do
so. That feeling he'd had upon returning, that his business didn't really need him, still troubled him. He felt
adrift, no wind in his sails, powerless to change course.
At least he'd managed to deal with the pressing letters
from solicitors, banks, and partners; the bare minimum
to keep everything in his well-oiled machine running.

*The bare minimum. How proud you should be.*

He needed to speak, or at the very least, write to his
friends. He'd had a stack of letters from Spencer, and
a few from Reid. The former sending news of his wife,
his stepdaughter, his mother, his life. Asking for news
in return. Asking for a visit. Telling him to come by
his London home when Freddie returned, before they
left for Yuletide. The latter, also sending morsels of
news of his wife and babe, along with enquiries about
investing in Walton Shipping. Some notes, from Mary,
simply too, asking for news and a visit.

But what was he to say to them? Not that he said
very much generally; they had pleasant conversations
about everything and anything, but right now, he had
no desire for small talk. Rather, he felt the terrible and
unfulfillable urge to speak as he never had. To lay all of
it, his sorry tale, his current predicament, every doubt,
every fear, every sin, at their feet, and ask for counsel.
He couldn't; he knew that. Friends though they may be,
a witness to some of their most private happenings he
may have been, the truth was, he was scared. Scared of
losing their good opinion, and their friendship. It wasn't
that he didn't trust *them*, it was that he didn't trust *any-*

*one* with his tale. Didn't trust anyone not to repudiate him; upon hearing his own story he wouldn't be able to do anything but cry *foul*.

Which brought him right back to Mena.

The most vital thing on his list, for his silence was preventing them both from living. These past days, living in that house, but not allowing himself to see or speak to her, for fear of begging for her love, begging her to stay and sacrifice a future beyond him… He'd had too much time, to think, to remember. He'd thought it might help, to identify the moment when he'd fallen in love with her. He'd thought, if he could, he could perhaps kill it and allow them both to move on. Only he hadn't found *it*. Every day, every night, he'd thought on the past, on all they'd shared—and hadn't. And rather than find answers, he'd found more questions.

*What happened to Mena's family? How did she come to be in London?*

He knew bits—that they were gone, that she was alone, that she'd come here—but no more. Why hadn't he ever asked? How many times had they sat in that parlour, or kitchen, together? And he'd never thought to ask? Just as he'd never asked why she kept her hair short. Why she didn't like Keats even.

*Because you thought you could keep her at arm's length.*

*Avoid…this very entanglement.*

All that time, wasted with talk of the business, of their days, of food even. *That* small talk meant more to him than a thousand meaningful conversations; still, why had he thought that a lack of meaningful would preserve distance? He'd fallen nonetheless, and now he felt *cheated*. As if he'd had a chance at something, and let it slip through his fingers. A chance to truly know her, though he knew her heart, and it was incredible, but he wanted to know it all, and—

*There is still time. A little time.*

Yes, perhaps there was. He couldn't end it, not like this. Not…at this time of the year. Their season.

*One last season together. One last Christmas to keep me warm for life.*

A deadline. Those were good. He would set himself the New Year as the deadline for this. He would enjoy as much of this season with Mena as he could, lap up her warmth and presence as if he were shoring up water to traverse the desert, and he would ask his questions, and get to know her, *properly*, and then, he would…

*Let her go.*

A solid plan. It would be a trial, it would hurt, to be with her, and remain silent, but this whole business of staying away was surely worse. And if these were to be their last together, well, he could ensure they would be memorable ones.

*Days to last a lifetime.*

'Ah, there he is! Finally, Marshall, you found him!' cried a slightly worse for wear Spellman, much louder than he needed to, even to be heard above the din of the dockside tavern. Freddie waved vaguely and forced the hint of a smile to his lips as he surveyed the private dining room filled with the pack of wolves that were his fellow men of shipping.

Ship owners, company owners, some agents, and builders too; all men that made up a circle of his *associates*. At least insomuch as he associated with them— apart from Marshall, an agent he sometimes worked with, the one who had dragged him here to begin with when all Freddie really wished to do was make good on his resolution and go *home*—he didn't really work with any of them. He wasn't really sure what to call them, he thought vaguely as he went round the room, shaking hands and nodding his head majestically, or importantly, or whatever it was he was doing.

Technically, he supposed most should be called *competitors*, as most of them ran companies like his. Then there were those who ran businesses concurrently, merely men of the same general trade. But even those technically considered *competitors*, well, that wasn't quite right. Because Freddie, not to crow, had worked hard to ensure his business was, *unique*. With his rigid rules for those he did business with, that which he shipped, and where he shipped it to. He, unlike others, didn't simply ship anything in large quantities indiscriminately from and to anywhere. It was a constant source of jest and sometimes jealousy.

Settling down in a vacant seat in the quieter corner by the window, Freddie nodded at the man across from him as Marshall disappeared, then reappeared to slap a tankard of ale in front of him.

'Henderson,' Freddie greeted. A man slightly younger than he, with fair hair, eyes, and skin, he was jovial, and well-natured, if at times bumbling. Though he was generally as mild-mannered as Freddie, tonight he seemed to be, as the others, past tipsy. His cheeks had taken on a bright red hue, and his eyes were slightly glassy. 'How are you this evening?'

'Rather well,' Henderson smiled, raising his glass. They toasted, as Marshall luckily settled a few seats down to enjoy the livelier conversation, his purpose apparently fulfilled. 'Business is steady enough, there are a host of parties this winter, and I am to be married in the spring.'

'Congratulations are in order, then,' Freddie said, raising his glass for another toast. 'Who is the lucky woman?'

'Northerner. Mill-owner's daughter. Miss Tweed or Miss Field or something equally as telling,' Henderson laughed; Freddie refraining.

Not solely on behalf of the man's fiancée, but also because he was shocked; he'd never seen Henderson so casually cruel.

*Perhaps the drink simply brings out the worst in him. As it does in many.*

'Not a love-match, then.'

'Certainly not,' Henderson scoffed. 'Mother found her. She'll do quite well; she's charming and all she should be.'

'He means she has buckets of money!' Spellman cried from the other end of the table, and everyone erupted into laughter. Spellman reached for some cheese hidden amongst the remnants of drink and tossed a piece into his mouth. 'And don't let Henderson fool you, his coffers need it, or didn't he tell you about those ships he lost in the storm last month?'

Freddie glanced at Henderson, who was currently grinding his teeth, seething into his cup.

'We all suffer losses at some time or other,' Freddie said placatingly, raising a brow as he surveyed the table. They could laugh of Henderson's misfortune, but he knew every man at this table had lost a ship, workers, or even partnerships. 'What matters most is how we continue,' he added, giving Henderson a meaningful glance.

'We heard you lost a valuable supplier in America,' Royston, an older owner who specialised in timber, said, a knowing and rather mocking smile on his lips.

'Rather, I decided to end our partnership as our principles had diverged.'

'It is a wonder you still have anyone to do business with, Walton,' Spellman agreed. 'With your morals getting in the way of so many excellent opportunities.'

'I shouldn't think them excellent if it means doing business with people who merely profit from the misfortune of others,' Freddie bit back, bitterly, his anger shining through despite himself.

'Yes, well, not all of us can have your rigid morals, Walton,' Royston sneered.

'I don't ask anyone to share my philosophies. But the world is changing. Those who refuse to change with it will find themselves as many before them: remnants of the past.'

The room quietened for a long moment, the only roar that of the public rooms and streets below.

Unwilling to sour their evening further, Freddie turned to the window, allowing them all to return to their idle chatter.

*Why on earth did I allow myself to be dragged here?* he wondered, staring down at the huddled masses, trudging through dusty white muck.

The world was down there. People from every walk of life, every corner of the world. And here… Why *had* he come? It was always the same. Inane talk of the weather, finance, speculation, and then this taunting of his own practices. Had it always been this way? Or had he not noticed, because when he'd first met them, he'd been trying to make connections, and learn everything he could of the city. He remembered too; they would speak of progress, of innovation.

*No more, it seems.*

Perhaps he was simply soured because he wished to be elsewhere.

'You seem far away, Walton,' Henderson said gently. He still cradled his cup, but it hadn't been touched since Freddie had last looked, and somehow the man seemed sobered now. 'Are you well?'

'Quite well.'

'I don't mean to be cruel,' Henderson said, looking down at his cup, contrite. 'Only somehow... I thought my choices might mean I would have freedom.'

'You still do,' Freddie remarked, leaning in slightly, to keep their conversation from the others. Not that he needed to, the others well involved in their revelry, but he sensed Henderson meant for this to be as private a conversation as it could. 'Marriage to an heiress will replenish the coffers, but there are other ways.'

'There is failure.'

'There is... A moment of lesser success,' Freddie shrugged. 'It would require sacrifice, and years of rebuilding, but it is possible. How many did you lose?'

'Nearly three hundred souls.'

Henderson's reply wrenched Freddie's heart; the mere fact that he responded in that way told him all he needed to know about the man.

As did the guilt in his eyes. Once, Freddie had lost a crew of nearly a hundred in a storm, some five years back. He remembered that pain, that weight, well. The only thing that had got him through, had been Mena.

*Always Mena.*

'A passing ship found a boat with twenty men, from one of the wrecks, some three days later. All others were lost, including my best captains.'

'You took care of the families?'

'Of course.'

'That's all there is to do; believe me I know. It is a dangerous business we are in. All we can do is keep the ships in order, and make sure we hire the most capable men to run them. Beyond that… The sea is a violent, vicious mistress.'

'Never stopped you from going off, did it?'

'Always with the knowledge I might not return.'

Henderson nodded, and leaned back in his chair, glancing out the window.

'One day soon, you'll have to give it up.'

'How so?' Freddie frowned.

'When you marry, I shouldn't think your wife would appreciate you being so careless with your life. And with an alignment such as yours, there are expectations beyond what will even be required of me.'

Freddie stared at the man for a moment, dumbfounded.

Apparently he was going to be married?

*I should've thought my knowledge of the matter might've been a prerequisite.*

'Henderson, what the Devil are you on about?'

The man looked about as equally confused for a moment.

'I'd thought… That is… Well, there are rumours.'

*Mary. Of course.*

He might've been used to this too—only he hadn't realised things had got so far. People were always thinking an alignment between Freddie and Lady Mary Spencer was only a matter of time. Apparently the world couldn't comprehend, or countenance, friendships between unmarried men and women.

*Something else to deal with…*

'I'm not getting married,' Freddie hissed, careful not to be overheard. The last thing he needed was to give the fools more fodder. 'Not now, not ever, and certainly not to Lady Mary.'

'Sorry,' Henderson mumbled.

'Marshall and Spellman are determined bachelors, why does no one pester them?'

Sighing, Freddie turned back to the window.

'What about becoming a broker?' he offered after a moment, a gesture of goodwill. It wasn't Henderson's fault after all that rumours spread like wildfire; and that he was in a grim mood to begin with. 'You have the skills, the knowledge, the contacts. You could sell the company, lease a warehouse—like that one, where is it…? A few streets north of my wharf? After a few years, you could start a new company if you wish.'

Henderson blinked at him, looking…

*Panicked?*

Quirking his head, Freddie studied him, wondering what the man had against becoming a broker, especially if it saved him from what sounded a less than enticing match in any regard but money.

'That warehouse is let,' Henderson squeaked after a moment. *Literally* squeaked. Shifting, he cleared his throat, and began again. 'The warehouse is let.'

'Then another,' he said slowly, still wondering what it was about that warehouse that threw the man off-kilter.

'I'll think on it, thank you,' Henderson smiled, and Freddie nodded.

He remained with them all for a short while longer, until the noise, the inanity, and the heat of the room became too much to bear.

Unfortunately, by the time he made it back to Holly Street, his return slowed by the rather peculiar evening, Mena had already retired. So, he ate the portion of roast and carrots she'd left for him, feeling lonelier than he had in a very, very long time.

It was made worse for the fact that he knew, soon, his life would be even emptier.

## Chapter Eight

Time was running out for her to tell Freddie everything. She felt it, as a tangible thing, sand in an hourglass, slipping through her fingers; the ticking of the clock in the parlour upstairs remorselessly chipping away at this great big thing called *time*. Nine days until Christmas Eve, and with every passing hour, it was becoming not only harder to conceal it all in practice, but, also, in her heart. Her excuses—that he was always home late, that she barely saw him—were naught but that. And they too were running out.

*Deluded coward.*

That was what she'd allowed herself to become. As a girl, she'd never been afraid. Even when she'd had to face the world head-on, alone, she'd been fearless. Some might say because she had nothing left to lose, only she had. She'd had life, and though it was hard, she hadn't ever truly wished to end it. Even throughout the darkest of circumstances, she'd had a will, a hope, which she knew were things not everyone had. Perhaps, given the chance, she might've lost all that too; but she'd been lucky, and not reached that point. Freddie had taken her in before she might.

Ironically enough, that is when the fear had come to live with her, a constant companion. When she'd found safety, and security, *that* is when her greatest burden had come, taken her by the hand, and prevented her from doing so much. Paralysed her. For so long, she'd been living, but not truly lived.

Until she'd learned to accept that demon of hers, slowly, with help, and patience, and kindness to herself. She'd not conquered the fear; however, she'd not been ruled by it. Now… Now, she was again.

Fear, of all that might happen, once she told him. In her mind, she could picture only the worst. The recriminations, the disappointment. The uninterest even, or the vile words others might shout pouring from Freddie's mouth. Though she knew him, knew the kind of man he was, she couldn't help imagining those terrible futures, because she knew, that in the end, it would be an end. And that terrified her most of all.

Where once her love for him had comforted, bolstered her, given her courage, and strength, now… It felt corrupted. As if her own selfish heart had corrupted it. Because her greatest shame—the secret she dared not even voice most days to herself—was that part of the reason she'd built Nichols House had been to prove she was deserving of *his* love. To show herself, that perhaps, a shared love wasn't such an impossible dream, but that if she could only become the sort of woman who built incredible things as he did, there would be a chance. If she could be his equal, perhaps he wouldn't go off and build a life, a family, with another. She would be a worthy opponent to the woman who, if he married her as the entire town seemed to think he would, bring him prestige, and connections.

It was twisted, and despicable, and she hated herself

for it; only it was the truth. It lived in that dark, hellish little corner of her heart along with the jealousy she couldn't ever quite rid herself of for the woman who would, in time, be Freddie's wife.

*Lady Mary.*

The Marquess of Clairborne's sister, with whom Freddie had been friends since the first time she'd come to the shop, four years ago. She still remembered that day perfectly.

Autumn, November. A gold, glittering sun streaming in through the windows, packed with crystal sets. This paragon of English beauty had stepped in, so bright, and delicate herself, sporting the most incredible dress of gold and burgundy silk and velvet. Mena herself had been blinded—so it had been no surprise that Freddie had too when he'd happened to come down for the account books.

The two had spoken a while, the woman's smile never fading; Freddie's neither. He'd walked with her around the shop, telling her everything there was to about every object therein. When finally it had come time for the woman to make her selection, she had, and paid, and been so *kind* to Mena. Not looked down at her; acknowledged her, even introduced herself. As Freddie had escorted her to the door, she'd heard Mary's promise to come again. And Mena's heart had twisted so brutally she'd barely been able to breathe. Because she'd known in that moment, the delusion she'd lost herself in, that it would be her and Freddie for ever, was over.

Lady Mary had returned a few times after, until she'd never come again, meeting Freddie in much more respectable, intimate places. Meanwhile, Freddie's business had become more than successful, growing until he was a leader in the trade. He had so many ideas for the future, for the business, for the industry. He would continue to rise. And to do so, he would need help. Connections. Marriage to a marquess's sister…would be a perfect match. Though Mena couldn't quite be *happy* for him, she was resolved. That all would be as it was meant to.

The worst of it all was, she *liked* the woman. She was beautiful, kind, and not at all superior, and—

Mena frowned, her thoughts startled from the self-destructive track they were on by Hawk's growling. She paused in her washing of the dishes, her hands stilling in the warm water, as she glanced over at him. He was at the top of the stairs, growling, and yipping angrily, all the hairs on his back raised.

A shiver passed through her, even as she told herself it was likely nothing but a rat.

'Hawk,' she called gently, but the dog did not move. 'Hawk!'

In answer, he barked shortly, and that shiver slithered down to her gut, pooling there, becoming uneasy dread.

'Hawk, what is it, lad?'

Another bark.

Mena glanced up at the windows, hoping to see something, whilst also dreading it. The moon, nearly full, illuminated the courtyard, but there was nothing. At this time of night, the only thing it could be was someone come to fetch help or who knew what, but then, they would knock, and make themselves known.

Another bark, sharper, and more viscous.

Though she really didn't want to, Mena knew she would have to look out there. Repeating that it was nothing at all—maybe another stray—she wiped her hands on a towel, and went up to meet Hawk, stepping back down a moment later to grab a knife, though she intently ignored the increasing thrum of her heart.

*'Tis nothing at all.*

'Hello?' Mena called, once again before the door. 'Is anyone out there?'

Nothing.

Grabbing hold of Hawk's collar with one hand, Mena awkwardly unlocked and opened the door whilst retaining hold of the knife with the other. A rush of frost and snow burst in when she did, but nothing else. Hawk sniffed the air, still growling, but not tearing off after anything either.

*No rats, no strays, no one.*

'Hello?'

Her voice echoed in the silent night, but nothing else.

'See, Hawk, there is nothing,' she reassured them both.

And for a moment, she was right, and felt better.

Until she began to shut the door, and then, there was a laugh. A chilling, harrowed thing. That was when she glanced down at the snow, and saw the footprints. Hawk tried to break free, barking madly, but she pulled him back, and slammed the door shut, hurriedly locking it, the knife tumbling to her feet in her bumbling, sweaty haste. She didn't know what that had been—*who* that had been—but it was nothing good. She could feel the malevolent intent, the unsettling and sickening intent to harm.

*Breathe.*

She did, leaning down to pet Hawk.

'It was nothing,' she told him. 'Nothing at all. It's gone.'

Except it wasn't.

Three raps sounded on the door above. Hawk slipped

from her grasp before she could stop him, bolting up the stairs, barking like mad. Mena took up the knife, and followed him, tripping and falling over her skirts, her own feet, and the steps, as she did. Flinging open the door to the shop Hawk was scratching at, she flew through it herself.

Together, they faced that great big, black door, which once had terrified her, but which tonight gave her protection, even in the darkness.

'Be gone, whoever you are,' she shouted through it, false courage lifting her. 'I'll have the Peelers here!'

There was another of those horrid, eerie, ghastly laughs, and then...

Silence.

Disturbing, full, and unyielding silence. Even Hawk was quiet, save for the deep sniffing at the bottom of the door. She wasn't sure how long she stood there, blood rushing in her ears, her heart pounding so thoroughly it felt as if it wasn't beating at all. Sweat pooling from every pore, the knife slipping in her grasp.

And then it was chaos.

Glass shattered. Hawk scratched and barked, growled and clawed, as Mena jumped, turning to the noise, retreating from the door back to the shop. Something large had been cast through the windows, with enough force to shatter them thoroughly.

*Bricks*, she thought stupidly, spotting them amongst the display of enticing treasures in the windows, now toppled, broken, and covered in glittering shards. Something small sailed past her head further into the shop, and though terrified of what she would find out there, Mena strained to see the street.

A lone figure stood not two feet from the window, cloaked, hooded, and wrapped in shadows as if born from them. Mena could feel hatred, and sick, demented joy, pouring off whoever it was, and she raised the knife.

The figure crouched, there was an odd scratch, and moments later, the demon raised a flaming jar. Mena glimpsed glittering dark pools, but nothing more before she jumped out of the way.

The jar flew in, sailing into the midst of the shop, as if slowed in time. It was almost beautiful, as it sailed across the room, spreading its slick contents in an arc before coming to shatter on a table of silks.

*No.*

The flames rose as if it were in fact a fiend who had cast them, and Mena knew she had mere moments before the entire house was engulfed. She raced to the parlour, Hawk's distressed cries underscoring her motions, grabbed some woollen blankets, and sped back out, trying to stifle the fire so she could go downstairs, and fetch some flour to fully extinguish it before it was too late.

Out of the corner of her eye she spied Hawk jumping onto the window.

'Hawk, no!' she screamed, even as he launched himself out of the hole after their attacker. Tears fell, her despair complete. 'No,' she cried, thinking of all that could happen to him.

The attacker would have no compunction in hurting him, and that was if he'd not hurt himself jumping out.

Mena had a choice then, to go after him, or quench the flames. She felt so alone, so desperately alone; powerless, and weak.

*But you are not.*

No. She would vanquish this evil, and once she saved this house, she would go after Hawk.

Relentlessly, she battled the flames until they were

tame enough she could fetch flour. She poured it over those remaining patches, and then, as darkness yet again invaded the room, the only light coming from the hearth in the parlour, she wept.

Out of fear, out of loss, out of desolation.

Freddie had been foiled again in his plans to go home, and speak to Mena, this time by a problem with the newest load of cargo. He was in the midst of reviewing it with his men, when the oddest sound caught his attention. Well, not odd; a dog's bark in these parts was the furthest thing from *odd*, but odd, because he recognised it. Only it couldn't be…

Striding from beneath the sorting shed, Freddie made his way across the wharf to the gate, and as soon as he saw that he wasn't going completely mad, his stomach fell to his boots, and he ran to close the distance.

'Open the gate, man,' he shouted, scrambling at the bars to reach Hawk on the other side. 'Hush now, Hawk, I'm here.'

The dog, seemingly relieved, barked one last time, then sat, waiting.

He knew something was wrong, so very wrong. The dog had blood on his leg, and soot. As soon as the gate was unlocked, Freddie surged through, dropping to his feet before the beast as he waved the guard away.

'Mena?' he asked the dog rather stupidly.

But perhaps not, for there was a whine then, a sorrowful thing, and Freddie lost all sense of rationality.

All he knew was that he needed to get home, now.

Scooping Hawk into his arms, he bolted. Without care nor concern for anything but his destination, his purpose, he ran, tripping and sliding, and bumping into angry sailors and rowdy late-night revellers as he went.

*What the Devil happened?*

Whatever it was, wasn't good. A fire of some sort, likely, though fire would bring neighbours, which *was* good. But how had Hawk got out? Got injured? What if Mena hadn't been so lucky? What if she'd been trapped?

*What if...? What if...?*

A thousand desperate and violent images assaulted him, even as he told himself she would be fine, because he couldn't lose her. It wouldn't be right. Fair. Not that that meant anything—not that it reassured him—still, it was the truth. He couldn't lose Mena, because there was still so much to say, and do, and she couldn't be lost to him now, before she even had a chance to live her own life.

They arrived at Holly Street blessedly quickly, and his greatest fears were realised. Only, there was no hue and cry—which had to be good, didn't it?

*Unless no one knew to come and help...*

The front windows had been shattered, and there was light coming through from behind the boards which had been put up to cover them.

*Someone cleaned up. This is good.*

Wasn't it?

Freddie ran up the stairs, and tucking Hawk under one arm, he extracted his keys with the other, and flung it open.

'Mena!'

Hawk was thrashing in his arms, so he dropped the dog, and closed the door.

'Mena!' he shouted, rushing in, only to freeze and gape when he saw the remains of charred tables, baubles, floors, blankets, and dusky flour. Yet it was good— because, again, this meant someone had cleaned up.

*After what?*

'Mena!'

'Hawk,' he heard her say from the other room. 'Hawk, thank God!'

'Mena,' he called again, rushing towards the parlour even as she came through to the shop. 'Mena...'

She looked...

*Horrendous.*

Haunted, terrified, singed. Her hair was a rat's nest, her clothes sooty and burnt, and he was sure there were tracks in the soot on her face. Her eyes were red, and puffy, and there was such sorrow in them... Still, she was the most beautiful, the most welcome, sight he'd ever seen. Because she was alive, and here.

*Have not lost her.*

'Freddie,' she breathed, fresh tears dropping, even as she swiped them away angrily. 'I'm so sorry...'

Shrugging she looked around at the desolation, and he blinked at her stupidly for a moment.

'I don't give a damn about the shop,' he growled, striding over to her. 'All I care about is you.'

The crashing of relief swept away what was left of his rational mind, and before he could think about what he was doing, he was taking her face in his hands and kissing her.

He just needed to touch her—*feel her*—beneath his own hands, know that she was real, and safe; and he meant to stop it there—it had been chaste enough, emotions were high, he could explain it away, and he knew he shouldn't be doing this, especially not like this—but then her own hands were on his wrists, holding him close, and she was kissing him back.

There was no artistry in their meeting, only pure, primal, unfettered need, and yet it surpassed anything he'd allowed himself to imagine in the darkest moments of the darkest nights. The kiss was messy, and unpractised, and devoid of any intention except to taste, and breathe, and *live* together. For a moment, a single, brief, unalterable and incomparable moment.

And Mena… She was life to him. Her scent, that unique essence of freedom and *home*, filled his lungs, and he could breathe again. Or perhaps, only breathe properly for the first time. Her taste…

*God, her taste.*

It was there too, the sea, the salt, and limitless horizons, and awe-inspiring sunrises, and the warmth that had no name but which he felt even in the harshest winter simply because she was with him. Their tongues tangled and meshed, and all he knew was that he needed more. It was as the poet's said—a hunger that could never be fulfilled. A hunger that gnawed, and set fire to your veins, and made everything ethereal *tangible*.

He needed more, but a twinge of guilt and rationality pierced through the haze of passion, and he drew back, breaking the incredible connection, leaning his forehead against hers and closing his eyes.

They breathed, or rather panted, together for a moment, and he kept hold of her because he couldn't make his body obey the command to release her just yet.

*Not ever.*

'I'm sorry,' he finally breathed. 'I shouldn't have…' *Mauled you without your consent. Kissed you like that after what you've been through.* 'Done that.'

Swallowing hard, he forced himself to slowly pull away, hoping that when he opened his eyes, and was no longer touching her…

*We can pretend this never happened.*

Only he never got that far. He'd barely lifted his forehead from hers, and her hands had gone from holding his wrists to grabbing fistfuls of his shirt. His eyes flew open and met hers, as inky as the depths of the oceans in the dead of night.

He could sink to the bottom of those too, he could—

'Don't leave me, Freddie,' she pleaded, her voice a harsh, cracking whisper. 'Please... I need this. I need you.'

Mena's need was there, plain to see, as was his own, he was sure, and what man in his right mind would not be undone by such words.

This was a gigantic, monumental, life-shattering mistake. They needed to talk, he'd let that go long enough, and what she'd just faced—

*Can wait.*

Because now she was pulling *him* in, or pulling herself closer; he didn't quite know who was moving how any more, only that their mouths were meeting again, just as ardently and earnestly as the last time. And one of her hands slinked around his neck, and held him close, and that was all it took.

What little was left of his mind, his good sense, left him, and he was a beast of pure instinct. His body called to be enfolded into hers, and so he listened. He snaked a hand around her neck, his fingers tangling in the soft tiny hairs, those silky strands he'd devoted far too much time thinking about, glorious and tantalising. His other hand caught her hip, and he pulled her as close to himself as he could.

Still, their tongues, their lips, their teeth clashed and met, until they could barely breathe but for simply being with the other. He felt himself moving forward until they could no longer, her back against the oak counter. Plastering himself to her, moulding their bodies together, he let his hands, and then his mouth, loath as he was to leave hers, roam where he could.

*The edge of her jaw, with downy little hairs.*

*The bottom of her ribs.*

*The sharp dip of her clavicle.*

*The ridges of her neck.*

*The soft mounds of her breasts, both above and below.*

*Her hip—the other this time—and beyond...*

*Her buttocks, her thigh...*

Her own hands strayed across his body, leaving trails of blistering light in their wake. Tangling in the curls at his ears, across his Adam's apple, over the muscles of his arms, even into the dips of his knuckles when their hands met again, ever so briefly.

Freddie had been with women before; there had been passion, and pleasure, but never this. He *was* folding into her, their essences seeping into the other's like smoke. He could feel it, a sort of relinquishment of himself, and he knew it was bad, and, oh, so *stupid*. But he didn't care. His mind was quiet, his heart was bright and alive, and singing, he would swear to it. Singing to Mena's tune, as if she were humming its rhythm herself.

And then her hands were at his trousers, and something, that little voice that whispered *last chance*, told him he could, *should*, end this madness here. Yet he couldn't. It wasn't an exaggeration to say she was life to him, and if he stopped this now, he would never have another chance to fully live again.

So he did the only thing he could.

He let her free him from his confines, and rucking up her skirts, he freed her from hers. An arm around her back to steady her, and he met her eyes. There was no doubt, no hesitation, only that same need, incandescent, the thing of dreams and angels. A kiss, swift, chaste, and he steadied himself before wrapping her leg around his waist, fitting himself to her, and plunging in.

Words failed him. Those were a creation of man, and what he felt went so far beyond that, there weren't any words. A cry tore from both their throats, her slick heat dragging him into herself, and it was the beginning and end of all things. He devoured her, reaching parts of her, *giving* parts of himself he never had, as he plunged into her, over and over.

She met his every thrust, her grip on his arm and shoulder tightening, her halted breaths and whimpers feeding the hazed frenzy they were both caught in.

Until it seemed all they were was one heaving, sweaty mass of flesh, and heart, and fire, and he soared and reached beyond anything earthly. Still, they clung tightly, united, together as one breathing life form—as they were meant to be.

For a brief, exquisite moment, he was *home*, and he knew the truth of the world.

And then, much like their ardour now sated, like the heat that melded them together, like a wave cresting, he came back to the cold harshness of reality.

Panic assailed him anew, different from before, because he had broken something so precious, so inviolable, he could never right it again. His eyes flew open, sweeping across Mena's familiar features that somehow now seemed invariably altered.

*What have I done?*

'Fuck.'

# Chapter Nine

The word echoed and rang in Mena's ears, slicing through her heart endlessly. She'd heard Freddie curse before, but never *that* word. It pierced through the cathartic, healing, incredible, sensuous, and awe-inspiring moment they'd shared, hooking her, and dragging her unwillingly back down to earth.

It had been a terrible idea, to let what had happen; to ask, *beg*, for it. She'd known that, known it would never change anything, certainly not Freddie's heart. But she hadn't lied. She had needed it, to feel him, with her, part of her, if only once. After what she'd been through tonight, her heart, her emotions, her mind, even her body, mashed through some terrible engine designed by devils, she'd needed *him*.

After stopping the flames, she'd forced herself to clean what she could, and board up the windows before going after Hawk. Luckily, no one nearby had seen nor heard anything. For that, she'd been grateful, because if anyone had come, she'd have lost all her strength, and just sat on the floor, and cried. So yes, she'd been grateful for the solitude, fuelling her clean-up with rage.

Rage at the man who'd attacked them without reason, at least that she could see. Rage at herself, for being so afraid. For not doing *something* more than what she had; and most of all, rage at herself for wishing Freddie was there. To protect her, to stand *with* her, against the malevolent presence that came for their house. She was angry at herself for needing him so much; when soon, she would, as she'd always known, have to face the world alone again. It had been that anger which had driven every nail through every board that now hid the destruction inside from the world. She'd been about to finally go after Hawk when he'd appeared, and then Freddie, and then...

*This.*

Where moments ago, there had been such care, and heat in his eyes, such *relief*, for her, now, there was sheer, blind *panic*. She knew it well—how many times had she looked at herself and seen the very same? Only in his eyes now, it was an ice storm, raging around, shards of its frosty knives cutting her a thousand times over. It was more than rejection—rejection, she'd expected. She didn't expect to hear declarations of undying love. He cared for her, she'd never doubted that, and he'd feared for her. And what had happened was a release, for both of them. A need to feel alive, to feel human, and a little less alone. She understood that much. If there was one thing she'd *always* understood, it was her place. In Freddie's life at least.

But this... This new terror that filled his eyes, it made her feel sick, and shameful, and *unwanted*. Everything she'd promised herself—promised *him*—she would never feel again.

Freddie withdrew from her slowly, in every possible way, putting himself somewhat together as she forced herself to push it down—*all of it*. She would not be ill.

She would not cry. She would take the handkerchief he offered her now, refusing to meet her eyes, and clean him off herself, *and you will not cry*. No. She would stand tall, and face whatever came next with the one thing she would never relinquish again.

*Grace.*

'Mena…'

'Don't,' she warned him, stowing away the soiled handkerchief to clean it later.

*Along with myself.*

'What's done is done. I have no illusions, Freddie,' she said, and it sounded steady to her own ears. 'It was a mistake.'

He finally looked at her then, and she might've sworn the same heart-wrenching pain she felt was in his eyes; that stormy sea-green which was familiar and yet so different from any she'd seen before.

'I…' Inhaling deeply, he raked his fingers in his hair, and searched the room a moment before starting again. 'I shouldn't have… I went too far.'

It wasn't what he was going to say, she knew, but she would ignore it.

*Along with so much more.*

'Nothing will come of it,' she reassured him coldly. He may have lost his reason, and she may have been close, but something inside her was always mindful of that kind of *complication*. 'The timing alone should ensure there will be no consequences, but I will take other precautions.'

Freddie nodded vaguely, and whatever he was feeling, he kept it well hidden.

*As always. Though now it will be worse.*

He would pull away, as he always did when things

became personal, and what they had broken tonight could never be put back together.

'We should report this, in the morning,' he said flatly.

'I will tell you all I know. I need to tend to Hawk,' she told him, smoothing her skirts, and her hair. That should've been the first thing she did, instead—

*Let be.*

'And there is something you need to see.'

Raising a brow, he studied her, and rather than subject herself to that, she moved.

Moving would keep her grounded. She went to the kitchen to retrieve supplies to clean and bandage Hawk, then returned to the parlour, and knelt down before the dog, who had patiently waited by the fire. He leaned into her caress, and her heart swelled with emotion again; this time in thanks for the pup who had defended her, and gone after Freddie.

*With you I shall never be alone.*

'On the table,' she told Freddie, when she could speak steadily again.

As she began her ministrations, she heard him go and pick up the tiny note that had been fastened to a rock, thrown in before the blaze. At first, it had made her think Father Bartholomew had been the one to visit them tonight, but thinking back on it as she'd cleaned, she'd known, those were not his eyes. She hadn't recognised those terrible eyes; and she knew she would've.

Shivering, she shrugged it off, and glanced at Freddie.

*Oh, no.*

Her stomach flipped again when she saw his stony expression—and face paler than she'd ever witnessed. The note meant something to him, something…

*Grim.*

It had crossed her mind, but she'd denied it, because…

*I was terrified of that possibility.*

*This* possibility.

That a simple Bible verse would be a harbinger of doom, as it was now.

*For thou hadst cast me into the deep, in the midst of the seas; and the floods compassed me about.*

'You know who did this,' she breathed. 'Tell me.'

Even before he opened his mouth, she knew he wouldn't.

This, like everything else, he would keep to himself. Even though she deserved to know—even though she wanted nothing more—because whatever was coming was dangerous, and he would face it alone.

She knew that too.

'Freddie, please…'

'I'll take care of it,' he gritted out.

Mena remained silent; what more was there to say?

Really, she wanted to rage, to scream, to pound her fists on his chest, and demand that he tell her everything. That before the end, he tell her all he never had of himself, of this mysterious danger that now stalked them, *him*; that he release her somehow from her own heart.

Instead, she swallowed the gaping hole inside, letting it become part of herself, and returned to Hawk. After a while, Freddie stalked out, pounding up the stairs, then, moments later, back out into the night. When she heard the click of the lock, she finally let more tears fall, hoping their release would help her heal. For a long time, she sat there, crying silently, petting Hawk, letting the flickering flames lull her into a place of, if not peace, then quietude. And finally, when no more tears fell, she left a note for Freddie telling him she would tend to fixing the shop, went up to her room, cleaned herself, and curled into bed.

Not that Mena found sleep, nor comfort, there.

The wind had turned bitter, viciously so, and even uncovered as he was—no overcoat, no hat, no gloves— Freddie couldn't feel it. He couldn't feel anything. Walking on, to nowhere, anywhere not *back there*, he passed through street after street, like the shade he felt he was. Part of the world, and yet, not quite. Unable to be, because of all he'd done, and could never free himself of.

The note that told him just that was still clenched in his hand, and it alone provoked feeling, burning his palm. A mark, to remind him, of what was coming. Of what had already come, for Mena.

This—*this*—was precisely what he'd been terrified of, *dreaded*. His past returning, not only to haunt him, but to harm those, *the one*, he cared for most. Years he'd spent keeping himself at arm's length, from her, from friends, from the world, for fear of sullying them with his own black deeds, and yes, for fear of it all coming back to drag him to Hell. Somehow, deep down, he'd known it wasn't over. That it could never be.

*That you did not die that night, Uncle.*

That night of reckoning, twenty-nine years ago, came crashing upon him, and Freddie stumbled, catching himself on a streetlamp as the numbness fled, replaced by *everything*. Guilt, pain, despair, anger, fear. It filled his chest that not hours ago had been full of light, with rancid, rotten, *rotting*, knots that twisted and scraped like thorny vines, opening gaping wounds in the furthest reaches of his heart and soul.

Yes, he'd known somehow, sometime, his past would come for him, as surely as a horseman at the end of days. Was it not what he'd felt these past days? The gnawing, the pricking at his neck. Yet, that wasn't what tore him open now, so that he could barely breathe, barely stand. It was what had happened tonight. What he'd allowed to happen to Mena by sheer fact of keeping her close; and worst of all, what *he'd* done.

How gravely he'd hurt her—he wasn't blind—he'd seen it in her eyes. The carelessness with which he'd taken, because he needed, and she asked, and he'd gone *too damn far*. He'd treated her… Abhorrently.

*And you would claim to love her. No.*

He'd been deluding himself. What he felt… It wasn't love. Not right, and true. You didn't use someone you truly loved, and discard them; put them in harm's way, cut them down, and anguish them, and—

Sucking in a breath of biting air, Freddie pushed off the lamp, and continued his walk, *run*, march, further into the depths of the city. He saw nor heard nothing, conscious only of his own thoughts.

How had he ever believed he loved her? How could he ever believe he was *capable* of it? What the Hell did he know about love? The general concept, what he read, what he'd seen in his friends.

*That isn't enough.*

How could he love if he'd never felt it?

*You can't.*

He'd loved his parents surely, once, but nothing was left of them, in his heart, or in his mind. Their names, the knowledge of their existence, that was all. He'd wanted to make his uncle proud; he'd *wanted* to be loved by him, but he never had. Even then, as a child, he'd known that much, long before he knew the rest. And Mr Walton… He'd cared for the man deeply. Been grateful to him for all he'd taught, given, him. Was that love?

*Perhaps a form of it.*

Still, it wasn't, it couldn't, be enough. How could he know what it meant to love—if he'd never experienced it? Particularly not romantic love. Desire, passion, longing, that's all it had been with Mena. Right? He wasn't built for love, he'd never been taught it, and most importantly, even if he had been, he didn't deserve it.

*Never did, never will.*

And there was nothing to be done about that.

Somehow, the thought brought him a settling, peaceful emptiness. He'd been a bastard. A fool. Now… He could…move on? Do what he must to see this mess through to the end, to clean up his affairs and put his life in order before…

*He comes for me again.*

For a moment, he thought about leaving, at the very least, leaving Mena, but his uncle was a cruel, devious man. Leaving would not protect her; neither would sending her away, though that thought flitted through his mind too, the idea of sending her away to Spencer or Mary an unwelcome image. No—either option would only serve to tell his uncle she meant something to him. For now, all the man knew, all he *could* know, was that she lived and worked at Holly Street.

*And so it must stay.*

He would put measures in place, hire men to search for his uncle, see if perhaps he could meet his fate head-on, and he would hire some to keep an eye on the shop. Discreetly—lest he tip his hand. However, it would be up to him to keep an eye on Mena otherwise; men following her about, no matter how discreet, again ran the risk of being noticed. Well, he could do that. He would simply…go on as before. Pretend everything was…fine. For it was.

*Will be.*

Yes, he could manage that, he told himself, slowing as he gazed around, realising he'd taken himself to the Inns of Court. He would work, and live, as if nothing were amiss; and he'd make sure everything was prepared for when he met his end. Until then, it would be nothing at all to be around Mena; that whole love nonsense had been just that.

*Nonsense.*

His need for her had been satisfied—*liar*—and he could go back to the way things had been before he'd wracked it all to ruin.

*Liar.*

Turning back to the east, Freddic told the voice to quieten, and when it did, he felt most satisfied that he was right about it all.

*I can simply soldier on as before.*

## Chapter Ten

The store hadn't been this empty since before they'd opened it. If Mena hadn't known better, she'd have thought she'd managed the impossible: gone back in time. For a brief moment, she wished she had. Gone back to *before*, when the mess of her life hadn't seemed so insurmountable. Back to when things were simpler.

Just her and Freddie, fulfilling the potential of this place.

*Fulfilling our own potential.*

Days ago, the future had seemed…*bright*. Full of un-tapped potential again. Now, not even her grand dreams had colour. Everything felt…tainted. Even this shop.

Casting her eyes about the nearly empty room, she felt…*angry* at it. For recovering so swiftly, practically invisibly, when she was still a fragile creature of fear and heartache. When it felt like she *had* travelled back in time—to when she'd been too afraid to step outside. Looking at the shop now, less than a full day after the attack, one wouldn't guess what had passed.

The glaziers had come and gone, spending the day replacing the windows, arriving first thing, before she'd even had a chance to finish clearing out the remains she hadn't tended to last night, too heartsick to do anything but curl into bed. Then the workmen had arrived, right after the glaziers, to fix the floorboards, take out the debris and lost furniture, and replace it all.

Regardless of the note she'd left, Freddie had made the arrangements. She wanted to be angry about that too—but she couldn't manage it. Because truth be told, it had felt soothing, a suffocating weight lifting, to have nothing more to do than put a notice on the door for the customers, clean, and make a plan for restocking the shop. She'd also sent a note to Susie, asking her not to come in. In it, she wrote a little of what had happened; word would travel fast—already neighbours had come by, intent, Mena was sure, on reassuring and taking care of her, only she hadn't opened for them. She just… couldn't face anyone. Not just yet. The workmen had given her a wide berth, and thankfully Susie hadn't come—though Mena *had* outright begged her friend for time alone.

Pretending—for anyone, which she would, not to burden them, not to see pity in their eyes, not to hear the supposedly reassuring words which did anything but—to be fine, was not something she could manage. She would break, scream, shout, and cry, and then where would she be?

*Nowhere good.*

She just… Wanted to feel safe again. To feel solid ground beneath her feet. It had taken so long, so much strength and fighting to have that for even a second, and now, it had all been ripped away in one fell swoop. With the attack—and all that had passed with Freddie in the aftermath.

Mena hadn't seen him since last night—she'd heard him come home at some point. She was enraged at herself that hearing him return had made her feel safer, calmer. Allowed her to sleep. How ever was she to manage when he was no longer in her life at all?

*Strong, independent woman indeed.*

But soon, she would have to be just that. If last night told her anything, it was that whatever status quo there had been, had been upended. Freddie couldn't give her what her heart cried for—he couldn't even trust her with himself—and so she had to move on. It was time. The house would be ready, and she would…

*Begin again.*

Sniffling away useless, angry tears, and thoughts, Mena forced herself to look at all the boxes and crates she'd brought down to fill the shop again…hours ago. It was evening now, and still it remained as empty as it had been this morning. Taking a deep breath, she began unwrapping some of the decorative pieces in the box at her feet, hoping for inspiration. For so long, unwrapping each silver tea set, or glass ornament, would bring her joy. The artistry, the stories each object carried, inspired her. She was never at a loss of precisely where to display them—knowing instinctively where they would best catch the eye of whoever was meant to take them home.

*Not today.*

'Would you like some help?' came Freddie's gentle voice.

Mena started slightly, but recovered quickly.

His voice soothed her—only that made her want to throw the tiny porcelain vase painted by a Dutchman called Jan at the wall. So she could see it as shattered as she was.

For a moment, she considered telling Freddie to take himself far away, that she would do it herself. Facing him… It wasn't what had passed between them, but the after. The reminder of the lack of trust—of what could never be.

Problem was, facing him was still less of a trial than not having him nearby.

'If you like,' she said softly.

When she turned to face him, the anger, the fear, that had kept her alive all day faded.

He looked…as raw as she was.

He gave her a small smile, removed his coat, and found a box of his own to undo. For a time, they worked in silence, the air changing from tense, and heavily laden with unsaid words, to comfortable, and comforting. Mena was glad of the silence, for after all, what was there to say? Freddie never said anything he didn't mean, and she wasn't sure she wanted to hear any more of *what* he had to say about the previous night.

Again, it felt as it had at the beginning, and the shop came alive as it had then, albeit quicker, as shelves and tables were laden with wares.

*See? All can always be rebuilt.*

'I'd forgotten what it was like to do this,' Freddie said finally, breaking the pleasant silence. Mena glanced over to find him smiling, almost restored. Though the sadness, guilt, and darkness about him now, it felt as if they would never leave him entirely. 'But even then,' he continued, huffing out what might've been a laugh. 'I didn't do much of it. It was always you. You've always had the better eye,' he added swiftly, turning back to his box to uncover more, not that there was much space left now.

Mena wasn't entirely sure what this new mood was, indeed, what this conversation was, but perhaps it was an attempt to return to the normality of their friendship. She could take the peace offering, or reject it.

*Accept it. It is not the end quite yet.*

No—she would know when their end came. She would know it in her bones.

'Your mind was always on the larger picture,' she offered, going to move his coat so she could fill the table he'd laid it on with fine linens. 'This shop…was my world. And the world passed through it.'

Something clattered to the ground as she moved Freddie's coat, and frowning, she leaned down to pick it up, hardly believing her eyes when she recognised it.

'You kept him,' she whispered, more to herself.

The rather grotesque carving of the tiny little sailor with a hammer, fashioned by her own hands, three years ago, after some whitling lessons with Mr Simpson, made her heart skip a beat, whilst it also filled it with immeasurable sadness. The little *Klabautermann* was a reminder of the Christmas spent without Freddie— the Christmas she'd known would change everything.

*The Christmas which truly woke me from dreaming.*

'Why wouldn't I keep him?' Freddie asked after a long moment studying Mena as she turned the figure over in her hands, noting, he knew, the marks of wear from all its journeys. He wasn't sure why the little figurine brought such sorrow to her eyes, dimming the light he'd just managed to get back into them, if only slightly, but he didn't like it.

How could such a treasure bring someone such sadness? He didn't understand it—how a gift *she'd* made for him, with all that care she put into everything, could bring such pain.

*There is so much I don't understand about her.*

It was all his own fault—he knew that. He'd not slept, turning the previous night's events—Hell, the

past twenty-nine years—over in his mind remorselessly.
All day, from the time he'd made arrangements for the
workers to come—banging on their doors at inappro-
priate hours and throwing money at them, figuratively,
not literally, so Mena would have one less concern—
to the moment he'd stepped foot back at Holly Street,
he'd tried to be...*useful*. Tried to make up, in some way,
for all the ill he'd done, particularly to her. He couldn't
lessen the hurt, but he could prevent her from more,
even if it was only hiring men to fix the shop, and others to watch it, not that she would know about *those*;
or the ones hired to track his uncle.

Even returning to Holly Street had been in an effort
to return to the safe normality of *before*, for her. Despite
his decrees to himself, all he'd *really* wanted to do when
he'd found her was to kneel before her, and beg forgiveness. For all he'd done; and failed to do. He'd wanted
to hold her, and tell her his darkest sins, and he'd even
moved towards her, his body failing to answer to commands again, when the light had glinted off a piece of
silver, and shocked him back to himself. He'd instead
asked to help, and by agreeing, she'd done what he was
meant to be doing.

*Pretended everything was fine.*

*Grateful* wasn't the word for what he'd been; however, he liked to think it was. That it was gratitude, to
her, for being the sensible, strong one, and simply pushing it all behind them. Only working in silence, making the shop itself once again, as they had once, had
reminded him instead of all the years they'd had together. Of all *they'd* had together; and hadn't.

Though resolved now that what he felt for Mena
wasn't love, with every new object he uncovered, his
mind couldn't help but wander through the years, try-

ing to find a reason for it all. For thinking he *did* love her; and *why now*. Doing something he hadn't for years, made him wonder what had changed so much since then. Since the time when working, and living, and speaking of nothing but the present, the tasks at hand, and the mundane of life, were welcome, not detested for their lack of *substance*. Of meaning.

What had changed so much that now every time he opened his mouth he wished to say, ask, discover, all that hadn't been before? What had made him finally open his eyes to the fact that Mena was beautiful, and desirable? What had made him see all he'd wasted?

He'd not found an answer.

It was possible that returning and realising his own unimportance to the business he'd made his life, his sole focus, had made him think he could have something more. Something he'd always known was not for the likes of him. Something he'd never even dared to think on.

It was also possible that seeing Spencer, one of his *only* friends, married, and happy, and in love, when the man had always scoffed at the mere ideas, complaining ceaselessly about his mother's haranguing and match-making efforts, was a contributing factor.

Perhaps it was the fact that he'd felt the impending return of his past, and all the change that would bring. Perhaps he'd only seen in Mena a hope for something different. As if she were some sort of mirage, the oasis to the man dying of thirst in the sands.

*Mena is no mirage. Mena is…everything. Past, present, and future.*

That was about the only firm conclusion he'd come to. Because any time he looked at her, no matter his guilt, his concern, his self-hatred, when Freddie looked at Mena, he saw it all.

*Not that any of it matters.*

No, it didn't—because nothing about the circumstances had changed. He was still who he'd always been, danger still circled, and all must return to how it had been if they were ever to have a chance at...*surviving this*.

Still, Freddie had to know why that little wooden figure brought Mena so much pain, when it had only ever bolstered his spirits and heart.

At the very least so he could prevent anything from doing so again.

'Why wouldn't I keep him?' Freddie repeated, frowning slightly, daring to take a step closer even if it was far from the wisest thing to do. His mind might've accepted that he didn't love her, but that didn't mean his body didn't still want her. 'He's sailed with me, attached to the mast of every ship, keeping me safe, as you said he would.'

A Finnish woman at market had told Mena that— it's why she'd made it for him, or so she'd said when she'd given him the carving for Saint Nicholas Day, three years ago.

He'd never forget that night, not that he could forget any of their Saint Nicholases together, but that one more so than any other because it had been so bittersweet. After their gift giving—his to her a scrimshaw carving of a boat and sea monster, done up by one of his new recruits, a veteran whaler—he'd told her of Spencer's invitation for him to spend Christmas at Clairborne House.

He'd not wanted to go, but he'd left it too long to deny the man with his attempt to ignore it altogether. He'd hoped, he remembered that now, that Mena

might've asked him *not* to go. Given him an excuse—
*any* excuse—not to go. Instead, she'd repeated the same
words Spencer's sister, Mary, had said.

*'You should go. It is a good connection, and you
should do all you can to foster it.'*

As if he hadn't known. As if he hadn't known that
having friends in the highest circles would only help
*him* rise higher. Only that didn't matter to him—it never
had. He wasn't, never had been, friends with Mary,
or Spencer, or anyone because of what they could do
for him. He should, he wished to be successful, but
that way... It felt too much like using people—which
is something he'd sworn to never do again.

He'd wanted to tell Mena all that that night, only, as
always, he hadn't. He'd nodded, or something equally
as benign. Rather than tell her the truth—all of it—
including that he didn't want to be anywhere but at
Holly Street, with her, particularly at Christmas.

*Always.*

*Moot point—for you cannot.*

'It's a terrible carving,' Mena said, not tossing, but
not gently placing either, the *Klabautermann* on his
coat, and turning back to her work. 'Barely better than
if I'd given you the stick he was made from.'

'Don't say that.'

'Why not? It's the truth,' she scoffed.

'What did the poor fellow ever do to you?' he asked,
trying to infuse some lightness in his voice, as he sought
to discern where Mena's bitterness stemmed from. Was
it merely latent hurt from last night, or something else?
Perhaps she too was reminded of that night—and of that
Christmas spent, not alone, but apart. *Could it be?* 'I
didn't want to go, you know,' he said seriously. Why?
Well, that was a *damned* good question, and not one he

would answer. Because answering it would be admitting he was doing the furthest thing from *returning to normality* that he could be. Mena stopped, and he pressed on, knowing he'd touched on something...*important*.

'When you decided that I should go, all I wanted was to ask you to come with me,' he whispered.

'What point would there have been to that,' she said bitterly, refusing to look at him.

Slowly, ever so carefully, he approached, until there was barely a foot between them.

He knew she could feel him—he could feel her, breathe her, breathe *with* her, and God did it feel right.

'We both know I wouldn't have been able to go,' she continued, and it sounded as it was both the plainest truth, yet as heartbreaking to her as it was to him. 'Even so. I had no place there, no business in such company.'

'Because I do?'

'Yes, Freddie,' she sighed, a well of sadness so profound in her as she finally turned to meet his eyes, it caught his breath, and twisted his heart. 'You earned yourself a place in that world, a long time ago.'

'I never wanted it,' he breathed.

*I only ever wanted—*

'Still, it is yours. You and I both know that,' she whispered.

Mena raised a hand, the braver of the two of them, no longer afraid of what touch would tell them.

Gently sweeping it along his left ear, with her thumb she circled the long-disused hole where once he'd worn an earring. The message was clear. Once, he'd been a wanderer, a man of the seas; the earring he'd worn symbol of that. He'd removed it as he rose into more *refined* circles, and that choice had been conscious; he'd known what he was doing, and why. *Who* he was becoming, and why.

Though he'd never realised Mena had noticed; nor cared as much about that change as she evidently did.

'I will finish this tomorrow,' she said after a long moment, breaking the connection. 'You'll forgive me if I don't prepare dinner; there is ham, bread and cheese.'

'Mena—'

'Goodnight, Freddie,' she said firmly, already on her way upstairs.

'Goodnight, Mena.'

There was so much more he wished to say, only he didn't.

Because maybe, just maybe, he was done being a selfish bastard, putting his own needs before her own.

*And she needs to be free of me.*

## Chapter Eleven

'Oh! Good morning, Freddie,' Mena said, not bothering to hide her surprise, though why she should be that he was here, in his own home, at this hour, was a mystery.

*Perhaps not a mystery.*

No, perhaps not. He'd been…

*Avoiding her again.*

Well, not exactly. He'd been *trying* to hold fast to his decree that things should go back to the way they'd been, that he *could*, ignoring the gigantic and proverbial elephant trampling about his house.

After that evening, that *moment*, they'd shared in the shop the day after the attack, which he still couldn't make sense of, not that he wanted to—*liar*—Freddie resumed his typical schedule from before his return, albeit with a few more visits home. In the evenings, they'd sit together at table, eat in silence, then wish each other goodnight.

There had been no news from the men he'd hired, not that he'd expected any, and so the days had been a strange balancing act between watchfulness and distance. Walking a line between restoring safe distances;

and protecting Mena, because if anything happened to her…

*My soul will shrivel and die.*

Only it was blasted difficult to keep a watchful eye when *she* seemed determined to, not so much avoid him, but *sneak*. He'd never known Mena to *sneak*, and yet, that was precisely what she'd been doing. Amidst the normality he'd tried to restore, amidst her own apparent return to the status quo, he'd noticed this new development.

Even as she expediently readied the shop, he would notice her disappear like smoke, citing *errands to run*, though he knew there weren't that many *errands*. Today, the shop was open again, though she'd left someone else in charge; not that he minded, but it was odd, because he'd thought she would want to remain safe in Holly Street. It worried him. She was hiding something, and all he could think was that it was somehow related to his past. Even if it wasn't, whatever it was couldn't be good.

*Mena doesn't sneak.*

'You seem surprised,' he said, thinking it was better to face these things head-on.

*Some things. Fine, just this one thing.*

'I… Thought you already gone,' Mena stammered out, her hands worrying the edges of her scarf, as she stood there, ready to waltz out the door, yet hesitant, because of him. *What is going on?* Freddie narrowed his eyes and Mena smiled what was meant to be a bright smile, but ended up rather terrifying. 'You've stopped going to the wharf so early.'

'I don't really need to be there. I thought… Well, we still haven't made arrangements for Christmas, and despite what passed between us, Mena… I should like us to have good Yuletide.'

Not what he'd meant to say—but then, it was the truth.

A truth as chilling as a trip to the gallows to Mena, apparently. Her eyes were wide, she'd paled, and was swallowing rather convulsively.

*Something is definitely wrong.*

'Mena…?'

'I should like that too, Freddie,' she nigh-on whispered, and *is that guilt in her eyes?* 'I… Have errands to run,' she said, surer now, though her eyes were studying the bottom of her skirts, and her fingers would not cease worrying the damned scarf. 'I… When I return, we will speak.'

'Mena—'

'I have to go.'

In a rustle of skirts and rush of frigid air, she was gone.

Freddie glanced down at Hawk, as confused as he was with this business.

The beast sounded a short bark and glanced at the door.

'How right you are,' he told the mongrel, wasting not one moment before he slipped on his coat, grabbed his hat, and strode out after Mena, Hawk on his heels, still limping. 'You stay here, I'll take care of this,' he told the dog, shooing him back inside before going after his quarry.

It took a moment to find her, her own strides as long as his, but as her head topped many, he spotted her easily in the crowd. Following at a distance, he told himself to remain calm, and rational, until he got answers. There really was no use in expending energy fretting about the possibility that his uncle had blackmailed her, or threatened her more than he already had.

*Really no use*, he told himself as he reflexively fisted and released his hands. After all, it likely something innocent. Perhaps she was shopping for a Christmas surprise. Though he wasn't sure why she would've needed so much time recently to do so… Or even that she would *want* to.

*Could be.*

It could be that she was meeting someone. How had he not thought of this? Perhaps, she was meeting someone for…

*A tryst.*

No. It couldn't be—

Before he could finish the descent into Hell that was that line of thinking, Freddie realised they had…arrived. Across the street, Mena disappeared into the old warehouse he'd been speaking to Henderson of—what now seemed eons ago. Only now…

Now it bore the name Nichols House.

The fear he'd tried to dismiss, the churning of his gut, transformed, as he stood there, thick petals of snow threatening to make him an ice figure. Except he couldn't feel the cold again. His mind struggled to make sense of this…bustling hive, of those faces all greeting Mena with smiles. The churning of concern transformed into the roiling sea of anger; incomprehension becoming painful understanding.

If someone had strode up to him and struck him, it might've had the same effect.

Probably why he didn't notice the figure before him until she spoke; and then he felt the icy cold, freezing the unshed tears and magnifying the painful daggers of emotion in his throat.

'Finally told you, then, did she,' the figure said, and he vaguely registered curls. 'I'm Susie by the way, we've not been properly introduced, but I recognised you and thought I should say hello.' An outstretched hand was before him now, and he shook it, and forced himself to blink away the frozen pain, and look down at this Susie. 'Pleasure, Mr Walton.'

'Susie… You work at Holly Street,' he managed dumbly.

'That's right,' she grinned. 'And here, when I can. 'Tis a wonder what she's done, isn't it?'

'It is… Something.'

Perhaps his tone gave him away, or perhaps Susie registered his turbulent expression.

'You didn't know,' she breathed, eyes wide, not with fear, but with compassion.

'No.' Susie nodded, and looked ready to say something soothing, but he cut that short. 'Where is she?'

'Third floor.'

A sharp nod, and he was off.

The crowds milling at the front parted for him, and Susie must've waved off the men guarding the doors, for they too gave him a wide berth. On he went, seeing, nor hearing, no one but the unsteady rhythm of his fractured heart.

*How could she?*

*Lying fool*, Mena chastised herself as she went to see Josephine. *Devious little liar*, her heart taunted her. The truth, and only that. She knew it. Meeting with Freddie this morning… It had completely thrown her.

These past few days, they'd been both doing so well, at pretending all was…*fine*. The fresh, raw, and gaping wounds in her heart remained, but they were concealed. She kept on, as she always had, because crumbling, succumbing to her desire to confront Freddie, and tell him all she truly felt…

*There be dragons.*

What use would it be? Someone, *likely me*, would merely get hurt some more. There would be no resolution. He thought what they'd done a mistake. Despite her words, she didn't; never could. A fundamental difference of opinion.

Though they both agreed that no matter what *care* they might have for the other, their paths were diverging. Already had begun, years ago. Pretending all was well, until they *did* finally part, was all either of them had.

Only this morning, Freddie had upset that deal, speaking of Christmas. How was she meant to just… out with all her secrets there and then? They'd barely found balance again… She couldn't just *confess*. He had…more important things to deal with.

*You're just as scared as before—more so.*

Naturally. His rejection, though expected, had cut deeper than she'd ever imagined anything could. Telling him about her plans and facing more rejection, anger… was more than she had the stomach for. Just now. She still had time.

*Five days until Christmas Eve…*

'Morning, Josephine,' Mena called, stepping into what now resembled an office, complete with a desk. She smiled, a small but true smile. She'd been grateful for all there was to do here the past days. It kept her busy, and out of that house that somehow didn't feel so safe anymore.

*At least when Freddie isn't there.*

'Are those papers you need signing ready?'

Josephine opened her mouth to respond, but no words

came as her eyes travelled beyond Mena's shoulder. Something in the woman's expression told her before she turned who stood at her back.

'A moment alone with Miss Nichols, if you please,' Freddie said sharply, and Mena nodded to Josephine, who wasted no time in making herself scarce.

*This is a good thing*, she told herself, before taking a deep breath, and facing him. *Really, it is.*

Though Freddie's face, his entire countenance, told her otherwise.

'What are you doing here?'

'I followed you,' he said grimly, scowling, looking as quietly enraged as she'd ever seen him.

*This is what comes of keeping secrets.*

'I thought you were in trouble,' he laughed mockingly, his tone biting. 'With all the skulking about. I realise now I was very mistaken.'

'I can explain.'

'I've a pretty good idea already.'

Mena sucked in a deep breath.

This wasn't how she'd imagined this, not by any means, and she understood his anger stemmed from the hurt her secrecy had caused. All they'd done recently, it seemed, was hurt each other.

Freddie raised a brow, waiting.

'I shouldn't have kept this from you,' she began, taking a tentative step forward. 'I am sorry for that. It was to be a surprise. I was going to tell you.' A muscle in his jaw ticked, and his fists clenched and unclenched. She had to fix this, and his silence now was perhaps the only chance she would have. 'I'm not sure what you've guessed—seen already.' *Stop babbling.* 'This place… is to be a haven. A place of learning, and industry, for those who have nothing, as I did, once. Not a poorhouse, workhouse, or even an alms-house,' she explained, in-fusing her voice with the passion that had helped her build it. Glancing around, she willed him to see all that was to come, as she once had, in the empty room that had become their shop. 'People who cannot work, can have a home. Those who wish to learn, can. About the world, to become whatever they wish. Trades too. We will use those skills others already possess. We will sew, build...we already are... There will be room here for anyone, to be safe, and there is even a doctor. A trust to manage it, and there are no requirements to stay here, other than kindness, and respect. We have agreements with businesses across the city who are investing in this place, in its people, ready to welcome workers or goods next year. For Christmas, we shall have a feast, and games, and dancing, and all shall be welcome. It's everything we could've dreamt of.'

Mena was smiling, broadly, her excitement, her con-viction, filling her heart.

It was the *only* thing that had kept her going re-cently—knowing that no matter how terrible the ache, how bad the fear, she would always have this place.

Only, Freddie wasn't smiling. He was standing there, staring at her, with dark resentment. He wasn't excited, he wasn't proud, as she'd desperately hoped he would be. He was just, *angry*.

*This is why you couldn't bring yourself to tell him.*

Her heart sunk at the realisation that no matter what, it would never be...*enough*. Her throat tightened, and she willed the tears to stay at bay, taking another step closer to him, willing him to say *something*.

'Everything *we* could've dreamt of,' he said flatly, so quietly, and yet it felt as if he were yelling. 'You say that, and yet, you kept me deliberately out of it. You've solicited businesses, and help, from across the city, from men I know, or at least so I posit, since Henderson was quite coy when this place came up in conversation, and yet, to me, you breathed not a word. You went behind my back, and now you dare use the word *we*?'

'Freddie...'

'Eight years, Mena,' he seethed. 'Eight years, we have worked, and lived, and fought, together,' he raged, his indignation now on full show as he paced the room. 'And you couldn't trust me with this? You couldn't ask me to help you build this, *your* dream?'

Mena swallowed hard, but it didn't unclog her throat. And, oh, how her eyes burned. He was right, but he didn't understand—

'After all this time,' he said, calmer now, or at least, not raging. 'All we've been through... You might've had the decency to be honest. To tell me you were leaving.' He walked to the window, and stared out into the courtyard. 'Eight years, Mena... I thought you trusted me.'

That did it.

Mena's despair shifted to hurt, and yes, anger.

Anger at herself, in some part, for having made this mess, but also at him, for his hypocrisy about *secrecy*, and yes, for not knowing her a little better.

*Anger at not seeing the rancid truth, the selfish motives behind the selfless ones.*

'You see everything so clearly, Freddie,' she retorted bitterly, catching his attention, his expression turning from anger to surprise. 'You understand people so well. Except those closest to you. Except what's right in front of your face.'

With that, she left him, striding out to find something useful to do with her hurt, and pent-up ire.

## Chapter Twelve

*December 25th, 1824*

Typically Freddie had no difficulty coming by sleep. Years of working docks, ships, a year here now, in Holly Street, making this house into a shop and liveable home, whilst also building his other business, had forced him to snatch good, if small, patches of sleep when he could. Typically, he could fall asleep as soon as his head hit the pillow, and wake when needed. But tonight… Tonight he found no rest—and not for lack of trying, for hours now.

*Or perhaps only one—for I cannot seem to keep track of time either.*

Another thing which his mind and body did well usually. It had been a long time indeed since he'd laid like this, staring at the blackness above, unable to simply shut his eyes and have dreams, *or nightmares*, as had once been the case, come crashing forth like waves in a storm. It was curious too—for if anything, one would expect a day such as he'd had to be propitious to restful slumber. A day such as he'd not had in a very long time. As he'd never thought to have again.

*A proper Christmas—full of good cheer, and warmth.*

And it was all Mena's doing.

Over the past year, the woman had come into her own. Together, they'd scraped, saved, washed, scrubbed, rebuilt, organised, and learnt, until the house and shop were ready. Mena had learned to read, write, do her sums, and so much more. They'd seen business take off already, and they'd made plans for the future. Mena had gone from the urchin he'd found in the rubbish heap, a cautious, but strong-willed woman, to a strong, competent partner. Despite some difficulties in the months after her arrival, which they'd been working through together, their time so far had been...*good*. She never balked at anything she was asked to do, and slowly, she had let her true colours shine; particularly when it came to keeping him in line.

They took care of each other, and so when she'd tentatively asked if he didn't have any plans, if she could make some food, and perhaps go to church, naturally, he'd said yes. After all, she was an independent woman, now earning her own money—of course he would pay for whatever she wished for—but she could do what she pleased.

More out of curiosity, or perhaps nostalgia, he'd gone with her to Midnight Mass last eve. For one, he wasn't quite keen on her going out alone, particularly at night, not when she was just beginning to be able to go out again *at all*; and then he'd thought it might remind him of his youth. Of those cold nights in church as a boy—with his uncle and cousin—which at first had not seemed so cold, with all the candles, and people come together to hear wonderful stories. That had been before he'd seen the hypocrisy of it all; before he'd lost his faith, in God and man. For as he'd grown, he'd come to know the priest was just as guilty as the rest of the congregation;

and he'd known one night a year in church couldn't save your soul if you didn't live a life of honour, and respect for your fellow man.

Mr Walton had been a fervent, but reasonable believer, and Freddie had always gone with him, out of respect. A good shepherd herded their flock with wisdom, and inspiration; and such was the type of sermons Freddie had always encountered with Mr Walton. Last night's service had been along similar lines—goodwill and peace to all men—though there had been some moralising which had been amusing only in that Mena's nose had wrinkled each time, as if she neither was quite impressed with what *code of conduct* was being touted.

She was certainly interesting. A country girl, hard-working, and yet, with the most inquisitive mind. Not that country girls couldn't be inquisitive. Rather, he'd made an assumption, based on facts, and she'd completely destroyed those preconceptions. She seemed to do that at every turn—surprise him.

As she had today, with a feast of food—not extravagant, but crafted with exquisite tenderness, and...*love*, he supposed. A perfect goose, some parsnips, potatoes, and even a plum pudding. The woman had even got him a gift—silver cufflinks in the shape of compasses. Where, how, *when*, she'd found those, *why*... Well, those were all questions best not asked.

It had been a strange experience, living with her, sharing this house, this *life*. There were sometimes temptations, to intimacy, of the mind, and yes, of the body, but he knew he couldn't ever allow them to cross those lines. They had—*were still*—marking up boundaries, where the other wasn't allowed to go lest there be danger; lest their relationship, their tenuous impersonal closeness, be broken. His past was one thing he was continuously tempted to share—and yet one which he knew he never could.

So yes, this whole Christmas business, with gifts, good food, and holly hanging about his house, and quiet little fireside songs, and games of cards, well. It was…

Lovely, and dangerous. Though he felt it was the one thing he couldn't deny her—or even himself. It almost seemed a fitting celebration to their own meeting a year ago—a sort of reprieve. A moment in time when they could—

*What the Devil?*

Frowning, Freddie perked his ears, listening intently. Someone was creeping in the house. He recognised the creak of that floorboard near the top of the stairs— just as he'd recognised the squeak of that doorknob— *Mena's*.

Slowly, so quietly that he might've been a ghost, Freddie crept out of bed, and went to the door. There was the unmistakeable sound of her descending slowly, and curious as to what she was about, Freddie followed, mindful to follow her pace so any noise he made would be covered by her own footsteps. On they went, at what felt a snail's pace, until finally they reached the kitchen. Freddie remained in the darkness at the bottom of the stairs, and watched as Mena lit a candle, then rustled about the room, gathering pieces of their remaining feast, and wrapping them into a parcel.

*Perhaps she is…hungry again?*

But then why wouldn't she…eat? Why would she be wrapping it, when he himself often wandered down in the midst of the night to steal a morsel of bread? And why was she dressed? And taking a blanket too?

*Why is she donning her shoes, coat, hat, and gloves?*

He waited until the door was locked to follow, donning his own boots and coat. Swiping the spare set of keys from the mantel, he slipped outside, following her footprints in the thick snow, out into the courtyard, to the alley, then out onto Holly Street. He kept to the shadows when he spotted her lone outline, creeping along the silent and somewhat pristine streets. Then, about two streets south, he saw her duck down another alley, out of the streetlamps' light, and he hastened, wondering what the Devil this was all about. He wasn't angry so much as...*baffled*. It wasn't as if he thought her about any mischief, but really, who went about packing food and wandering the streets at one in the morning, he noted, as the bells tolled across town?

And then, he reached the alley, dank and narrow like so many others, this one home to boarded-up houses and shops. He peered down it, the moon no help as it was barely a quarter. Still, his eyes adjusted to the dimness, and he saw her outline slip into darkness, and into one of the buildings. Again, he crept and followed, until he reached the window where she'd disappeared, and then, he peered between the boards closing it off from view.

Inside, a lone stub of a candle burned, and there was Mena with...

Well, he didn't know. A youngish man, who seemed older for having lived. He was bundled in a threadbare coat, with boots that looked as if the soles would fall off, and no hat, but a wool scarf. There were old papers strewn about the floor in what resembled a *paillasse*, and then, Freddie understood.

All at once, curiosity morphed into... Something that had no name he could think of. His heart tightened in his chest, as he watched her smile, and the young man laugh, and the two behave as if old friends. He'd known of Mena's kindness, and generosity, if only for having experienced them himself. But to see her now, creeping about pinching food for another who was as they'd both been once… It changed him. Or perhaps simply changed how he saw her. Whatever it was, he couldn't have her believing she had to sulk about in the middle of the night to do such things as this.

And so, he waited for her to come out, which was a while, during which he learned of the man's youth in Yorkshire, and how he'd lost a hand at Waterloo, as he enjoyed some of what Mena had brought. He even learned that Mena had a great-aunt who apparently only had one hand due to a farming accident, and still had remained the best crocheter in the parish.

*I should've liked to meet her, I think…*

'Good morning, Mena,' Freddie whispered when she finally came out, though Mena jumped, startled, nonetheless. 'Shh…shh… I didn't mean to frighten you, I'm sorry,' he added gently, and she stopped backing away, recognising his voice. 'I couldn't think of a way *not* to startle you.'

'Freddie… What are you doing here?' she asked, still frightened, though not of a shadow in darkness, but of his reaction.

'Rather a silly question, no? I followed you.'

'I… I… Please, don't be angry.'

'Mena, I'm angry that you didn't think to trust me with what you wished to do.'

'I'm sorry,' she said, and he could tell she was bowing her head.

'Stop saying that, and come along so we can speak in some sort of light.' He took hold of her elbow, and guided her back onto the street, where they stood beneath a streetlamp. She looked…*otherworldly* in the dim orange glow, surrounded by now pristine snow—the flakes falling again, in thick tufts now. 'You should've come to me. You didn't trust me, and you might've put yourself in danger.'

'Daniel would never,' she objected immediately. ''E's a good man, a good soldier, who served this country, and lost everything when he lost his arm. They'd put him in jail with that new law—'

'Mena, Mena,' he said soothingly, reaching out both arms as if to take hers, then stopping himself. 'I believe you. But you were wandering the streets at night. Alone. If you'd have asked, I'd have come. And we might've brought your friend Daniel a little more, perhaps even some clothes and boots, if that was your wish, and his.' Mena stared at him with wide eyes, as if she couldn't quite believe what he was saying. 'I understand, as well as you and he, what it means to have nothing,' he reminded her, though perhaps it wasn't truly a reminder, for had he ever told her anything of how he'd come to be Freddie Walton?

*No. And not today.*

'Go tell him to come by the shop tomorrow, and we will outfit him for the winter properly. And if Daniel is interested, I can speak to Henderson; I think he has some work going.'

'Thank you,' Mena breathed.

And the way she looked…

*NO.*

'No thanks necessary. Off you go.'

With a blinding smile, she scampered back down the alley, and Freddie waited while she did as instructed.

When she had, they walked back to Holly Street, arm in arm, and Freddie thought, that in all the years, he'd never quite understood the meaning of Christmas as he had tonight. Mena had reminded him, of what the day was truly about.

And he thought, that perhaps, in future, if they were blessed with another Yuletide, perhaps, they could find ways to remember that lesson, together, next time.

## Chapter Thirteen

'What would Society say if they realised you are not so fashionable as they believe,' Freddie said chidingly, as he approached the undeniably *au courant* woman nestled at one of only two tables set by the diamond-pane bay windows of the coffee house, one of the last survivors of a bygone age.

Nestled in a backstreet between the Garden and Soho, on the very cusp of respectability, it was a quaint, cramped place of dark wood, miniscule tables and chairs, books, and the most delicious scents. It was friendly, welcoming, and remained steadfast in its purpose of being a place of amicable meetings, debates, and enlightenment.

Mary glanced up from the book cradled on her lap, and smiled.

'Meeting in a coffee house? Distinctly scandalous and *passé.*'

'Considering your company supplies said vestige of the past, Mr Walton,' Mary pointed out, raising a brow. 'I would've thought you'd appreciate the choice of venue.'

'How on earth do you know that?'

'Come now, Freddie,' she laughed. 'You more than anyone knows I'm far cleverer than I seem.'

'Indeed, I do. Good morning, Mary,' he said, taking her hand, and kissing it, before settling across from her.

'Good morning, Freddie,' she replied daintily, mischief still sparkling in her eyes.

She turned, nodding to one of the serving women, then turned back to him, resting her elbows on the table, and cradling her chin in her hands, waiting for him to disclose the reason for this meeting.

*Clever indeed.*

It wasn't that they never met like this. They were friends; close in a way Society and, well, any onlooker might misconstrue. *Had* misconstrued. He was rather certain Mary's brother had similar thoughts—though he'd been lucky not to be questioned or encouraged by said brother. Likely because they'd often discussed their shared disinterest in marriage—though neither delved into the precise reasons. And then the past year and a half Spencer had been rather preoccupied himself, running away to Scotland, discovering long-buried family secrets, and acquiring a wife and daughter of his own.

Freddie knew his friendship with Mary could potentially lead to trouble for them both, but the fact was, she was his oldest friend other than Mena. It was Mary he'd befriended first. She'd been a constant ally and friend, who'd then introduced him to her brother in the hope of helping him rise. And he… He'd become *her* confidant too. They had a natural affinity, in mind, and in spirit, which made their conversations…easy.

There was so much more to Mary Spencer than met the eye and he knew he was aware of barely half of it. Out of necessity to some degree, having been roped in last year when she'd gone after her brother, discovering secrets that had changed *her* life. He was part of her life as much as she was part of his. Thinking on it now, it might've been easier, to agree with what the world saw when it looked at them. *A couple.* More than friends. Mary was not only clever, and kind, she was beautiful. Long golden curls, blue eyes speckled with silver, a form anyone would deem pleasant. And yet. It might've been easier, but it wasn't right. Even if he could convince himself he was worthy of *anyone*, extraordinary though Mary may be...

*She isn't Mena.*

And there was the crux, the reason he was here.

He waited as coffee was brought and poured, then took a sip for courage, glancing out the window, watching passers-by tighten cloaks and hold down hats as the torrent of scrappy flakes poured down.

'How is your family?' he asked, turning back, buying himself a moment.

'Ah... So we are doing this first,' she said, settling back into her chair to enjoy her coffee. 'They are all well, up at Clairborne House now. Spencer was quite disappointed not to see you before they left.' Mary raised an eyebrow, but Freddie refrained from responding, so she continued. 'I think he wished to tell you in person; however, I shall tell you now that he and Genevieve are expecting.'

'My sincerest congratulations.'

'Hopefully you will convey that yourself before too long.' Freddie nodded. 'Mama is thrilled of course, as is Elizabeth to be a sister. The news quite distracted from her distress at going to Clairborne House rather than Yew Park and seeing Gawain—oh, yes—Spencer purchased a companion for Galahad despite vowing never to have another goat. However, Christmas at Clairborne House is tradition as you know, and this year again, Reid, Rebecca, and Hal will be joining them.'

'But not you,' he realised.

'I was helping a friend when they left. I could try to face the roads, but I am neither sure whether I would arrive in time, nor in one piece. So I shall be remaining in the town house; there are some parties I shall likely make an appearance at.'

Mary gave him a small smile as she sipped her drink, but her whole demeanour was subdued.

Though he knew she and her brother had suffered a distance between them over the years, as both children had with their mother, they had always been stringent about spending Yuletide together. Just as he had, for years, consciously and unconsciously, with Mena. The one year they hadn't… Had been a strange sort of torture.

However, in Mary he saw not disappointment but… relief. He knew last year's revelations had changed much for her, that she'd changed somewhat, in her outward gaiety, her outward facade, becoming more pensive, almost hard at times. He didn't know if that was the reason for this separation, after all the family had not parted since as far as he knew, but something told him it was more than that.

Regret, jealousy perhaps even? That her brother had settled, with a family of his own? Unlikely, considering Mary had never been anything but open and content with her unmarried status, her seemingly now, incontestable spinsterhood, but then, there had been that moment, at Christmas, those few years ago, when she'd made him an offer. One he'd refused, naturally, though there was nothing rational or natural about it.

*Unless one takes Mena into account.*

'Is everything well with you, Mary?' he asked, clearing his throat as he cleared his mind of the past.

'Things are… Trying, at times, Freddie, I shan't lie,' she admitted softly. 'And no, there isn't anything I should like to speak of. Not… Now. Perhaps someday. Only, not today. Today,' she said, with a determined nod, straightening in her seat. 'Is about you. And how you fare, which I can guess isn't all that well, considering how you look. Is Mena well?'

'Perfectly,' he ground out, that bitterness of hurt spiking into him again, along with the bitterness of his own lie.

*She is not well—we are not well—that is why I'm here.*

Ever since he'd discovered what Mena had been doing behind his back two days ago, he'd been…festering. In anger, self-recrimination, regret. He'd tried to sort his mind out himself, tried to make sense of the turmoil, even as he fought the fear of his past lurking around every shadowed corner, but to no avail. He'd known he needed help, to at least untangle some measure of the twisted web he'd caught himself in, and desperate, he'd reached out to the only person he could trust.

*Mary.*

'Ah… Then am I to surmise she is the reason you are out of sorts?'

Freddie managed a half-grunt, half-mumble of agreement.

Again, he wished he could lay it all out—but he couldn't. Alienating her when he needed help…would be as idiotic as the rest of what he'd done recently. No, he would focus on the main problem, the one he'd discussed with her so many times before.

*Mena. Mena. Mena.*

'Would this have anything to do with that incredible endeavour of hers?' He started, narrowing his eyes. So everyone in London knew of Mena's plans? As if reading his thoughts, Mary shook her head disapprovingly at him. 'Yes, I knew, and no, she didn't tell me. The only times I've met Mena have been at the shop, with you there,' she said flatly, as if he needed to know, which, his heart seemed to cry, he did. 'I heard about it from friends, who thought I might be interested in contributing, which I did, anonymously. It was my understanding that Mena did not wish for you to know. It was therefore not my secret to share.'

'She didn't tell me.'

'You discovered her scheme before she could?' He nodded, his words caught by the lump in his throat. Shifting uncomfortably, he glanced back outside, hoping the sights of the city would calm him, as his friend was doing anything but. 'And it did not go well, I presume?' Freddie shook his head, Mary's tone making him squirm; her stark understanding and clear censure neither what he expected, nor needed. 'What did you say to her, Freddie?'

'The truth.'

'That she has done extraordinary work, and that you are very proud, and happy for her?' Was he blushing?

*No, this is shame burning your cheeks.*

'I thought not.'

'I accused her of going behind my back,' he admitted begrudgingly, staring down at the remnants of dark liquid in the cup he hadn't realised he was cradling. 'Of not trusting me. I was—I *am*—hurt. She betrayed me, *lied* to me—'

'*Betrayal* is a strong word, Freddie. I would caution you in its use.'

With a sigh, he nodded, running his fingers through his hair, and setting the cup back in the saucer before he did something like launch it across the room.

*It is only yourself you are angry at. For what you did to Mena.*

'Did she tell you why she kept it from you?'

'No. Only that she was going to tell me, and then she accused me of not seeing what is right in front of me.'

Mary snorted, most unladylike and startling.

'Well, she is right,' Mary shrugged, offering him a beseeching smile, as if to say, *admit it.* He rolled his eyes, doing just that. 'Have you finally admitted to yourself that you love her, Freddie? That you are *in* love with her?'

*Inconceivable.*

Were all the women in his life able to read his heart and soul so easily?

*No. Only the ones who care for you. And I don't... love her.*

'I'm not in love with her,' he mumbled, unsure where his conviction from the other night had gone. 'I...don't know what that even means.' Mary frowned, and he shook his head, unwilling to delve further in *that.* 'Even if I did, we're not... We can't be.'

*Keep telling yourself that, even after what you did...*

'All these years, she's been working for me. Helping me build *my* business. I couldn't see it, what I'd taken from her, until I came back. She deserves a choice, to make her own life. She cannot do that if she stays with me.'

'She has done very well building a life of her own already, Freddie. Or is that precisely what bothers you?'

'I should've helped her. I should've been the one to stand by her and help her build her dreams,' he explained rather loudly, checking himself when he noticed other patrons glancing pointedly his way.

'Perhaps that is what lies at the core of this mess,'

Mary said gently. 'You must not forget what Mena has now, thanks to you. Her life, her education. I think, she might've wished to prove she could do something on her own. Just as you once did.'

'But I didn't do it alone.'

'I know that, Freddie. However, think, if you were Mena, would you want to owe more to the person who you might already feel indebted to?'

Freddie took in a deep breath, and poured them both some more coffee.

'I don't want her to feel indebted,' he said, realising then that was precisely the core of the matter. 'Ever.'

'Deny it all you like Freddie, you are in love with her. Even if you were better at hiding it, even if I had paid no attention to you these past four years, all you've just said, would tell me precisely that. Wanting what is best for another, to help them build their dreams, even if it takes them from you… I think that is what love truly is. And I believe, that what you fear, is the possibility she might only return your feelings out of gratitude,' Mary offered sagely.

Leave it to her to sense everything so immediately when it had taken him a long time to sort through his *own* heart.

Not that he had, really. Up until about five minutes ago, he'd been prepared to live in the land of denial where he *didn't* love Mena. He still wasn't convinced he knew how to do so properly, one had only to look at how he'd behaved, *like a careless, wanton, brutish boor*, but he couldn't refute anything Mary said, and when *she* said it, it sounded…*right*. And there was that unextinguishable fear he felt any time he thought of losing Mena. So yes, maybe, he'd been right at the start. Maybe he did love Mena—only not properly.

Because he had no idea how to do that.

'Or is it that you believe whatever feelings she may already harbour for you are born of the fact you saved her life, and kept her with you all these years?'

'I don't wish for her to have tender feelings for me at all. I don't wish for her to love me,' he whispered, feeling more vulnerable, and eviscerated, than he had in… *A very long time.* 'I wish for her to be free of me. Before it's too late.'

Mary frowned and, etiquette be damned, reached out and placed her hand on his, concern marring the usually clear depths of her eyes.

'Too late…? Freddie, are you in trouble?'

*No.*

*Yes.*

*Always.*

*For ever.*

'I only meant before it's too late for her to have her own life,' he lied.

His friend looked as if she were about to argue, and pry further, but instead she nodded, unconvinced, but knowing better.

Removing her hand, she crossed her arms and looked out the window for a moment.

'Why did you come to me, Freddie?' she asked after a long moment, the clear, fading light of winter flickering across her face. 'What is it you needed from me?'

'I don't think I'm even certain.'

'Well,' she smiled, turning back to him. 'In that case, general advice. Fix what you have broken, before it *is* too late. Apologise, and support her. She will understand, I am sure. After all, she knows you best of all, I think. Despite whatever it is you keep from everyone.' A pointed look, and she continued. 'I would also counsel you to open your heart, to tell her all you've told me, and let the woman have *her* say, but I know that would be a lost cause.' Freddie huffed out a bitter laugh—*right again*. 'Whatever the future holds for you both, you wouldn't want what you have to end like this. Even if your paths diverge, make it right before they do.'

'You are a very wise woman, Lady Mary,' he said softly, gratitude in his eyes, beyond that which he could express with mere words.

'I know,' she grinned shamelessly.

'Mena is planning a large celebration for Christmas,' he said after a moment. 'At her new…house. You should come along.'

'Thank you, Freddie. I would… However, I think you both need some time, together, *alone*. And, well, so do I. A quiet Christmas will suit me just fine this year.'

'The invitation stands, should you change your mind,' he said, even then knowing she wouldn't.

Whatever was on Mary's mind, he understood that she needed time for herself to sort through it. If and when she needed to talk, she would come to him.

He knew that too.

'Perhaps after Christmas, we can go for a show,' she suggested. 'Depending on how things stand with Mena, perhaps she could come as well.'

'Perhaps,' he agreed.

It would be a lovely thought, but there was so much…
*So much yet to come.*

He smiled, and they spoke a while longer, of life, of the city, of her family. Finally, he took his leave, and slowly wandered back to Holly Street. Wondering, all the while, how precisely to make things right.

*Before it is too late.*

## Chapter Fourteen

*M*ake it right. That became Freddie's mantra, as Mary was undeniably correct. Come what may, diverging paths or not, he wouldn't see things end with Mena this way—no matter how much easier that might be.

*A clean break.*

Only, it wouldn't be. It would be a break which festered and ultimately killed; at least for him. Perhaps for her too. His idiocy, his cuts, would likely make it so; at the very least.

The danger over their heads still loomed. Freddie knew that. His uncle had waited twenty-nine years for vengeance—he wouldn't just *relent*. However, with the men he'd hired at his back, Freddie felt confident, if not to let down his guard, to at least trust that they would keep a watchful eye. Besides, he had a feeling his uncle would wait—let him remain on tenterhooks for a time. Let the fear and anticipation build. He might've feared a greater scheme altogether, but events so far led him to believe his uncle had discovered him only recently, and hadn't had time to put something far worse into place. If his uncle had even been capable of such; he was a mean, spiteful man, but not someone ever capable of seeing larger possibilities. A schemer, not a planner.

*Bastard either way.*

Yes. Both of them were.

In any case, Freddie knew he had some time to attempt and mend what he'd shattered. How... Well now, that was the question, wasn't it?

Though an apology was obviously in order—he was still working through precisely what and how to say it all—he also knew words would not be enough. If anything could ever be enough. This...*grovelling* demanded action. It demanded he demonstrate, *prove*, that not only was he sorrier than words could ever express, but that he *was* immensely proud. That he did, and would always, support Mena, in any way she'd let him. That his hurt was not merely from her deception, *surprise*, but at himself. For having imposed a policy of separation. A limit on intimacy and sharing. That he'd been so blind, so as not to see he'd been holding her back; or rather, that he'd not even paid enough attention to see that she was already moving on. He couldn't quite relinquish the policies on separation and intimacy, he couldn't reveal all he felt, but perhaps, he could...*relax* it.

It was all well and good to come to such conclusions, it was entirely another to put it into action. The day after meeting Mary, Freddie managed to track down Susie, and after a rather long speech demonstrating his contrition, he convinced her to help him. Somewhat warily, she laid out Mena's plans for Christmas, and together they devised ways he could be useful—without stepping on Mena's toes, and without being discovered. Which led to some rather comical moments, as it was quite a challenge considering Mena spent half of the remaining days until Christmas Eve at Nichols House. There

were some rapid retreats under tables, and quick dis-
simulations behind other persons.

However, she did save him from having to avoid her
at Holly Street, as she did that herself. She still ensured
the shop was open, and well-tended, she still prepared
every meal, and kept the house as she always had, but
she was like a wisp of smoke, disappearing from one
moment to the next. Not that Freddie didn't understand.
God knew he understood. Had the situations been re-
versed, he might have wished to never look upon his
own face again. In fact, as it was, he couldn't quite stand
to look at himself at the moment.

*I will make it right.*

And so it was that Freddie found himself with the
building crew, finishing the house, notably the offices
which had been left until last. He thought he might get
exposed by Mena's accountant, but when he pleaded
for her secrecy, she laughed, and declared it would be a
great lark. At least someone found amusement in all this.

Along with building, Freddie found himself making
wreaths and strands of greenery with a collection of
Scots. He cooked and baked until he was pastry himself
with a group of Portuguese, Prussians, and Russians.
He collected the extra crockery and blankets donated by
an old boarding school in Essex. He swept, he sewed,
he basted, he wrapped small gifts and prepared games;
he did anything that was needed.

Every minute he spent in the halls of Mena's creation,
his admiration, and his love, for her grew. She was in everything; and the smiles on even the most tired and hag-
gard faces told him her care had infused everyone. The
popularity of the place—it was bursting at the seams—
considering it wasn't yet officially open, was staggering.
Though he knew Mena would no sooner have turned

away someone in need on pretence of being *unready*, than she would've kicked a child.

This place… It was her dream. And perhaps it was also *their* dream, one he'd never thought to have, but was at the heart of them. At the very least, it was an extension of their own traditions.

Every year, since he'd discovered Mena squirrelling victuals to her friend Daniel, who still worked at Henderson's warehouses, Yuletide had become a time for them to give. It had begun small, opening their doors, and serving food to those Mena could find nearby, and convince to come. Ten, perhaps twenty, would come to the kitchen door, and either come in to sit by the fire, and have a meal, or simply take something and go, as they wished. Each year, it had grown, until the past year, they'd welcomed nearly two hundred over two days.

Some they helped find lodgings, or work if they wished, at nearby shops, at the markets, at the docks. Others in Holly Street helped, leaving baskets, or coming to help Mena and Freddie cook and prepare parcels of clothes and blankets. And Christmas wasn't the sole time of year they did what they could to help others; Freddie supported charities which best aligned with his and Mena's principles of *giving without conditions*, and she continued assisting those she met every day in what ways she could. But Christmas…

That had always been a special time.

Freddie hadn't quite realised how much so until he'd gone to Clairborne House. It had pained him, physically, but he'd listened to Mena and Mary, when they'd said it would be for the best, that it would forge stronger relationships with a powerful family. It had been a pleasant enough time, though very strange when he and Spencer had finally gone to Thornhallow Hall. Except it had seemed so cold to him, that Yuletide. Not solely because of the separation from Mena, but because he'd been in such a formal, quiet, and lonely setting. There had been all one could ask for—except what fed Freddie's heart.

There weren't people from every corner of the earth, every walk of life, milling in and sharing stories. There wasn't laughter, and warmth, and a sense of *togetherness* with his fellow man. There weren't children playing in the snow of his courtyard, making angels, and there wasn't a sense of being right where he should be. After that time away, Freddie had sworn he would never miss Christmas at Holly Street again; though Spencer had asked for his company again. He'd never told him why, never felt comfortable sharing all those feelings with the man; though after last year's events, he might've. Mary was the only one who knew of Mena, and even she didn't know what happened at Holly Street every December.

Not telling Spencer, or Reid for that matter, of Mena, was...*explicable*. Her own reluctance to meet new people, to go to places Spencer or Reid frequented, was an easy excuse to accept. Even if he might've brought either of them to Holly Street—for years he'd had the most successful and powerful men of shipping and trade there for dinner parties as he built up his own enterprise. He might've at least spoken of her to his friends; except he hadn't. Because...

*Because I was a coward. I wanted to preserve it all as it was.*

As if his life with Mena *could* be preserved. Like a ship in a bottle, untouchable by the outside world. Never to face the trials and turbulence of the open seas. Only he hadn't preserved anything. He'd wrecked it from the inside out.

*Which is why you will make it right. All of it.*

Yes, Freddie vowed as he finished tying his cravat, the last of his preparations for the evening. Glancing at himself in the mirror, he met his own eyes, and that vow ensured he could.

*Time to speak the words now.*

Everything was perfect; just as she'd dreamt it. The house was full to burst with people, who tonight were all smiling. Glowing, with joy, and hope, and it soothed her own broken soul. Greenery, banners, fanions, baubles, drawings, and sprigs of mistletoe and holly hung from every possible corner, wall, doorway, and banister. Candles and lamps illuminated the house, and a symphony of excited chatter in a hundred different languages and dialects echoed from the walls.

*Everything I dreamt of.*

It was. Weeks ago, months ago, years ago, she wouldn't have thought it possible. Yet everyone here had worked tirelessly to make it so. Perhaps it was frivolous, to accord so much importance to one time of year. To one celebration. Except that Mena had found something, in the darkest winter night those eight years ago. She'd found light, comfort, and hope; the most precious gifts of all. Civilisations for millennia had celebrated this time—the solstice, Yule, Christmas—and no matter what one believed in, the gods of old or the Son of God, it was a time when people could gather, and feast by the fire, and know, that soon, winter would end. A new day would come, and that *was* worth celebrating.

Tonight, and tomorrow, they would. There would be music and laughter, good food, games, dancing, and shelter from the frozen, snowy night. Respite, brotherhood, and *love*. Standing at the door to the mess hall,

Mena gazed upon all the souls gathered there, and let peace trickle into her heart, as people came and went, offering her good wishes and smiles, which she returned, though her mind drifted elsewhere.

These past days… These past days since Freddie had come, and seen, *said*, all those things, had been difficult. The blows he'd dealt had cut deep, and though she knew she should make things right, she couldn't find the courage. To say her own piece; to confront him, properly. To say all left unsaid. She had divided her time between the shop, busy with the season, and here. Not that they'd truly needed her here; everyone lent a hand to see that the celebration could happen, and that there would be space, and supplies, for anyone who needed either. Everything was organised and prepared without her needing to help; all she needed do was say the word, and things happened. She wondered if great lords felt that way; building this place had taught her that though money might not buy happiness, it could materialise dreams.

Not that she was one to simply give orders. No, she'd needed, always, to feel useful. To put her own hands to good use, and so she had. It had been healing, for her own heart and spirit, selfish though *that* might be.

For so long, things had been, if not simple, then… *steady*. There had been balance, understanding, between Freddie and her, connection and support. She'd allowed herself to be entranced by the simplicity of it, to become accustomed to it, and the safety it offered. Even as the outside world, as reality, pierced through at various intervals, seemingly leading up to this, when everything would be upheaved.

*When I fell in love with Freddie.*
*When Lady Mary walked into our shop. His shop.*

*When he spent Christmas in the North.*

*When he went hunting with Mary for her brother.*

*When he returned this year, though I cannot say why.*

Every time reality pierced through the illusion of their life, through the illusion that it could last for ever, Mena had ignored it. Swatted it away like some troublesome fly, so she could cling tighter to her fantasy. Until she'd clung so tight every inch of her soul hurt; and she'd made nothing but a tangled mess. If there was one thing she would regret when she died, it would be that she was a coward. A fearful thing, unable to relinquish her fear because…

*I know it too well.*

There was safety in it too. Safety in keeping to the same streets, in keeping to the life she knew. In not disturbing the balance of her life with Freddie, so as not to lose it altogether.

*And yet I have.*

That was the crux, wasn't it? What she'd truly wished for tonight, selfishly, was for Freddie to be here, with her, to share this. For them to celebrate, as they always had, surrounded by others. She knew it would end someday, that he would go on, rise, live his own life, but before he did, she'd wanted to share this with him.

*One last Christmas, as was our way.*

Well, she would not mope. She would enjoy this, and find what she wished to give others.

*Joy.*

Taking a deep breath, she smiled to herself, and made to step into the room, but before she could, a hand appeared on her arm.

'Susie!' she exclaimed, slightly startled, before she looked over to find her friend looking lovely in a dark gown of burgundy wool, and a crown of holly. *'Joyeux Noël,'* she said, folding the woman into her arms.

'And a happy Christmas to you!' her friend returned, taking her hands, and looking her up and down. 'My, my, you look *resplendissante.'*

Mena smiled at the compliment, though she never truly accepted them.

She appreciated it though, having made an effort with the more daringly low-cut navy-blue gown, and gold ribbon in her hair, which was neatly pulled back for the occasion, though that had necessitated quite a few pins. All topped off with the necklace Freddie had gifted her.

*Not that I ever take it off.*

'Thank you,' she said gracefully. 'You look *très belle* yourself.'

'Why, thank you very much,' Susie grinned. 'It is all like you imagined, yes?'

'Yes,' Mena lied.

'Well, I am off to find some punch, and upstairs some of the children will be performing a play soon. You should go to the front desk. Someone is waiting for you.'

With a slight frown, and a nod, Mena watched her friend disappear, then headed to the front hall, wondering who could need *her.*

After all, everything was well under way, and barring something unfortunate—

Mena couldn't have stopped the gasp which escaped had she tried. Her feet became rooted to the spot, even as groups of people milled around her. Tears pricked her eyes, and her heart sped up to an indecent rhythm, hope of a different kind swelling inside her.

*He came.*

Or at least, so it seemed, though she wasn't quite sure she could trust her eyes not to be merely conjuring up

Freddie, dressed in formal, but far from extravagant evening wear, his gaze firmly affixed on her own, his eyes shining with...

*Something else I don't recognise.*

All she knew, was that it made his eyes clear, a bright spring sky full of promise. Slowly, she made her way to him, and it wasn't actually that difficult when it felt as if they were the only two people in the world.

Still, she told herself to mitigate her emotions; for all she knew he could be here for any other reason than the one she wished for.

'You're here,' she breathed when she finally stood before him, after what felt like a century.

Only, he really *was* here; she could feel his warmth, and his scent met her nose, and he was smiling so brightly it was blinding, and studying her with those clear eyes as if he'd never seen her until now; quite as, she was sure, she was doing. So at least she knew he wasn't a figment of her imagination.

*That is something.*

'May we speak?' he asked quietly. 'Somewhere, less busy?'

Nodding, Mena shook herself from the hazy, magical dream, and glanced around, able to see it all again, though still somehow separate, enclosed in a warm bubble.

Spotting an unoccupied corner, she gestured, and together they slipped to it.

Not entirely private, but then, tonight, short of finding a dark alley somewhere, Mena didn't think anywhere in the house would be devoid of people.

*Full, as I wish it always to be.*

'Freddie...' she began when they stood before one another again, the words she'd tried and tested for days not so easy to *say* now.

'I'm sorry, Mena,' he said with a dead seriousness that pierced through her apprehensions. Meeting his eyes again, she found that whatever had been coiled up tight inside her these past days—*my heart*—unfurled. 'Truly, for everything. I behaved, abominably, though that word is hardly close to how despicable I was. Not only after what happened at the shop, how I treated you then, how I injured you... But here, when I saw what you'd built. I do not say this to excuse myself, but I reacted out of anger, because I was hurt.'

'Freddie—'

'Please,' he breathed, raising his hand. 'Let me finish. You accused me of not seeing what was right in front of me, and you were right. You helped me build my life, Mena, you must understand that,' he pleaded gently, taking a step closer. 'I care for you,' he admitted, as if it cost him to say the words. 'And it hurt, that when the time came for you to build something of your own, you did not come to me to support you.'

'I wanted to do it myself,' she whispered, her heart beating furiously, that he was here, that he did understand. 'I wanted...' God, why was it so hard to speak the words? To admit her selfishness? 'You gave me so much, Freddie. An education, work, a home. A future. The world... I wanted to give that to others, but the terrible truth is... I wanted to prove to you that I could do it. All on my own.'

*That I was worthy. Of you.*

That final confession, she couldn't make it, though she willed the truth to shine in her eyes.

'I know,' he smiled. And whether he did know *all* of it, well. It felt as if he did, and perhaps, that was enough for now. 'I do see that. It took time, and some help. But I do understand.'

Something worse than hurt raised its head inside her at the mention of *help*, for she knew well who he meant.

But it didn't matter, because he was here, with her now.

'You are the best friend I have in the world, Mena,' he continued, and the confession was both a balm, and a painful reminder of all that could never be. 'We have shared so much, and I... I know things must change, that things *have* changed. However, I would never forgive myself if we parted ways as we might've. Though I don't deserve to ask, I will ask that you forgive *me*. That we be friends, once more. I wish to spend this season with you, as we always have. I wish to be part of what *you* built here. These past days... I've spent them here, seeing all you've done. I am so proud of you. Inspired by you.'

The only words she'd ever wished to hear stole her breath, and her power of speech.

She nodded, her throat tight, and smiled, swearing she would not cry. She would not cry because he spoke of things changing, and parting ways, for that was the way of it, of life. A fact she'd always lived with, and she knew he was right. On all counts. Parting as they might've, with things fragmented, would've been torture, and something else she would regret always. Parting as friends, sharing one final season, knowing his care for her, not that she'd ever truly doubted *that*—it would be enough.

*It will have to be.*

'I am sorry too,' she managed finally. 'Things are changing; I've felt it for some time. And it terrifies me. I kept this from you for so long...*too* long. You are *my* best friend, Freddie, and I too should like us to spend the season together. Whatever life has in store for us, I think perhaps we should learn to speak of it a little better with each other. No more misunderstandings, no more of this avoiding each other. I have hated these past days, these past weeks, and I shouldn't like to repeat them.'

'Neither should I,' he agreed, though there was a tightness in his expression.

The warming of a fiddle, accordion, and various other instruments sounded loudly in the hall, breaking the tension, for which they both seemed relieved.

'I think that means it is time to join in the party,' she chuckled lightly.

And she did feel...*lighter*.

So much remained unsaid; so much likely would. A danger still lurked in the dark, Freddie's past hanging heavily around them like a storm on the horizon. Yet it was still on the horizon. For a time, they could be friends again, and share in the glorious bounty of the season.

*Joy, light, and good cheer.*

'Then let us join the party,' Freddie agreed, offering out his arm.

And together, they did just that.

# Chapter Fifteen

The past two days had been a fantastical, chimerical dream Freddie never wished to wake from. Full of radiant splendour. Mena and he had spent every waking hour at Nichols House, dancing, feasting, playing, cooking, serving, talking with hundreds of different people... It had been a Christmas unlike he'd ever known; and was unlikely to ever know again.

It was indescribable, what he'd felt there, always, it seemed, at Mena's side. Beyond peace, beyond warmth; it became something unutterable which filled him with...*completion*. A sense of belonging, of family, of *home*, which went far beyond what he'd ever understood they could be. Not something you were born without or without, but something which you could find, create. It was dizzying, *incredible*, and Freddie felt as if he was walking on air.

Even now, as they made their way to the back door of the Holly Street house, after a day full of more subdued celebration, and cleaning, tired as he knew he should be, Freddie felt alive. Electric. Capable of anything. And he knew who was to thank.

Mena stood at the door, bundled up against the unrelenting cold that had now firmly taken hold of the city. She glanced back at him, expectantly, and Freddie's mind rushed back to that night, eight years ago, when they'd stood almost as they did now.

How much had changed in all that time? How little? How much had they grown, together, becoming truer versions of themselves, without even noticing? How much had they shared, without ever realising? The Mena before him now, she was at her core the same woman to whom he'd offered shelter; knowing in his heart it wouldn't merely be for a night. And yet, she was so much more.

Flashes of her throughout the years, many of them from his returns after long voyages, darted through his mind's eye. A twinge of nostalgia plucked at his heart as he watched her become the woman she was now almost in an instant. It was then he understood there hadn't been *a* moment when he'd fallen in love with her. There wasn't any *one* moment to identify, because it had been the work of weeks, months, years. It was the work of a lifetime. To fall in love with her, to feel it, have it evolve and grow as they did; even as he hadn't known what it was. He'd felt it, living in his breast, with him every second of every day. It had picked him up when he'd thought he couldn't fight any longer; and it had kept him company on the farthest edges of the world.

Standing there in the light of the half-moon, the blanket of snow covering their courtyard that in spring and summer would be bursting with wildflowers and vegetables, Freddie felt—

'Freddie, are you coming?'

'Yes,' he chuckled, sauntering to the door.

Mena frowned, a smile playing at the corners of her

lips, a question in her eyes, but once he was beside her, she hurriedly opened the door.

Hawk yipped and hopped in excited greeting, and they both took turns petting him whilst removing their coats. Freddie slipped him a ham bone he'd stashed, and at once, the beast returned to his blanket by the hearth to chew on it. Mena threw him an *oh, so that is how it is* glance, and he shrugged.

Shaking her head, Mena finished divesting herself of her layers, lit a candle, and then they both stood there in the dusky kitchen, somewhat awkwardly, the dying embers and single candle the only light, though they illuminated all he ever needed to see.

*Mena.*

Or perhaps, she was the light. It surely felt that way. And he was no better than one of those moths that flew straight for it, for here he was, being drawn closer, without any recollection of allowing his feet to move. Together, they stood there, simply *looking* at each other, the candle between them, flickering with every breath. He wasn't sure what was happening, yet neither did he wish to make sense of it.

All he knew, was that something was, and if he listened to reason, and did as they always did—wished each other goodnight and left—he would regret it.

'Thank you, Freddie,' Mena whispered after a long moment, something shifting her eyes from deep blue back to the pale lightness he knew so well. 'For being there. All your help.'

'There's nowhere else I would rather be,' he admitted quietly.

'Freddie, I… Goodnight,' she said finally, turning to leave.

He knew he shouldn't—but he couldn't stop himself.

Gently, he laid a hand on her arm, and turned her back to him. There wasn't one, but a thousand questions in her eyes, which he couldn't bring himself to answer.

Instead, he asked one, reaching up to finger the silky strand escaped from the braids she sported today.

'Why do you keep it so short always?'

Her eyes widened, reluctance, and a plea not to make her answer, filling them.

Freddie gazed back, pleading in his own eyes.

An offering, to her; a prayer for her to cross this new line with him.

'I like it. But mostly, to remind me that I'm safe,' she said softly, her voice cracking, and he felt his heart do so too. He never wished to hurt her, never again, and yet he knew they would both have to face pain in order to break through to something...*else.* 'I sold it, when I first came to London. Got me a bed for two nights. Keeping it this way...reminds me I don't have to again.'

'You've let it grow these past months,' he frowned. 'You've let it grow these past months,' he repeated, understanding hitting him when she shrugged slightly.

Mena too had felt the shift.

*The divergence of our paths.*

He hated it. Hated that, if even for a moment, she *hadn't* felt safe. She'd built something extraordinary, where others could, and where she would go if, *when*, they parted, yet still, she'd not felt safe. That she would always have a haven here, in this home that was theirs; and it was his own fault. There was so much to tell her, yet he didn't have the strength for that.

Still, he could... He *wished*, wanted, with every fibre of his being, to make her feel safe. Protected, *loved*. In that moment, he knew that though he couldn't say the words, couldn't make promises, he could make her feel what was in his heart.

There was the distinct possibility that it would ruin what he'd just mended, attempting to cross this line again. That he would condemn himself to even more turmoil when this all ended, yet he couldn't walk away.

*Not unless she tells me to.*

'Mena… Would you let me stay with you tonight?' he asked quietly, barely above a murmur, and yet, it seemed the loudest, clearest thing he'd ever said.

If she felt any surprise, he saw no trace.

Instead, it seemed as if she'd already known he would ask; and known what her answer would be. Wordlessly, she took his hand, and no matter what mess would follow, he knew all would be well, because this rightness couldn't be a mistake.

*I may not know much but I do know that.*

*In for a penny, in for a pound as they say*, Mena thought, as she slowly led Freddie upstairs. In this case, it would be a pound of flesh in the shape of her heart. Then again, she'd relinquished that to him years ago, so really, it wasn't a matter of that at all any more. She wasn't sure what was happening, what this was beyond a physical intimacy they both needed; but she was tired of questioning.

Tired of hesitating, and considering all the possible horrific outcomes ceaselessly.

Yes, her heart would be broken; but that would happen regardless as two facts remained incontestable: that she loved Freddie, and that someday soon their lives would continue down different paths.

Yes, it would change their friendship; however, that had already been unarguably altered.

So, for the first time in a long time, she hadn't questioned the sense of his request, or her own answer. She'd leapt, headfirst, into…*whatever* this was. Not unafraid, yet master of the fear enough to know, looking into Freddie's eyes downstairs, that whatever they shared would be different. That he wouldn't hurt her, regret it as before; that he needed her as much as she did him.

These past days, this Christmas, had been all she'd ever imagined, and more. Being at Nichols House, sharing all they had—laughter, extraordinary moments with others—feeling supported and as if she had a true partner beside her, it had changed her. Or at least, shown her all she had in her life—with or without Freddie. And though she'd never doubted his care, his friendship, she'd always wondered what would happen when their lives finally divided. She'd doubted, that no matter *what* passed, they could, and would, remain connected. Now… She doubted no more. Her trust in him had surpassed the niggling, irrational fear that always lingered, despite all they'd faced, that one day she would find herself alone again, cast far from Freddie's light.

Though trials lay ahead, she knew, as she led the way into his room, not so different from what it had always been, merely populated by more books and clothes as the years passed, that nothing would break the bonds they had forged, not entirely.

And the other truth was, that if they faced the end of the road together, she wished to know him, in every way; experience what she'd let her mind only rarely ponder in the inkiest hours of the night. This night would be different from the night in the shop. There was a promise of care, of yielding, in Freddie's eyes—and though they might not *love* each other tonight, it would be something she would cherish until her dying day.

Setting the candle on his night table, she turned to him, and if there had been any doubt left in her heart, it would've melted. He was looking at her with what, if she hadn't known better, she might've sworn was adoration. It was as he'd looked at her Christmas Eve—only magnified to an almost unbearable degree. Perhaps he sensed her discomfort, for a moment later, he relaxed, if only slightly, and tamped down the intensity of whatever that was—though the desire in his gaze diminished none as he advanced slowly.

And then he was there, within reach, the flickering candle casting all but themselves into darkness. Illuminating the planes of his face; all those lines she knew so well she could trace them from memory. Instead, she traced them with her fingers, cautiously, gently, following the crinkles at the corners of his eyes, the invisible dimples, the rough stubble of his greyed beard. His eyes drifted closed as he leaned into her touch, absorbing it. He was as starved as she was of affection, of tenderness, of love, yes.

*And all those I can give.*

Closing the remaining few inches of distance, she kissed him, lightly, but with ever so much intention. It was so different from before, even when he opened himself to her, and they began a lazy exploration of the other. Not solely because this wasn't passion born of turmoil, of danger, for there was passion in this kiss. Passion to make her dizzy, and drunk, on his taste which contained everything from the ambrosia of the gods, the steadfastness of the earth, and that essence of home which she would never find again, anywhere. She could wander the earth for eternity and never find it, for it was all he was.

No, this kiss was different because of the intention, from both of them.

Her intent to show him love, and all she innately knew he'd never known, how, well, God only knew; and his, which she could feel. To give her pleasure, to care for her, to cherish and worship her. She continued to run her fingers across his roughened cheek, as her other arm strayed over his shoulder. He pulled her close, one hand cradling her neck, whilst the other curled around her waist and hip, so that they were nearly one again.

*Nearly, but not quite.*

They remained there a long while, learning, playing, teasing, tempting…their passion slowly growing until they were both breathless and unsteady; their grips tighter, and sweat beading and sliding where they touched.

Breaking the kiss, but not the connection, Freddie rested his forehead against hers, his thumb lazily moving back and forth against her hip.

'If you wish to stop… Tell me. I would only ask that you remain here, sleep beside me.'

'I don't wish to stop, Freddie.'

'If you do—'

'I will tell you, I promise.'

He nodded, then nudged her nose with his own playfully, beseeching her to meet his gaze.

'I have a French letter,' he said, and she might've sworn he blushed a little. 'I have never made use of it—this one, I mean,' he added awkwardly, and she chuckled, the talk somehow diffusing some of the tension, and expectation; though it didn't dimmish the passion.

'I think it would be best,' she agreed.

The timing would otherwise be risky, and though there were other options—the doctor had been surprisingly forthcoming over the years, thinking her Freddie's bedfellow from the first, and quite modern in his beliefs—she thought the French letter would be the wisest, surest solution to avoid consequences. Though nothing was infallible, they could do their best to take what precautions they could.

He nodded, dropping a swift kiss to her lips before reluctantly untangling himself, and striding to the chest of drawers on the other side of the room.

It took a few moments of rustling, before he found the box which held the letter, and all the while Mena let her gaze drift. Despite there being nothing personal—no portraits, no baubles, no decorations—the room felt uniquely his. In its spareness, its messiness—clothes flung onto the chair, mirror, and screen, books piled haphazardly along with papers, letters, and even a cravat. This was the one place he no longer allowed her to come, not for years now, since his last bout with influenza, when he hadn't had a choice in the matter. She never ventured in secretly whilst he was away—he cleaned his own room— and being allowed in now… It felt like a massive shift, that of mountains rising from oceans as da Vinci had purported; of land emerging for her to cling to. Freddie was opening himself, infinitesimally, and that meant more to her than anything anyone had ever given her.

Freddie returned, dropping the box on the table, and they were standing there, staring at each other awkwardly again, but Mena smiled. It wasn't that either of them were novices; though Mena hadn't been with anyone since she'd come here, Freddie had, she knew, indulged at times, in the early years, and sometimes when travelling. Only, she, for one, *felt* a bit of a novice, unsure of how and where to begin.

*Simply.*

So she did, reaching out and sliding her fingers against

his palm until he followed the gesture, his hand raising at her prompting so she could twine her fingers with his. She marvelled at the sight, the matching of their long fingers, the strength and grace of his, the bony narrowness of hers, feeling his eyes travelling across her face as if he marvelled at *her*.

Letting their hands drop, still entwined, she raised her other hand to unknot his cravat, and he let her, not moving an inch, watching every move, apparently fascinated. She'd never had anyone be fascinated by her. *Marvel* at her. Well, other than at her height, which had always made her feel awkward. This was new. Spurring, and emboldening.

The men she'd been with before... They'd appreciated her well enough, in terms of what she offered. She'd never felt shame for what she'd done, for the act; only when others had made their opinion of her actions known. It had been necessity. Survival. Sometimes there had a measure of pleasure, other times, endurance. So being watched, being given...*free rein*, it was novel, disconcerting, and empowering.

It allowed her to slide off the silky cravat, toss it to the floor as if she were some grand seductress dancing with veils. It allowed her to unbutton his waistcoat, then his shirt, until she could run her hand over the heated, smooth, and thick expanse of chest, peppered with black and silver hairs. It allowed her to run the pads of her fingers, then her nails, over his now erect nipples. A small intake of breath told her he enjoyed that, and she smiled up at him, proud of her little discovery, as his fingers tightened their hold on hers.

It allowed her to pull his shirt from his trousers, and explore his torso some more, the linen at the back of her hand an interesting contrast to the taut, somewhat ridged, and scarred warm skin beneath; except for that trail of hair there, leading to places yet to be explored. Touching without seeing, it was mesmerising in its own way, but also…

*I need more. I want to see.*

Releasing his hand, she looked up at him, and the fire in his own gaze nearly turned her into ash, right there. A muscle ticked in his jaw, but he waited, to see what she would do—so she showed him.

Calling on every ounce of the seductress she'd never known within her till now, she slid her hands torturingly slowly under his coat, over his shoulders, sliding the garment off, and letting it fall to the floor with a quiet thump. Their breathing grew harsher, louder, in the otherwise quiet room, save for the occasional creak of the wood beneath her feet as she shifted, and the crackling of the candle's wick.

His waistcoat and shirt followed, and Mena took a long moment then to gaze upon that which she'd uncovered. Freddie was… Stunning. All she'd imagined, and more; a feat considering she'd done a great deal of imagining, particularly in the days when they'd worked on the house together, him in rolled-up, sweat-soaked shirtsleeves… Even as a younger man, he was strong, and solid, but she'd never quite grasped how much more so he'd become. Or how attractive he was—in that he drew her to him, like an invisible force.

So he did now, and again, she let her fingers roam, drunk on how his breathing turned into harsh, deep pants, at how his eyes drifted closed, and his fists tightened when she traced the line of his hips, or the line beneath his breast. Her impulses were beyond her control now, and she stepped into his heat again, and kissed him, this time on his Adam's apple, watching it bob as he swallowed hard. She kissed and licked, and scraped her teeth along his collarbone, the curve of his shoulder, down further, taking his nipples into her mouth for a moment, eliciting a strange, echoing moan of growl, which she felt more than heard. She traced each rib, and the line which went from sternum to belly, and before he could stop her, or she could think better, she moved around him, turning her attention to his back; committing more lines to memory, feeling just what the ridges of his spine felt like; tasting the hollow at the small of his back. Not an inch was left by the time she finished; none of her sanity or awkwardness either.

All that was left were their breaths, so short they seemed continuous.

Hot, salty skin.

Lips afire, and a hunger, low inside her that asked for more.

*More.*

Still at Freddie's back, she slid her hands around his waist, and finished divesting him of his trousers, his undergarments, his socks, and his boots. Finally, she stepped back to admire all of him; the solid power in every inch. Letting her gaze rise to his once more, she let him see her appreciation, *her* hunger, and that is when he snapped into action.

'My turn,' he growled, stepping forth, his deep voice that normally soothed setting what little was left of her unharmed on fire.

Freddie had let Mena take the lead. Because he'd felt so adrift in happiness, and so *lucky*, overwhelmed to be alive, with her, at this moment, that he could barely breathe, let alone think; let alone plan what to do. For her; with her. He wanted to give her pleasure, to show her how he felt, to prove his worth, and his devotion, if only for one night. Except that standing before her, he'd felt… A green youth, with no idea what to do.

It wasn't as if he was; though his experience was limited, unlike many he knew. He'd sought out the experience when he'd first left Mr Walton—it seemed the thing to do—and then, he'd enjoyed some comfort over the years, until he hadn't. He'd longed for more— *what*, well, he hadn't known until he'd been with Mena that first time. No matter what had come after, standing here with her again, he knew it was love he'd been missing. Affection, tenderness, that he'd always craved and never known.

*Until her.*

Those gifts, they poured from her, into him, so yes, he'd been a bit dumbstruck. At first, Mena had seemed hesitant too—until she wasn't. He'd been fascinated by her, her quiet beauty, her attention, and care to *him*, and so he'd let her do her worst, and, oh, how she had. He was throbbing, not only his baser self, but his heart, every morsel of skin, and flesh, and bone, throbbing, for *her*, until he couldn't take it anymore, whatever it was she was setting him alight with, through every touch, and every breath. He had to see her, had to finally know what she looked like, *all of her*. He'd had that glimpse once—but it hadn't seemed right to ever ponder that, dream of that. He only wished to see her… As she was now. Willing, wanting, the same desire sparking in her now iridescent depths as was in his soul. Open to him, with all she was.

*I will take it—and keep it close to my heart.*

Without wasting any precious time, for now more than ever he understood how precious time was, how easily it could run out, he kissed her, everywhere he could reach; subjecting her to the same torture she'd subjected him to as he, rather deftly if he was being honest, undid the buttons at the side of her dress, and liberated her of it. Along with the rest: the corset, the chemise, the undergarments, stockings, and boots. It all joined his piles on the floor and furniture; she may have had the patience to divest him slowly, but his hunger to be with her as man had been at the beginning of all things was too deep to deny any longer.

Finally, *finally*, there she was, a light in the shadows, beckoning him. Long limbs, small, slightly low breasts with perking nipples begging to be devoured, between which hung the necklace he'd given her. Hips and buttocks to match, and that haven of curls he would happily live in. She let him look, truly look, not hiding herself, not dropping her gaze, merely blushing in time with his roaming eyes. It was a sight to behold. If he were a painter he would immortalise it in oils; a poet, in ink.

*If only...*

However, he wasn't, so he would make do with his eyes, and his tongue, and his fingers; he would have to make his body immortalise the sight of her within him. Slightly less controlled than she, he did just that; did what she'd done to him, until she was as on edge, and panting, as he was, trembling slightly beneath his touch, her arousal thick and heavy in the air, along with her scent, and his, mingling as they always should. Their scents completed each other, as they themselves did.

*Land and sea.*

'Freddie...'

Her breathy gasping of his name unlocked a door he hadn't known was shut. He rose from where he'd been, worshipping her buttocks and thighs, and spun her around to face him. Wide eyes, filled with pleasant surprise and heat, met him, and he had to kiss her, he just *had* to. So he did, their tongues meeting and mating in feral harmony, as his erect self found a warm cradle against her belly. He nearly lost himself then, and that thought, that he would not allow her to go unsatisfied again, pulled him back, though it was the last thing he wished to do.

Gently lifting her, he laid her down on his bed, kissed her once more, for good measure, then worked his way, not slowly, but indirectly, back down to the slick centre awaiting him. He made a rather long detour at her breasts, marvelling at the thickness of her pebbled nipples in his mouth, at their sumptuous taste; then he forced himself to move on, for now.

Nudging her thighs apart with his nose and chin, like some manner of beast, he watched as she opened, revealing the dewy bud and petals waiting for him. He glanced back up at her, catching the glimpse of hesitation in her eyes—along with a trust that felled him. It did, cut him wide open, until he wasn't sure he couldn't ever be put back together again.

*Perhaps this way I can.*

Setting his mouth to her, slowly, gently, calling on his reserves of strength and decency, to not lose himself at this taste, this nectar of immortality, he began his exploration, his gaze never leaving hers. A little unsure, she tensed slightly, until his tongue found the hooded bud, and then with a hitched gasp, her head fell back, her legs fell open, and along with them went he. One hand grasped her thigh whilst another travelled to her abandoned breasts, and hers grasped the blanket as he kissed her. Thoroughly, and without reserve, watching, listening, feeling, every ridge, every bump; until her body followed him, seeking his touch, and her

legs tensed so that he knew she was close. And yes…
There it was.

He didn't relent, but he watched, drinking her in as
he drank in the sight of her in ecstasy, and it was un-
earthly, life-changing, and it swelled his heart, and his
ardour, all at once, until he had painted that image of
her, mouth gaping, every muscle taut in bliss, into his
mind.

Calming his pace, he let her descend, and when she
had, he reached to the table and fumbled for a moment
as he slid out the French letter, then wrapped himself
tight. Sliding up her body, he let himself come skin to
skin with her, mindful to keep his weight off her. Fram-
ing her face with his forearms, he let his hands slick
back her dampened hair, and chart the lines and freckles with a feathery lightness until she opened her eyes,
returned from her travels beyond the horizon, back to
him. He smiled down at her, and felt the prick of tears
as he did.

*How will I ever give her up?*

Already his heart ached. Already he felt as if he were
drowning, the weight of water pressing down until he
couldn't—

Her kiss stilled and quietened him. It gave him breath
again, as her fingers wiped away the moisture at his
eyes. When she released him, siren that she was, he
found her smiling right back up at him. As if she knew
all he couldn't say, as if she felt the same, as if none of
it mattered, and they were, and always could be, simply, as they were now.

She nodded—and it seemed as if she were saying, *Yes,
to all that*—but he couldn't accept that, not just now, it
was too much; so instead he took himself in hand, and
positioned himself where he was meant to be, and with a

slow thrust, he was within her. Her long legs slid around him, curling around his own legs, and her hands grasped his waist tight, and there it was again, that need to kiss her.

So they went, thrusting together, and kissing, moving in such beautiful concert he wasn't sure who led, who followed; whose skin was whose, whose flesh was whose. They moved in tandem until all was slickness, and heat, and shining pools of a blue no ocean had ever been before. Until his heart was fused to hers, there, right there, where their breasts touched.

Until he felt her tightening around him again.

Another cry, another kiss, and he shattered within her too, her nails biting into the flesh of his buttocks as she held him tighter than anyone should by rights ever wish to.

*Never let me go.*

## Chapter Sixteen

It might've been minutes, hours, or even a lifetime that they'd been lying here. After that first time, when it had felt as if the marrow of her was being woven, and rearranged into something other, permanently melded to Freddie, they'd cleaned themselves, and the letter, but they hadn't made it back to bed before Freddie had taken her, taken her *with him*, again, there, against the wall between the hearth and the corner where his washing stand lived.

It had been more urgent, clumsier, and yet no less explosive nor *personal*. They had cleaned themselves again, this time in the small bathing room down the corridor that Freddie had put in when he'd had running water installed in the house. He'd said he wanted to be *modern*, but Mena had a feeling he also didn't want her constantly running out for water. When they'd finished cleaning up, she'd thought he might ask her to go back to her room, but instead he'd grasped her hand, and like naughty, naked children, they'd raced back down the chilly corridor and tumbled into bed. *Into*, this time, not on top of.

There had been some caresses, and some kisses, and then Freddie had settled as he was now, curled into a ball like Hawk was wont to do, his head on her belly, his arms encircling her as she toyed with his hair, her nails running lightly across his scalp. Tiredness, the physical kind, made them lazy, and stole some of the heat from their eyes and hearts, but both were wide awake, and Freddie still looked at her with that intense fascination, like now, as he studied the little hairs in the dip below her breasts.

So yes, it felt like a lifetime, living in this moment. A lifetime of happiness, and satedness, and utter completion that would surely bring her comfort in years to come. Her mind was blessedly blank, the warm, heady haze of pleasure, and the fire too, basking her in a cocoon of drugging safety.

*These moments will last me a lifetime.*

'Would you tell me of your life before?' Freddie asked, his eyes meeting hers, grey-green now, the colour of his hesitancy.

Even if she'd wanted to say no, his voice, reverberating through her, would have compelled her to answer.

'What would you like to know?'

'Anything. Everything. You came from the country? And lost your family, I think?'

He was trying to be gentle, but then, there were no words which made such losses any easier.

'Yes,' she nodded, letting her mind drift back to that time.

Memories of her youth had kept her company, and given her hope, of sunny days and bright colours when the world had come for her in all its ugliness.

Well, perhaps not all; she'd been lucky in so much.

'My family were farmers,' she told him. 'In Essex. For…generations. I might've been too, not that I minded. It was hard, but good work. Soil beneath your fingers, the

sun so bright some days you couldn't see but blue, and
the vibrant green of the fields. We had a happy home. I
had a sister, Helen, older than me by a year, and a brother,
Martin. Younger by five. He was the apple of all our
eyes. Terror, but a sweet one. In late summer, we'd sneak
into the neighbouring orchard, and steal plums from the
ground, the three of us.' Mena smiled brightly, remembering those wondrous days of unfettered childhood;
of bonds and love she'd never thought she'd find again.

*But I have, with Freddie, and all those at Nichols
House.*

'And then, a winter came, harsher than others. Crops
died, animals died, and people died. My family too, a
fever. I caught it, but I lived, and when I was well again,
there was nothing left.'

Staring out into the room, Mena remembered those
days, when it felt as if a great reckoning had come upon
their village; upon her.

Something biblical, though she hadn't had the words
then to describe it. Feeling forsaken, and alone, as if
there was nothing but frost-burnt fields of hard dirt, and
a hollow inside you that would never be filled again.

*Only it was.*

Smiling a wan smile, she met Freddie's steady gaze,
and continued.

'I sold what I could to pay off debts, took what was
left, and… Walked away. There was a boy,' she remembered. 'Well, almost a man, like me. We'd been courting,
and I think I would've married him. Until everything
was gone, and I…couldn't. It would've been the smart
choice to make, but something inside me… I felt, with-
ered,' she breathed, and Freddie nodded against her, as
if he knew precisely how that felt. 'I kept thinking, if I
marry him, I will be fed, and have children, and feel the

soil in my hands, but I won't ever bloom again. So I left. I walked, and I thought to come to London, find work, don't know why, could've gone anywhere, but I thought, London will be good.'

She huffed a small laugh, thinking on how strange it was she'd followed that feeling, in her heart, her gut, whatever it had been.

Something had called her to London, and though the old ways were supposedly dead, where she came from, they weren't. You listened to the earth, to the moon, to the birds, and you listened when they told you which path to take.

When the wind called you, you either denied it, or followed it, to see what you'd find.

'It was a hard road,' Freddie said, bringing her back to him.

*Where I belong. Where I was called to.*

'All roads which lead to good things are,' she shrugged. 'At the time, of course, it didn't feel that way. It felt a path leading to nowhere. Of walking, and rain, and mud, and fear. What little I had was stolen, and that's when I had to make due to keep myself going.' Freddie laid a small kiss on her belly, and the gesture of understanding, and acceptance, wrenched her heart. 'And then I was here. I tried to find work, I tried to find somewhere to go, but no one would have me. Those that would… It came with a price too high for me to pay. The workhouses, they wanted what was left of my strength, and hope, and I'd walked so far to keep them, I couldn't. Same with the churches, they wanted vows I couldn't make. I know that sounds foolish, like I should've taken what I could get, but somehow it seemed worse than what I'd already given to get here. And I had this feeling, like if

I went in, I'd never come back out. Not as me, whoever that was.'

'How long was it, before you came to Holly Street?'

'A few weeks, a month maybe. Lost track of time. Then it was Christmas, and no one had work. I begged some, managed to get food, but… If you hadn't opened your home to me, if I had made it through another night, I would've gone back to the workhouse, or the church, and given all I had left of myself. You should know that,' she whispered, her voice cracking.

'I am sorry for what the world took from you,' he said, quietly, but fiercely. 'But I am glad you walked until you found my door. I didn't open my home to you, Mena,' he continued, and she frowned, confused, and yes, hurt. Then, his hands found hers as he slowly shifted, uncurling, and sliding up her body until he had her nestled in his arms, his body shielding her from anything but his heat, and comfort. 'I opened my house to you. You… You made this place a home. And I need you to know, if you are certain of anything, be certain of this. You will always have a home here.'

Tears to match the ones which had fallen from his eyes earlier slid from Mena's and tumbled into her hair.

No sooner could she have stopped them than she might've stopped the sea washing ashore. She felt raw, scratchy, as if that same sea's waves had continuously lapped at her heart, eroding the protective stone that had kept her safe for so long.

They weren't words of love, she knew that. But whatever this was, at least she had the memory of his tears to comfort her a little, silly as that was. To reassure her, that whatever lines they were crossing were, as painful to traverse for him as they were for her. That whatever happened when it all ended, perhaps, she would not be alone in feeling *something*. Was it so wrong to think, to hope, that he might miss her when they parted? That he might remember this night, always? Even if only for the sweet pain of it?

Freddie leaned down, sweetly kissing away the trails of salt her tears had left, then her cheeks, her nose, her eyelids. Finally, her lips, delving into her mouth achingly slow; and that phrase she'd read in books sometimes, about people pouring emotions into a kiss, it felt like that. As if he were literally pouring himself into her, and so she let herself fall into the downy comfort of the bed, and him, the gentle cloud of it all, and receive.

When he had finished his offering, pulling back as slowly as he'd begun, he remained there, staring down at her, his thumb moving back and forth against the little curls at the edge of her hair that could never be tamed. And though she knew it might break the spell, force him back to his old habits, Mena found she couldn't resist the chance she was being offered now.

*The chance to perhaps know him a little better.*

'I know if I asked of your past, you would tell me nothing,' Mena said quietly, not startling him, but pulling him back from dangerous depths indeed. Gazing down at her, having her in his arms…a man could get used to this. *He* could get used to this. This feeling of utter completion, and peace, overriding all the turmoil, the doubts, the complications.

Overriding rationality.

Tonight… He'd never expected tonight. He'd never expected to have this opportunity, to learn, even the smallest thing, about Mena. To *be* with her; no expectations, no reserve. It was drugging, everything he learned.

*Her past. Her heart. How she looks when she reaches ecstasy.*

His heart had cracked when he'd heard her tale; all she'd gone through until she came here. Not only the bad, but the good too. Something akin to jealousy, and longing, had seeped into his breast when she spoke of her family, of beautiful summer days and childhood. If he'd had any of that, he couldn't recall.

And when she spoke of her journey here, to him... It filled him with something else entirely. Not only anger, at those who had profited from her diminishment, regret too, for her turmoil. That it had been the cost, for her to arrive here. There was fascination, for her; what she'd done to remain *herself* despite it all. To make choices which others would scoff at; and yet still to make them for they were hers. People as she'd been, as he'd been once, it was difficult for others to understand, and not judge. Not to say, *You should settle for scraps*, or even, *How strong you were to survive*. It was difficult to understand that not everyone's road to such circumstances was the same; and no road from there could ever be alike. To understand, that people were still people.

And amidst it all, as she told her tale, he'd also felt... *Hope?* That somewhere, something, eternal, and intangible, had had a hand to play in her tale; in both their tales. That the call she'd heard, the one to send her on her journey, had been to him. Perhaps he'd been the good she'd felt waited for her; he liked to think he had been. That he could be; for whatever time he had left.

*That I can make her happy, even for the briefest flicker of time.*

And maybe, for that flicker, he too could be happy. Could *let* himself be happy.

*Even if I don't deserve it.*

What he'd said to her, it was the closest he could come to fully opening his heart and confessing everything, including his love. Every word, every kiss, would have to tell her what was truly in his heart, for he could not. She was right; he couldn't speak of his past just as he couldn't confess his true feelings. Because though he may be, may have been, good to her, she deserved better than him.

It always came back to that.

'And I also think that were I to ask you of the future,' Mena continued, the ghost of a smile playing on her lips. 'You would not answer. But would you tell me something? *Anything?* A memory, or something of your friends?'

*Would you share with me as I have with you?* her eyes asked.

And considering he understood the impulse, the desire to *know* the other, considering the fact he'd never been able to resist those eryngo eyes, nor would he ever, not in a million years, he nodded, letting his mind drift over the years to find something to give her.

'I first went to sea when I was about eighteen,' he told her, and at once, he felt, and saw, any tension within her disappear. Her eyes widened, as if she needed them open to take all of him in, even his words. 'Older than most, but still so fresh it took me nearly a week to get proper sea legs under me.'

Mena smiled, and so did he, remembering that time.

How annoyed he'd been at his own body, for refusing to match his determination. How exciting it had been, despite the grief, to bid farewell to England's shores and venture out into the horizon he'd gazed at for so long. How much of a boy he'd still been, despite playing at being a man.

As he perhaps always would.

'The ship was called the *Marie-Héloïse*, and we were bound for South America,' he said, returning back to the present. 'The voyage was everything I'd imagined— endless sea, a sky of a blue so bright, you'd never believe it for seeing it. Hard work, and I got the worst of it, new as I was. I will let you imagine what that means,' he grinned, and Mena chuckled, the sensation rocking through him in more ways than one. 'I loved every second though. My hands were raw from working the ropes and climbing aloft; my feet became leather. My skin turned red and peeled, and my lips cracked, but it felt… extraordinary. One early morning, those of us who'd never made such a voyage before were torn from our beds and marched up onto the deck. Awaiting us was Neptune himself,' he laughed, remembering the sight of the older, sea-hardy Spaniard dressed up in the costume that might've rivalled those the *ton* wore to masques. 'I had no idea what was happening—I was passed from hand to hand, water was launched at us, then we were smeared with…well, I don't even wish to know what, then rinsed again by being tossed into the sea. When it was all over, they presented us with pieces of parchment, that marked our first line-crossing.'

'Do you still have it?' Freddie nodded. 'Will you show me?'

He needn't be asked twice; that was the way of things now.

*Always.*

What Mena wanted, Mena got.

It took him a few minutes, to remember where he'd stashed it, but finally, he extracted the folded parchment from a book on South American flora, and settled back in bed, letting Mena curl into his chest, then handing it to her.

He watched as she, with the utmost care that was inextricably woven into her, unfolded, and read, the parchment, her fingers dancing over the ridiculous drawings of maritime beasts, and his name, drawing each letter as she had when he'd taught her to read. His hand tightened where it rested on her hip as emotion flooded him; from the memory, and from this new one.

Had anyone ever asked him, Freddie would never have said he was a creature of emotion. He would've said he was a man of determination, anger, and guilt. The softer ones—tenderness, love, bittersweet happiness—he'd never really experienced them enough to be able to say he knew how, or even what they were. Excitement, pride, yes, but nothing like what he felt every time he was with Mena. Like he was fully formed; *human*.

Perhaps that is what came of opening yourself to another. You learned. You cared. It had happened with others too—his friends. Never before might he have made friends as he had with Mary, or Spencer. Never, would he have known when his friends were in pain; or what to say to help them, or push them. And of course, it had happened with Mena; albeit reluctantly, even till now.

The paper in her hands, it was nothing. Why he'd even kept it… But giving it to her—he might've given her the world.

*Perhaps I am. A piece of my own world.*

'Thank you,' she breathed, folding it back up just as carefully, and sliding it onto the table, where the candle was now nearing its end.

When she settled back into his arms, he could feel her desire to ask more; and her decision not to.

In another life, he might've been the sort of man to

give it to her, to open the floodgates, and say, *Have at it! Have at my soul, Mena mine.* Only, he wasn't that man. He was the man who kissed the top of her head, and blew out the candle, and lay there with her until she was fast asleep.

*In another life.*

## Chapter Seventeen

The days which followed were so unreal, Mena felt as if she was stranded at the edge of the cosmos, out of time. Routine returned to the house as Christmas's pause ended— albeit with some modifications.

They both returned to work, keeping the schedules they had for years—not those which had emerged when they'd avoided each other, or whatever it was they had done— though Mena also spent time at Nichols House. Now that the festivities had concluded, it was time to get everything in order for the official *opening*; and besides, the winter, and growing cases of cholera, meant the house was at its busiest.

They would both return home for supper, after which they would read for a time in the parlour, talk a little, of the weather, of work. When it came time for bed, well, that is when things changed visibly.

The night after St Stephen's, there had been a strange, awkward sort of discussion about *the hour growing late*, and *the impossibility of reading any longer*. Together, they had wandered up to their rooms, with a final farewell to Hawk, who now kept to the lower floors with his leg, and at their doors, there had been some mumbling, and shuffling, and general reluctance to actually *enter* their rooms. Until they'd finally turned to each other, and Mena had crossed the corridor, and instead entered Freddie's room.

There was no more talking, not as they had that first night; still, there was the physical connection. The passion, the soft tenderness; the wonder and pleasure. It all grew, in those three nights, along with a peculiar frenzy, as if they both felt the ticking of time. As if whoever had given them the gift of togetherness had turned over the sand glass, and its rushing could be heard through the walls.

Had Mena not been prepared, she might've feared it, as she did so much else. She might've screamed in protest, begged for more time. Perhaps it was the haze of pleasure that kept her docile, that gave her the gifts of peace, and acceptance. Perhaps it was simply growing older, and wiser. Whatever it was, she was not so foolish as to not be grateful.

Just as she was grateful for the ease that now lived between her and Freddie. An ease, to touch, whenever they wished. To kiss, to hold hands; or each other. An ease to laugh, to *be*, to breathe together. It was as if a weight had been lifted, a suffocating weight that had kept everything in her heart locked up tight; but which had also kept her merely existing. Now, she could let loose with action at least, if not with words, what had lived, and grown, inside her for years. That too was dizzying, freeing and thrilling. It reminded her of youth, when she'd been allowed to ride to town on her own, and off she'd gone, tearing down the lanes, bonnet flying off her head, laughter, and excitement in her heart.

Just as there was now, as they both stood side by

side, her washing up, he drying their breakfast dishes; and Freddie leaned over to kiss her cheek.

Mena smiled, knowing she was blushing, but a knock on the back door interrupted them, and they separated as though they'd been caught doing something naughty.

'I'll get it,' Freddie said, doing just that, his own smile, and the light in his eyes, gone. 'Ah, good morning, Susie.'

Shaking herself from the line of self-destructive thoughts which that observation threatened to send her down, Mena finished up the plates, and smiled as Susie stepped in from outside, Hawk rushing past her to investigate his water bowl, his leg stiff but improving daily.

'Good morning, Mr Walton, Mena,' Susie said, knocking her boots one last time before descending into the kitchen.

'Good morning, Susie,' Mena replied cheerfully. 'Am I late?' she asked, realising her friend never came in this way—nor knocked.

'Not at all, and apologies for disturbing you. I was out front, but then Hawk came bounding back from his travels, and I thought I might follow him in. It was getting rather frosty out there,' Susie laughed, divesting herself of her coat, hat, and gloves. 'It's turned even more bitter; that wind from the river is mighty strong.'

'Of course! I've told you a thousand times to come this way.'

Susie merely shrugged, and the three of them stood staring at each other until Mena moved into action and began preparing tea for her friend.

'Are you to the house today, Mena?' Freddie asked, apparently not quite ready to be on his way.

Almost as if he were making an effort to spend time with *her* friend.

*His employee, dimwit.*

*Quite so.*

'This afternoon. This morning, Susie and I are changing things a bit, giving everything a bit of a once-over before the New Year.'

'Well, you know best,' he said, looking at her for a beat too long. 'I… I was thinking,' he added after a moment, glancing between the two of them. 'Some of the things which those at Nichols House make, the carved wooden boxes, the quilts, even some of the preserves… Perhaps we could have a selection here. I think people would like some finely, locally made things which support a worthy cause.'

Mena and Susie glanced at each other, and the latter shrugged, as if to say, *I'm not the boss.*

'Freddie… You don't have to—'

'I want to,' he assured her, a little of that light returned—though perhaps that was merely the warm winter sun streaming through the windows. 'It is good business.'

'Then we would be delighted,' she agreed, her heart all warm and fuzzy, because deep down she knew it was not about *good business.*

'Excellent,' he grinned, diminishing it slightly when he glanced at Susie and seemingly remembered her presence altogether. 'Thank you for the marmalade, by the way. Most excellent.'

'Glad you liked it.'

'Well, I am off now,' he said, putting on his overclothes. 'Remember, I won't be back for dinner; I have that party with Marshall and the lot.'

'Of course,' she said, only recalling it just then, hoping her disappointment didn't show.

*Only we have so little time—enough.*

'Have a good day, Freddie.'

'You two do the same,' he smiled, affording her one last private glance before stepping out that held...

Well, she didn't know what, and she was exhausted trying to decipher it all.

*Just live.*

*Quite so.*

Turning back to her friend, she found her pouring her own tea, and settled at the table, waiting. More for something to do, Mena poured herself a cup, and settled across from her, thinking she really should make conversation before things became...*odd*, but Susie beat her to it.

'We should clear a space for items from Nichols House today,' she said thoughtfully, though Mena knew her friend hadn't missed one detail of that whole...interaction. Something relaxed inside her. Speaking of what was between Freddie and her... Hearing any manner of judgement, or even observation, might completely disrupt that gentle peace she'd managed to find. 'Since we're already changing things about,' Susie continued, and Mena smiled, nodding. 'Perhaps you should come to mine for dinner too, since Mr Walton will be out. I can try out that fish pie for you.'

'I'd like that.' She would. A night away from Holly Street, with a friend, would be...*a pleasant, welcome change.* 'I will bring a pudding.'

'I should invite Mrs Wilferry. See what she thinks of my execution of her recipe.'

'Good idea.'

The two women smiled at each other, and Mena silently thanked her friend, for everything.

They sat there a while with their tea, until the time

had come to get to work, which they did, with alacrity, and a strange giddiness.

*Just live.*

'A toast! To another year of swift voyages, lower taxes, and soaring profits!' Spellman shouted to the room, raising his champagne so high and swiftly, some tumbled over the edge back onto the crowded table. Not that he noticed—nor minded. There was plenty more to be had; in fact, it seemed that tonight, food and drink were in endless supply.

There was a chorus of *'Hear, hear!'* from all those gathered—the same bunch as always, along with about twenty more men of the trade who Freddie knew only by either reputation, or sight—and Freddie made a show of adding his voice to the crowd, along with a smile.

Tonight, they'd all gathered in Spellman's home, a rather impressive mansion at the border of Kensington and Mayfair, that would, and did, rival that of any aristocrat. Though the evening so far had been pleasantly informal, a buffet of culinary delights, and a constant stream of alcoholic offerings to satisfy any taste, to Freddie, the house was cold, impersonal, and far too grand for Spellman, a committed bachelor, and he couldn't deny the wealth that poured from every inch of the place, including this dining room, with its high ceilings, and abundance of gilding.

It made him long for the simple warmth of Holly Street—though, to be truthful, everything did. Everything tonight made him long for home, for Mena, and just as he had during that luncheon what now seemed a lifetime ago, he wondered why he even bothered to come; why he continued to force himself through such… pageantry.

*To foster connections, and keep good relations with your fellows.*

And if he was being *completely* honest with himself, he needed out of the house. He needed something vastly different to remind him what life would be like without Mena— if he got a chance to ever live it. Which was, in itself, doubtful.

These past days, he'd allowed himself to be consumed by their relationship. Their ease, the wonder of it all. He'd allowed himself to dream that it could always be like that. Perhaps it was the pleasure he found with her—it fogged his mind, made him forget how this was all bound to end.

*Exactly how I deserve it to.*

Everyone sipped their drinks, or emptied them in some cases, and the concerted movement tore Freddie from the unwelcome, souring thoughts. Glancing around, he spotted Henderson, and strode over to the man, who looked decidedly better than the last time they'd met.

Henderson smiled as he approached, nodding, and raising his glass.

'Walton.'

'Henderson,' Freddie greeted, clinking his glass against the other man's. 'I apologise for not finding you earlier. Marshall had me cornered since I arrived, and was insistent on introducing me to a brace of gentlemen I'm afraid I don't even recall the names of.'

'I noticed,' Henderson laughed. 'One would think this was his party, rather than Spellman's.'

'Isn't it?' Freddie jested.

'Point taken.'

This may have been Spellman's house, but Marshall had been the one to invite and organise them all; they all knew that.

Not that Spellman minded, quite the contrary. The two had been friends since school, and thick as thieves. Really, they were good sorts, at the core, and for all Freddie's griping and moaning, he might've had a harder time starting out had they not done as Marshall had this evening, brought him into the fold and introduced him to others who could help him build his business.

Clearing his throat, he returned his attention to Henderson.

'How are you?' he asked seriously. 'You look...better. If that isn't insulting.'

'If it were, would it stop you?' Henderson commented, grinning mischievously over his glass. 'You are always frank, Walton. It's something I, and many others, appreciate, when it doesn't cut too deeply, that is.'

'Glad to hear.'

'In answer to your question, yes. I am, better,' Henderson said with a true, grateful smile after a moment. 'I took your advice. I had a rather, enlightening conversation with my fiancée, and she is that no longer. Our parents were not thrilled, to say the least, but, well, neither of us liked what our lives would be should we do as pleased them. She did me the honour of jilting me, so there is that. I am selling the business, and have already spoken to some brokers who have agreed to assist me in my transition.'

'I am happy for you.'

'And I must thank you. Had you not said what you did, I might've made a grave mistake.'

'You don't—'

'Do cease skulking in the corner, you two,' Spellman exclaimed, cutting in, his inebriation again on full display—though the man was boisterous without aid. 'This is a party, do behave as such!'

Spellman contrived to get between Freddie and Henderson, and put an arm around each of their shoulders, the drink in his hand miraculously empty enough not to provoke any accidents. As he steered them on towards a nearby group, Henderson and Freddie exchanged a defeated but amused glance; when the man was like this, there was no arguing.

'So, what do you think of my house, Walton?'

'Very grand, Spellman, very grand. Much…more than the last one,' Freddie said, a bit at a loss of what else to say, as he'd preferred the old house, in Cheapside; modern and with much less of, well, *everything*. 'Perfect for such gatherings.'

'Yes, quite a party, Spellman, thank you for having us,' Henderson agreed.

'You boys should follow my lead, and get yourselves a place like this,' Spellman said as they joined the group he'd steered towards. 'Lord knows you have the coin. Well, you do, Walton.'

Freddie threw a worried glance at Henderson, who merely shook his head, fully at peace with his circumstances, which Freddie thought suited him much better than miserable with the prospect of an heiress's dowry.

'We're all moving out here now, Walton,' one of the men said—Landry or some such. 'Soon, Society itself shall have to move to make room for us *merchants* to come and have their family homes. No surprise with the lot of them having pockets to let because they cannot be bothered to but look down on trade.'

'Hear, hear!' someone cheered.

'Things are changing, mark my words.'

'As long as it is for the better,' Freddie agreed diplomatically.

'Why don't you find yourself a place here?' Marshall asked, turning the conversation back to a place Freddie certainly did not wish to go; not that he seemed able to stop it lest he walk away, and insult them. Which, despite his reluctance to be part of their group at times, was not something he wished to do. 'That house of yours was good when you were starting out—we all have fond memories there; however, now you must make a show of it, of how you've risen. Society must see what industry can do for men like us.'

Freddie gritted his teeth—taking the point, yet not in the mood to have this conversation, and was about to reply something trite and deflective, when someone beat him to it.

'You know well why he hasn't left Holly Street,' Royston said pointedly, and the gaiety of the group chilled in an instant.

There was a glint in the man's eye that sparked Freddie's anger, though his mind didn't process quite as quickly what the man was doing.

'Of course,' Marshall laughed, grabbing his attention, his mind apparently quicker on the uptake. Freddie frowned. 'Fear not, Walton, you could bring your mistress here; it certainly wouldn't be the first time someone set one up a doorstep away—or even in their own home! Though you might prefer to keep her in Holly Street—closer to the wharf—easy access during the day.'

Marshall laughed.

And laughed, and laughed, unaware of the look on Freddie's face—which everyone else saw instantly, and which kept them silent, and wary.

Freddie had never experienced this variation of anger

before. This white-hot rage that clouded the mind and sent him spiralling down a dark path where the word *hurt* echoed against sharp walls.

'Mistress?' he managed to growl out, and still, Marshall did not waver, carrying on as merrily as before.

'That woman of yours,' he clarified eagerly, before turning to the others gathered. 'You all remember her, the one who'd serve us when we'd dine at Walton's! Pretty thing, no meat on her, but whatever your preference, Walton.'

The white-hot rage turned to red-misted bloodlust in an instant.

Years, Freddie had strived to turn his mind, his life, from violence. But in that moment, wrong as it was, despicable though it made him, he couldn't stop. Shrugging off Henderson, and the variety of other hands that came to stop him, he launched himself at Marshall, punching him so that the man stumbled and only managed to avoid the floor by being caught by others in the circle, though the glass he'd been holding fell and shattered.

A gasp, and cries of protest, erupted from the room as Marshall staggered back to his feet and met Freddie again. Blows flew and the men grabbed and scratched at each other until enough came to and managed to pull them apart.

Both breathed heavily, blood flowing from lips, eyebrows, cheeks, and hands.

'What the Hell, Walton?' Marshall exclaimed, tearing himself from those holding him back, wiping a trickle of blood from his nose, more confused than hurt.

'You don't speak of her that way,' Freddie hissed. 'You don't ever speak of her that way.'

'Walton, I meant no insult,' Marshall told him seriously, daring to come closer. 'I… We all,' he continued, gesturing to the room. 'Thought her your mistress. There is no shame in it, half of us have one of those,' he laughed, shrugging. 'I see now we were mistaken. And so I beg you to accept my apology.'

Marshall held out his hand, true contrition, and forgiveness of his own in his eyes.

Those restraining Freddie let him loose, not moving too far lest he decide to behave a beast again. He waved them down to reassure them; the initial mindless state passed—he was returning to himself. Though the anger still burned bright, so did the shame, at what he'd done. How he'd behaved.

*As I promised never to.*

'Forgive me,' he ground out, taking the man's hand. 'Too much drink, I think.' Marshall nodded. 'I think it best if I excuse myself. Thank you for the welcome, Spellman.'

Nodding to the latter, he strode out without another word.

Hushed voices and murmurs followed him, but all he knew was that he needed to get out. Thankfully, the servants already had his things waiting—likely warned that he would be leaving soon by those inside.

Grabbing them, he rushed outside into the bitter cold, ignoring Henderson's cries for him to wait, until finally, they faded away too, and Freddie was alone in the frozen streets, with only his shame and anger for company.

## Chapter Eighteen

The evening had been just the ticket; a gentle, but necessary reminder of life beyond Holly Street. Pleasant, relaxed, with good company and conversation, as Mena hadn't known often. Her own doing, she knew. Fear had paralysed her for so long, and even when she'd been able to go out into the world again, in some measure, she'd kept things as they'd been before. There was comfort and safety in what was known. In habits, and the familiar.

It wasn't as if she'd deliberately avoided making friends—there were plenty of people who'd been kind acquaintances—only she'd contented herself with her own company, and Freddie's when he was home. There was nothing wrong with that; one's own company was good, and she was glad to be someone who was happy in solitude. She'd never really known loneliness since she'd been at Holly Street, *felt* the solitude; only very rarely these past few years when, yes, she missed Freddie. But that was loneliness of a different sort.

And Mena didn't think she'd ever be the *extremely* gregarious type, but evenings such as this, with friends, and the most entertaining stories from Mrs Wilferry, who'd had quite the collection of lodgers, well, those could be good too. Smiling, and humming, Mena let herself into the kitchen, and as soon as she stepped inside, a chill came over her. Something felt off—

Hawk whined, and she started when she saw the dark figure at the table.

'It's only me,' Freddie growled.

'I didn't think you'd be home until later,' she said, her eyes adjusting along with her heartbeat as they made out his form. It was so dark—only embers in the hearth—why hadn't he lit any candles?

*Perhaps he's only just returned.*

*Quite so.*

'How was your evening?' she asked cheerily, divesting herself of her coat and accessories, though she couldn't shake the feeling something was *off.* 'What is Spellman's new house like?'

Freddie had told her about the purchase when he'd mentioned the invitation; it had been one of those unwelcome reminders of what his own life should, and *would*, look like.

*A fashionable, grand house. A wife. Children.*

*Enough*, Mena told herself, as she went and stoked the fire, adding some fuel. Once the flames grew again, she turned back to him and gasped.

'Freddie!'

He was…a mess.

Hair dishevelled, lip split, a blistering bruise forming on his cheek, and his knuckles… Bloody and cut, as they cradled an untouched measure of whisky. There was blood on his crisp white shirt, and likely elsewhere. Hawk was at his feet, whining again, and she understood the feeling.

'What happened?' she asked, rushing to him, trying to get a better look at everything she hadn't seen.

*More cuts, more bruises.*

Had whatever evil which visited them set upon him again? He might've been killed, he might've— 'Freddie!'

'Looks worse than it is,' he said flatly, flinching away as she made to touch his cheek. 'It's nothing.'

'It doesn't look like nothing,' she bit back. 'Let me clean this up before it festers.'

He didn't assent; though neither did he *dissent*, so she set about gathering what she would need to clean and bind his wounds.

Fear was in her breast again—she didn't for one second believe it was *nothing*—but frustrated bitterness was gratefully overriding it, making her efficient. She knew how he was—constantly unwilling to share *anything*—but she'd thought they'd made it past that; enough at least for him to share what had happened. Enough to set her own mind at ease that whatever had come for the shop wasn't responsible. Wasn't some old danger that would take him from her for ever; or something else so terrible. Biting back her tongue, unwilling to cause a scene and *demand* answers, Mena set about putting him as right as she could, cleaning the wounds and gently dabbing clover salve onto them.

He sat there, unmoving, unwilling to meet her eye, his jaw ticking away nearly in time with the timepiece in his pocket.

'Please, Freddie,' she said, when her anger and hurt had calmed enough to restore a measure of clear-headedness. 'Just tell me what happened,' she pleaded, wrapping his hand. 'Whatever it is… We can face it, together.'

Freddie looked up at her then, his eyes full of disgust, shame, and guilt.

Something told her this wasn't about their previous attacker.

*No... This is something else entirely.*

'Freddie?' Mena asked again, her voice full of concern, and pleading. Her eyes, so full of confusion, and worry. So trusting, so...*desperate*. Desperate for him to be honest. Freddie knew she wouldn't let this go. And as much as it pained him, galled him to say it out loud, for how it might hurt her, at the same time, he realised she deserved to know what was being said about her.

*About us.*

'He called you my mistress,' he grumbled, turning away, unable to look her in the eye.

'What?'

'Marshall. Right prat. He called you my mistress.'

'So you...'

'Punched him, yes,' he finished for her. Why didn't she sound...indignant? Revolted? Insulted? Why did she only sound...*more confused*. 'A scuffle ensued.' Freddie raised his gaze, and finally met hers. She was frowning, incomprehension in her eyes, as if he'd just set a problem before her she couldn't solve. 'He had no right to speak of you thus.'

Sighing, Mena tied a tight knot with the bandage on his hand, then rose, taking the cloths and basin with her to the sink.

'Mena?'

Shaking her head, she turned back, crossing her arms, and leaning against the sink as she stared down at him with what felt like bitter astonishment.

Something—a blend of dread and confusion—churned in his gut, making him feel somehow worse than he had all evening; even stewing in his own shame and anger as he had been.

'Eight years we've lived together, Freddie,' she shrugged. 'Only just the two of us. What precisely did you think they all said? Of us—me? Do you think this the first time someone called me thus, or even something fouler?'

'You should've told me—'

'So you could beat up half of London?' she laughed. 'I thought you knew, and, like me, didn't care. Didn't grant it any importance, because we knew the truth of it. The thing is, now...'

'Now, what?' he asked when she trailed off into silence for a long moment, her gaze wandering to the hearth.

'I mightn't have been your mistress when the rumours started, Freddie,' she said, a hardness in her voice he was quite certain he'd never heard. 'But aren't I now? And if not your mistress, then what? Your servant? Your plaything? Your friend? The woman who lives in your house? What am I to you, Freddie?'

The pain, and desolation, in her voice, the crack of it, the sheen in her eyes, all of it, had him on his feet and before her in the blink of an eye.

'You're my partner, *God damn it*!' he exclaimed, taking hold of her arms.

He wanted to shake some sense into her, to pull her tightly into his arms, to make her see it.

*How could she not after all this time?*

So he'd not said it—not aloud, there was so much he couldn't—but she knew him better than anyone, didn't she?

'How can I be?' she asked quietly, and that was worse, than if she'd shouted, and screamed, and tore at him. 'How could I ever be your partner when I know nothing of you?' Tears trickled down her cheeks, but she did nothing to stop them. He'd done this. Broken her, broken his Mena, because he hadn't had the courage to see *anything* clearly. 'I can't do it anymore, Freddie. Live here, share this house, this life, your bed, all the while knowing you don't trust *me* enough, to share more than the tiniest morsel of your past with me.'

'My past isn't who I am.'

'It is part of you. If pasts don't matter, why did you ask of mine?'

She shrugged him off, and he let her. He knew what she was asking, but *she* didn't know what she was asking. What she thought of him, everything she thought him to be, it would change. She looked at him as if he hung the moon, but if he told her of who he'd been…

*She never will again.*

'I will gather my things, and leave,' she said, heading for the stairs. 'I will speak to the others; they can tend the shop until you find a permanent solution. Susie can be trusted with a key now, I think.'

'I'll go,' he declared.

'This is your house, Freddie.'

'No. It's not.' He heard her stop, and, well, he might as well tell her. As he should've the other night. He'd tried… Hadn't he? *Had*, in a sense. Best he could, at the time. Now, he would tell her *properly*; she could add it to the list of his sins. 'I put it in your name three years ago,' he admitted, turning to face her.

'This is what I mean, Freddie,' she cried, literally throwing up her hands in exasperation. 'You share *nothing* with me! You give me this house and don't tell me for three years? What were you waiting for?'

'For a time when I could let you go!' he shouted.

Not meaning to raise his voice, but he just…couldn't lose her.

They stared at each other for a long moment, both stunned by his outburst, *confession*, until finally, she sobbed, shook her head, and tore from the room before he could stop her.

*So much for not losing her…*

Breathing hard, he paced over to the fireplace, and leaned on the mantel, rubbing his eyes, hoping the gesture might chase away the burning. It didn't. It only grew, as he listened to her climb the stairs, and her door slam shut.

How had it come to this? Not a full day ago, they'd been…*happy*. And now… He'd made, not even a mess, no. It was much worse. He'd razed it all to the ground. All she asked for was the same trust she accorded him, and he couldn't give it. He couldn't trust her not to turn her back on him once he told her *all* of it—but what had that got him? He would lose her regardless. If she wasn't packing now, it would be a miracle.

Clearing his mind a little more, Freddie realised the anger he'd felt earlier, his innate reaction to the word *mistress*, hadn't truly been for Marshall, or anyone else there who thought as much. His anger had been at himself, for feeling as if Mena was so much more; and never doing anything about it. For years, he'd been blind to what was said of them, though apparently she'd heard it all—been forced to confront that every day—and still she'd continued with her head held high because she'd known the truth. How had he been so blind?

Even when he'd—*recently*—realised that he'd limited her options in life by never confronting their situation, he'd not thought for one moment what people might've said about them, how *that* might impact her chances.

What a wretch he truly was.

Perhaps he'd made himself deliberately unseeing because he liked things the way they were. Because he wanted Mena—even though he couldn't admit he *wanted* Mena. All of her. Only he couldn't claim she was his partner—he couldn't ask for all of her—if he couldn't give himself. She was right.

*As bloody always.*

Closing his eyes, he took a deep breath, and swallowed down the worst fear he'd ever felt—worse than the fear of death. The fear, of showing himself, and the potential of Mena casting him out into frozen desolation again. Then, when he was as ready as he would ever be, he lit a candle, climbed the stairs, and knocked on Mena's door.

'Go away, Freddie!' she cried, and it broke his heart a little bit more.

*Best to be prepared for when it is truly broken.*

'You want to know who I am?' he asked through the door.

*Speak now, or for ever hold your peace.*

'Then I shall tell you.'

There was shuffling, and the door was thrust open, Mena's face, red, and blotchy, before him. She was frowning, but there was also hope in her eyes; disbelief that he could be giving her what she'd asked for.

*Though you will regret it, my love.*

'When you've heard my tale, you will know why I've kept it from you. From everyone. When I've told you… You will see.'

*And I'll be damned—more than I already am.*

# Chapter Nineteen

The bone-chilling look in Freddie's eyes nearly made Mena balk. Made her promise never to ask again, about whatever was so ignominious he would look at her like that. A different man from the one she'd known all these years now stood before her, cold, implacable, and capable of... Well, that was the problem, wasn't it? She wasn't quite sure what this new man was capable of.

*Still, I will love him all the same.*

Yes, she would. The realisation gave her courage, to face whatever secrets he'd kept all this time, from her, and from the world. To stand beside him, and face whatever they would mean.

*Even if only for a time.*

Because no matter his words, what they seemed to suggest, whatever they *were*, whatever they had been, partners, friends, lovers... Whatever he'd said but never said, done but never told her... One day, it *would* end. Until then, she would be there for him, as they'd been for each other all these years. She had thought about leaving, truly, up until he'd made that revelation about this house. Even then... When he'd refused to say more, *reveal* more, she'd come up here to think. To decide. Half dressed, half undressed, she'd been debating packing up and leaving, caught between love, and anger. Between fighting, and conceding defeat.

Now, the decision had been made for her. He needed her; she saw that too, the need to finally speak of whatever he'd hidden. So she would listen, and she would know.

*I will know him before the end.*

Mena stepped aside, and let Freddie in. He didn't even look around, merely strode to the hearth, set his candle on the small table before it, and sat in one of the chairs. Mena followed, and after a few quiet moments, Hawk could be heard clicking his way up, and after some sniffling at the door, he settled at it. It was perhaps what Freddie needed to finally resolve himself to do what he'd said.

The fire casting deep, dark shadows across his face, he met her gaze, and with a bleak, but steeled look, he nodded.

'I was born in the Romney marshes,' he began with a deep, heaving sigh. His shoulders dropped, as if resigned to face her condemnation, and rejection already. 'My parents died, sometime before I can even remember. I was taken in by my uncle and raised along with his son. My cousin, Malcolm. We didn't have much, lived a simple life—or so I thought for as long as my childhood lasted. I was raised to know the sea, the land, the marsh, everything. I loved it,' he smiled weakly, pain, and a desperate yearning for understanding, in his eyes. Mena longed to reach out, and hold his hand, but she couldn't. Not yet. He would stop, push her away again, for *her own good.* 'Until one night, my uncle woke me. I must've been… Five? Six, perhaps? It was a full moon. I remember that.' His jaw clenched, and his eyes unfocused, seeing the moon, the night before them, rather than her, this room, *this* night. 'My uncle told me to dress. To follow, and not make a sound. I still don't know how I hadn't seen it… Seen what he, and so many where we lived, were.'

'Smugglers,' Mena whispered after a long moment of silence.

Freddie nodded, back from the memory, for now, at least.

'Such a simple word,' he breathed. 'With so much meaning for others, but for us… It wasn't just a word. It was a way of life. It wasn't about thieving, and killing, or so I was led to believe. It was about surviving. Living a good life, despite what the king and those in power dictated. Despite what wars across the sea meant. It kept children from starving, and men from turning to worse crimes.'

Fervour had taken hold of his gaze now, and Mena nodded, not understanding, for she feared no one having not lived it could *understand*, but still, comprehending.

'Honour in dishonour,' she said quietly.

Freddie snorted out a breath that sounded like a mockery of a laugh.

'Yes. I believed that for a long time,' he told her, harsher now, anger at his own self colouring his voice. 'To be honest… I still do,' he shrugged. 'Only… Not as my uncle, as his…*pack*, did it. They were everything you read about in penny bloods. Murderers. Wreckers. Blackmailers, and thieves. Pure greed drove them. It took me a long time to see it. To see what I'd become at their side. Come to think of it, I don't quite know where I learned right and wrong. Wasn't as if we went to church if not to store goods in it.'

Again, he laughed, a cold, cruel sound that made

Mena's insides twist. She couldn't even begin to imagine what he'd gone through—what he'd been forced to do as a child.

And still, she knew there was more.

'I was somewhere around thirteen, I think, when I couldn't take it any more. When it all weighed…*so heavily*.' His eyes misted, and Mena couldn't help herself any longer, her heart writhing in her chest. Scooting her chair closer, she laid a hand on his, and he took it, desperately, as a man clung to a life raft. 'I knew who the law were, the true law, not the ones on our side. Took me a full day to get to them. But I did. Told them everything. They made a plan, to come on the next run. Another full moon. It was December. Cold, and biting, like this one. So like this one… Snow on the sand. Such a strange sight…'

Mena held his hand tighter as he disappeared into his memory again.

'It all went wrong,' he said. Bluntly, sharply. 'The war was on with the French again, and it wasn't only goods coming over. People too. 'Twas good money, they would pay whatever it took to get away from the fighting. And we…took advantage of that—used their grief and terror to *make money*. There was this couple, in one of the boats. Fancy—couldn't hide it. Though they tried to hide this box… Mal, he called my uncle over… They killed the man, and my uncle, he was about to shoot the woman… So I took the box, and I ran. I knew, my uncle, he would follow me, and the woman might live—I don't know what I was thinking…' Freddie shook his head, took a deep breath, and continued. 'That's when the law appeared. It was chaos. I didn't stop. I just ran, and I ran, as I never had, off the beach and into the marsh. I could hear my uncle, shouting. It echoed off the ice, and the mists, and I knew I couldn't stop. I passed this church, St Symeon's, and kept running, deeper, and deeper, into the marsh, thinking I could outrun the moon or something. I couldn't hear him anymore, and there was this old tree, a marker, we used to navigate by. I dug, and I put the box in there, and then I ran some more. Then he found me.'

The terror the little boy had felt, the regret, the guilt, she saw it all, freshly on Freddie's soul as if born only yesterday. She took his hand into both of hers, and he looked down at the sight, as if it were the most incongruous thing he'd ever seen. And when he met her eyes again, she let him see all she felt in her heart. Hurt, for the boy he'd been, for what he'd been forced to do, by his family, and by his own conscience.

And love, unfettered, unwavering, love.

'I'd never seen him like that,' he whispered, eyes red with unshed tears. 'I'd always been good, and loyal, but he looked at me as if I were an enemy. To be hated. He raised his pistol, and I knew he would kill me. I should've died that night.'

'But you didn't,' Mena reassured him.

Some part of him had, yes, but not all of him.

Not the goodness, not the strength, not the soul.

'Do you believe in ghosts?' he asked quietly, emotion replaced with a strangely stark curiosity.

'I've never given it much thought,' she admitted.

'I never did,' he told her, as if *that* were what he needed her to know most of all. 'There were always these stories… Hanged highwaymen roaming the streets, and apparitions in the marsh. My uncle, he was superstitious. A lot of the older ones were. Deeply. The stories, they gave me shivers, but I never believed. Not till that night.' Freddie swallowed hard, waiting for her to jump up and leave him at this, the presumably most absurd part of his story.

*I won't leave. I believe you*, she willed him to see.

'I was standing there, waiting for him to shoot, and this woman, all in white, she just...*appeared*. From the mists, from the marsh, from the moonlight. And she raised her hand as if to stop him, and he *did*. He blanched, and froze, and shook, and I ran again. He shouted. Once more. And then, there was a splash. He cried out to me for help but I didn't move. There was nothing more after that. I waited,' he told her. 'The only thing I heard were the law coming, and... I left. I should've met them, gone with them, but I just kept walking until I couldn't any more, and then, I went on a little farther. It's strange... I've never thought much about the guilt; I've not wallowed in it, but I've carried them all with me. The people we hurt, every one of them, they've been with me, all my life.'

'That night...' Mena began, unsure of how to tell him all she felt. How sorry she was for him, for what he'd faced; how stupid he was for believing this could ever change how she saw him. How it didn't change one thing about the man he was. 'The night you offered me a place here,' she began again, clarifying. 'You spoke of sins on your soul. You believe what you did with your uncle... were sins. You were a child, Freddie.'

'A man by anyone's standards,' he said fiercely. 'They have younger ones working the mines.'

'And you fight against such practices. You were a child, Freddie,' she insisted, leaning closer, so he would see the truth in her eyes. 'And what you did... Calling in the law on your own family, because it was the right thing to do... No child—*no one*—should ever have to do that. But you did. You are the man I've always known you to be. This tale… You thought it would change what I see, but it doesn't. Just as my past didn't define me. You refused to judge me, and so do I. Except to judge that you are kind, and loyal, and generous. And *good*.'

'Anything good I've ever done has been penance,' he retorted bitterly.

'Liar.'

He was staring. He knew he was, yet he couldn't stop. If Mena's intention had been to shock him from his stupor of regret, memories, and guilt, heavier now than it had ever seemed before, she'd succeeded. With the tiny hint of a smile on the corner of her lips, and the sheer starkness of the veracity in her pronouncement.

The despicable secret of his past had been laid before her. He'd hoped, in some measure, to drive her away. To let the choice to turn away be hers, because he couldn't seem to be trusted to do it, even if he knew every second she spent with him put her further in danger. Risked not only her life, but her *life*. Risked her being dragged down into the dark, dank depths of his existence; risked the bright future she'd made for herself.

Only, she wasn't running. She wasn't looking at him in disgust or crying, *Murderer!* as she should. She was looking at him as if she truly could see him, all of him, his soul, and *didn't* find him wanting. Didn't find him any different than she ever had.

It was that same absolute trust, and cutting knowledge in her eyes, along with that undefinable thing he couldn't name…

'Liar,' she repeated, her hands tightening their hold, challenging him to deny the charge. Only he couldn't—because, perhaps, despite what he'd always believed, that it had all been penance, perhaps it would, *could*, be true. He wanted to believe it, desperately; more than anything he'd ever believed before. 'You gave me the world, Freddie. I told you that once; still, you don't see it. Not only did you take me in, you gave me so much more. You didn't have to. It wasn't penance.'

'It was,' he argued.

*She has to understand...*

'I spent days walking after that night. Until I no longer had any idea where I was. I laid down in a ditch, never intending to leave. What point was there? I had nothing, *nothing*, left,' he told her vehemently, knowing she knew well the feeling, of being alone, with nothing. 'An old man, Mr Walton, he found me. Nursed me back to life, gave me what I gave you. He was an old navy man, a bachelor, with no one to provide a legacy. So I became his son. And he was… Everything to me. Until he too, passed on, leaving me with a small fortune. And I swore, to put it to good use. Make a legacy he would be proud of.'

'So you did.'

'So I did. But you see, Mena, you *must* see, it was all for him,' he told her. 'Everything I've done, was to repay the debt owed. For what he taught me. What he gave me.'

'You can fool yourself into thinking that is the only reason you ever did anything good, Freddie,' Mena said, shaking her head as if he were the dullest man on the planet. 'I know it isn't. You might've lived well, and lived well by others, and still honoured this man. You might've saved my life, in exchange for the one given, and given me an education, as repayment for yours. But everything you are, your heart,' she smiled, laying one hand on the offending organ. 'It was already an incredible, generous thing. You knew what was right, and what wasn't. You might've fought to build something which would never take advantage of people, as your family once did, but you never had to. You *chose* to. That is your goodness, not penance. Treating me with respect, when I was nothing more than dirt to some, that is *goodness*. Helping your friends at every turn, standing by them when they make difficult choices, that is goodness. Mr Walton might've shown you the way to live an honourable life, given you the means to do so, but it was there, in your heart, always.'

'You can't know that,' he croaked.

'Perhaps not,' she shrugged. 'But you can. Examine your heart, *objectively*, Freddie, and tell me again your life has been penance, and penance alone.'

He did as instructed.

Eyes locked on hers, he delved into his truest self, opened himself to it as he never had; as he'd been too terrified to, ever. For a long time, they sat there, Mena not abandoning him, steady, and anchoring, as he sank to the deepest depths of his soul and returned again.

Without an answer.

Well, with an answer—but without certainty. He believed she was right. That over the years, he'd managed to convince himself any *good* deeds were done merely out of penance. Yet the truth was, he knew there had been times when he'd had to *convince* himself. As he had when he'd allowed Mena to stay. He'd had to find an excuse. So perhaps that meant, it was merely that.

*Convincing. Excuses.*

He still didn't think, *know*, that he was a good man. How could anyone? Was the mere action of thinking you were somehow *not* the behaviour of a good man? It was enough to drive him mad. All he knew, was that Mena, even with all he'd told her, believed him to be good. Or at least, *good enough*. He'd have to take her word on that.

Raising her hands to his lips, he kissed them, pouring his gratitude and love into that touch.

'That's what I thought,' she said softly, disentangling one hand to gently sweep back strands of his hair. They remained there for a long moment, and Freddie might've sworn pieces of himself he'd never thought could, healed with her touch, as if she were magic herself. 'He's the one who came after the shop, isn't he?' she asked what might've been a century later for all he knew or cared; and the question cast a harrowing chill over him, despite the lack of concern, or reproach, he deserved to hear in her voice. 'Your uncle.'

'Yes,' he told her honestly, unable to withhold anything anymore. 'I won't let him hurt you again. I won't let anything happen to you.'

'Neither will I.'

Before he could retort anything, tell her that was madness, and not for her to say, and there was no way in Hell he would let her ever get close enough to danger to protect *him*, she smiled, though the promise in her eyes was no less potent, and leaned over to kiss him.

Gently, ever so tenderly, mindful of the cut on his lip she had tended to what seemed so long ago, considering how far they'd come. She pulled away after a delicious, but all too short moment, and he searched her eyes, wondering if that was to be *goodbye*, or even merely *goodnight*.

It was neither. The same question he asked was in her own eyes—*stay with me?*

This time he kissed her, none to gentle, but with any ounce of tenderness he might have within him, learned, and stored up along the way that was his life. His lip hurt, and she tried to be mindful, until he proved he didn't need her to be. That sting was the very least of the pain he felt, and only she could soothe it. Any of it.

She must've sensed that choice, for in a second she was devouring him, rising to stand between his legs, and it felt as if she was determined to prove she still desired every inch of him. That she...

*Don't.*

Sucking his tongue into her mouth she cut off his ability to think. He rose, grasping her tightly, and vaguely registering that there were barely any clothes on her. Her underthings, and a dressing gown.

*Good.*

He led her back in the direction of her bed, or at least where he assumed it would be, stomping in as he had, focused on one thing alone. Well, two. Her, and his sorry past. She grasped him as tightly as he did her, and by the time they made it to the bed, all but his trousers, and shoes, and her stockings, were gone.

He saw to that issue swiftly once he lay her down, and then he leaned over and stole another deep, soul-searing kiss. As he did, he swept his fingers through her womanly curls, groaning as he found her already slick, and ready. It wasn't that he wished to rush this, but right now, this fire between them, this desperation born of scarring healing, it needed to be quenched.

It didn't feel as if a lifetime of hurt, guilt, loneliness, and self-loathing had been miraculously, and instantly, healed. It didn't feel as if he were a better, stronger man than he'd been—it felt as if he were quite the contrary. Raw, scraped, until nothing but his truest, most vulnerable self remained. Scraped as skin was by barnacles. Left aching, and pulsing; bleeding and open for all to see.

In another time, that might've sent him running, terrified. Not tonight. Because Mena was here. With him. She'd not abandoned him, not repudiated him. She saw his wounds, and welcomed them, as he did hers, for they were part of who they were. And that gift, *that* miracle, it was the greatest thing he'd ever known—or was ever likely to.

He rose again, taking her thighs in hand and bringing her to the edge of the bed before widening them. She nodded, almost imperceptibly, except not, because he was watching her so closely. He saw it all—as she did—and he would never look away again.

Placing himself where he desired most to be, he sank in with a heavy groan. Mena let loose a half gasp, half whimper that undid him, her arms flying back to grab hold of the edge of the bed as she arched forward, and into him, rising and grasping hold of him with her legs.

They knew this dance well—they excelled at it if he could say so himself. There was a harmony born of their newly gained physical knowledge of each other, and he revelled in it. He let the wave carry him, as he drove them, higher, and higher; until all they were was sound, and heat.

*Land and sea—meeting again.*

A sharp cry, and her back was arching further off the bed, her legs clenching him as tightly as her inner muscles, and he held on tight to her hips, biting his tongue so as not to follow her, despite that being his deepest desire. He wouldn't… Force that choice on her.

*Any choice.*

And so he watched, and held, until she was floating down, and then he left her body, taking himself in hand for the final two strokes before he spilled himself on her belly. She watched him through half-closed eyes—and that look alone might've allowed him to do so without aid.

Spent, he leaned on the bed a little, and when he had enough strength to lower himself without losing use of his arms, he did so, taking her mouth again, drinking all she gave to him until he was breathless.

When he had, revived by her taste, he kissed her nose, then rose, and felt around for his shirt in the half-light, the candle long extinguished and the fire dimming. He wiped himself from her body, then gathered her in his arms, and settled them into bed properly.

Much remained to be said, but for tonight, enough had been. He hadn't lost her—not yet. And though he knew none of this meant he could keep her, Freddie fell asleep comforted by the fact that, at least for tonight, he didn't have to let her go.

*My heart never will.*

## Chapter Twenty

*Light. Endless, soul-warming light.* That was what Mena felt she was basking in as she awoke, nestled deep in the comfort of her bed that now not only bore her scent, but Freddie's too. Streams of decadent, glittering sunlight poured from the window; she'd always had the most of it in this room—despite its position at the back. She had a feeling Freddie had known that when he'd given it to her.

Smiling, she stretched lazily, unwilling to rise and move, though she knew she would have to soon. If the sun was this bright, it was quite late. Only she couldn't bring herself to care—that she was being a lay-abed, that she was late, any of it. Last night… Last night had been gruelling, harrowing, in so many ways. Yet somehow, they'd found a way through—*together*. Freddie had given her what she'd craved and prayed for most.

*Himself. Truth. Trust.*

It was the most beautiful gift he'd ever given, and though much lay ahead, and nothing was truly fixed, the day did seem full of promise, because he'd done what he had. Revealed what he had; given her who he was.

Inhaling deeply as she prepared to get out of bed and

wash, face the day, Mena frowned, catching the hint of something unexpected.

*Breakfast.*

Pulling herself up to sitting, she found a tray of delectable-looking food on the table before the hearth; and Freddie, standing not so far away, his back to her as he stared at the wall. A wall, full, as every other was, as every inch of her room was, covered in traces of him. Drawings he'd made, rocks and twigs and dried flowers he'd given her, framed, or in little glass cases.

The world she'd never seen, that he'd brought her.

'Why?' he asked, his back still to her.

Mena pulled her knees up to her chest, hugging them tight.

There was something in his voice... It sounded like desolation. Disappointment. It broke through the joyful haze—telling her that not only had he discovered *her* deepest truth; he was far from pleased.

She'd expected that, really, she had. Though she'd hoped for perhaps a moment that the adverse could be true—and better yet—that it *had* been love in his eyes, that they could have that, together, well. Her heart had known better. He'd never said the words. He'd called her his *best friend*, and his *partner*. Said that she made his house a home. Said that he hadn't been able to let her go. He'd bared himself to her—but that was all. And maybe, if she hadn't expected it, she might've felt true heartbreak in that moment.

Yet she didn't. She felt...icy freedom. In time... In time, the hurt, the regret, the longing, the heartbreak, they would come. But for now, she was free—the knowledge, certainty of where they stood, somehow shocking her back to the reality she'd always seen in her future.

Mena knew she could lie. Make it...better, perhaps.

More palatable for him. Reassure him that not all was as it seemed, and that he was safe from her clinging to him, asking for more. Except she couldn't will herself to do it. Lying outright was not her. She might've *dissimulated* truths, but lying would be poison; and it would kill her soul just as surely. This freedom she felt now, it gave her courage. To say the words, at least once. To give them voice, and breath, and to put them out into the world. To liberate them from her heart, where they'd lived for so long.

*And to reassure him I know where we stand.*

'I love you, Freddie,' she said, unwavering, with all the strength she had. 'With all my heart. I have, for a long time. And I think, I *know*, I always will. But you need not fear, I know...you don't feel as I do. I won't ask anything of you. Still, I am grateful. For the time we had, the life we had. For what you gave me last night.' Closing her eyes, and taking a breath to centre herself again, Mena continued before she could say no more. 'I will sign the house back to you as soon as I can get my solicitor to do so. I will move into Nichols House after the New Year.'

'The house and the shop are, and will remain, yours,' he said after a long moment, still refusing to turn, to at least grant her one last look.

*So this is what it feels to be cast into eternal darkness, then.*

'You may do with them what you wish, go where you wish to.'

*I don't care*, he didn't say, but it was there, visible like flaming words between them. That was when she heard the first crack in her heart—the sign of impending doom—and she swallowed hard, drowning it out. She

wouldn't, *couldn't*, let him see, any of it. She would re-
tain her grace until the end even if it killed her.

'You need not fear my uncle; I said I would take care
of it, and I will. There are men watching the shop; I will
instruct them to make themselves known should you
need them. I will be out tonight; Mary has invited me
to the theatre. You have the day, Susie has opened the
shop, and I've given her a key. Enjoy your breakfast.'

With those inane, banal words, he strode out, not even
sparing her a glance.

All she caught was his profile as he left; stone-cold
and closed off to her for ever now.

*'Enjoy your breakfast.'*

As if she could.

The icy freedom was still enveloping her; however,
she also felt ill. Of all the…

A thousand times she'd imagined what their parting
might look like.

In the better versions, they shook hands, smiled, and
every so often, he would kiss her cheek. They would
bid each other a fond farewell, and wish each other the
best. Sometimes, she would glimpse him, years later,
as fulfilled as she would be, perhaps at a party, and she
would meet his wife, and his friends, and then she and
Freddie would smile at each other, safe in the knowledge that the connection had not been lost, and that their
friendship would live on for ever.

More often than not, their parting would be cold, and
professional. A *thank-you* for services rendered, and a
*good day*. In the worst versions, there would be tears.
Chasms of loneliness and avoidance. It would look much
like those days after his return would; or like the fights
they'd had, only they'd never get the chance to make

things right. It would be full of bitter resentment, and festering wounds.

In all those times, she'd never once imagined this.

The clicking of Hawk's nails sounded in the room, and then his warm body was curling up next to her. Mindlessly, she stroked his rough fur, and a tear slipped from her eye. She didn't swipe it away; she let it, and its companions, fall freely.

Despite everything, she'd thought she'd known him. After eight years, she'd thought she understood him. Even more so now, with all the pieces clicking into place, all those unanswered questions answered. Now, she saw that she didn't. Perhaps never had. She couldn't make sense of him, of his casual indifference and kindness. It was a special brand of cruelty that cut to the quick.

Bringing her breakfast, decorating the tray with that sprig of holly she could see peeking from it.

Being so utterly devastated that she should love him.

Telling her of men he'd apparently hired to watch the house; whilst also telling her of his evening with Mary.

Saying, in not many words, that he didn't care for what they'd built together any more, that he was starting anew.

Last night… Last night, fool that she was, she'd thought they'd moved past what he'd kept to himself all these years. She'd thought they'd, not freed him, but perhaps rendered less terrifying the ghosts that haunted him so. She'd thought, perhaps, that his opening to her, giving her *trust*, had been a harbinger of a new beginning. Not an ending.

*Not an ending such as this.*

Though, perhaps it was a beginning. For Freddie, at least. For her, perhaps in time she could see it so.

*Not yet.*

For him, however… Maybe revealing his past had been the first step. Maybe his past had kept him from opening himself to what awaited him with Mary. Now that he'd told his best friend, well. He could tell his other friends. His future wife. They would help him through whatever danger he still faced, and help him begin anew. Perhaps he was as free as Mena was now.

*For I am free. To…move on. To live.*

In time, she would convince herself. And no matter how much it hurt right this moment, in truth, she was glad for him. That he'd found a way to happiness. That he'd found his way to the life he deserved.

*As I always knew he would.*

*Quite so.*

Mena remained there all morning, stroking Hawk. She let herself grieve what had been; and what never could. Finally, she forced herself to eat, dress, and then, she returned to bed.

Susie came in some time later, with more food. Her friend said nothing, merely helped her dress further and wash, and they ate together, and when they had finished, Mena went down to the shop, and made herself useful. She tried very hard not to think how very fitting this ending was after all.

*A sad ending to a sad tale.*

## Chapter Twenty-One

It was a very good thing he couldn't see himself properly in the antique, curved copper which had served as a looking glass once, and which he was using for that purpose again this evening. Before, it had simply been an object that he liked, that he thought looked rather nice in his office, reflecting the light into it as it did. Tonight, it was a tool which enabled him to be the coward he was.

So yes, he was grateful for the distorted reflection, the bare bones of his appearance only. He didn't have the stomach to look at himself, to see the guilt and shame at what he'd done again, worse this time, in his own eyes.

*Hurt Mena.*

But then, he didn't have the stomach for much after what he'd done to her. He'd known that this morning, known as he'd walked out of her room that he couldn't go back to that house. So he'd gathered what he would need for a few days, gathered this evening dress which felt a farcical costume, bid Hawk to go find her, and walked out before he could change his mind.

Change his heart.

Of all the terrible things he'd done, it was likely that tearing her heart out and stomping on it, as he'd known he had, would haunt him longer, and more viciously, than the rest. Perhaps, because as Mena put it, he *had* been a child then. Unable to fully comprehend what he was doing. What it did to others. Whereas this… This he'd done in full consciousness. He'd made the rational decision to hurt her; so that in breaking her heart, he might stomp out the ridiculous notion of love she'd held therein.

It was his own fault, allowing this to happen. Being so stupid, and blind, and selfish, so as not to see what was happening. What had already happened. He'd imagined the possibility, certes, he'd discussed it with Mary, but tender feelings were one thing. The love she held for him… That was another entirely. And he'd gone and made it worse by succumbing to his own desires; his own inability to *let her go* as he'd always known he must.

Tying his cravat, he thought again on that morning; he hadn't really stopped all day. He tried to understand how he hadn't seen what she claimed to feel for him before; even though looking back now, he had. He'd at the very least felt it—in every touch, every caress, every kiss. Especially last night. What he'd called *tenderness*, and *care*, it was love.

He'd never known it before; maybe why he'd not recognised it. Yet it was that very same reason, his own actions up until now, which demonstrated what he'd always known deep down. He may love her, but he didn't know *how* to love her, and certainly, not well. All these years, he'd stifled her, kept her close, and kept her to himself. When he'd seen her room this morning…

A sabre through his chest might've been less jarring. Last night, he'd been so focused on himself, *as always*, to pay attention, and he'd risen before the sun, determined to bring her breakfast, and lie with her a while, and give her a day all to herself as she'd not known for some time. To give them a day, to…revel in each other. He'd thought it was easy, and uncomplicated, that despite his feelings, they could share time, and then bid each other a fond farewell, and though it might cause some pain, though they might miss each other, they would not…be heart-broken. Or that she wouldn't be.

And then he'd seen her room. Covered in mementos he'd brought or made for her. Lovingly cherished, framed and displayed, as if they were the most precious things in the world. As if his memories were. He'd stared, for hours, maybe, until she'd woken, and though he knew the answer—it had been one he'd always dreaded—he'd had to ask.

*'Why?'*

*'I love you.'*

Three words. Three words that could change a life—or in this case, destroy it. There was no doubt in his mind that her love, what she *believed* to be love, had de-stroyed her life. Kept her from so much more, so much better. It didn't matter what anyone said—he knew the truth. She couldn't love him. Not after what he'd done for her, and not after what he'd done, full stop. He couldn't allow it.

Which is why he'd done what he had. Unable to look at her for fear of crumbling in the wake of pleading eyes he could *never* refuse, he'd been as cold, and cutting, as he knew how. For her to be free, she needed to know she was safe, that she had a future, hence mention of the house, and men protecting her; and she needed to know he was not, and would never be, an option for her. He'd gambled that if everyone else believed something was happening with Mary, then so would she. As he'd just received the invitation to the theatre, it was perfect.

*Just bloody perfect.*

In time, Mena would learn the truth, but by then, hopefully, she would've moved on. And he…would likely not be there to see it, but then, maybe that was for the best too.

Smoothing down his lapels, Freddie turned away from the mirror, and made quick work of throwing on his overcoat and hat. He was already late, and would be later still if he didn't stop turning over all this business in his mind. It was done.

*And hopefully it is not too late for Mena.*

With that prayer in his heart, he strode out and made his way to the street to call a hack. One mercifully pulled up almost immediately, and he clambered in. The bumpy ride was long enough to threaten his peace of mind, and by the time they reached the Strand, Freddie stopped them, paying the driver, preferring to walk the rest. Harsh balls of snow pelted against him, but he welcomed the boreal weather, the sting of it.

At the sight of the crowds gathered further ahead, chattering, and laughing beneath the shining lights of the theatre, Freddie was both grateful he walked, and annoyed that he'd ever thought this a good idea.

*A friend's company at the worst of times is always a good thing.*

He'd told Mary that last year—and now, he felt its truth. Excusing himself, slowly making his way through the various groups of tittering skirts and booming tailcoats, he finally spotted his quarry nestled near the doors.

Only, he never made it to her.

The click of a pistol, and the feel of it at his back, along with a hand on his shoulder, told him that his time had run out. Which was a blessing, really. Because he'd never have to experience life without Mena after all.

*What torture that might've been.*

'Come wit' me or she's first t'die,' his uncle hissed.

Freddie nodded, and smiled as he faded back into the crowd before Mary could see him.

'Lead on, Uncle,' he said. 'You'll have no trouble from me. I've been waiting for you.'

*For such a long time.*

## Chapter Twenty-Two

The sound of frantic pounding on the front door startled Mena from the self-pitying stupor she'd been in since Susie reluctantly, but finally, left, and she'd come to lay on her bed, unable to even undress. Hawk shook himself from contented sleep, and Mena's heart pounded, memories of the night they'd been attacked coming to the forefront of her mind as Hawk clicked downstairs.

*But there are men outside if I need them.*

Good, capable men who had come before the shop closed to introduce themselves. Still, she hesitated, listening to the knocking intently, trying to decide whether it was the same devil that had come that night, having dispatched her protectors and Hell-bent on vengeance, but when Hawk's bark met her ears, light, more of a whine, she determined that it was unlikely to be Freddie's uncle.

Grabbing a candle, she hastened downstairs, forcing deep breaths into her lungs, reassuring herself that all was well, and that there was no need to be wishing for Freddie.

*Ever again.*

'Coming,' she yelled, taking the last few steps, and

unlocking the door to the shop, before gracefully gliding around the obstacles therein. 'Hawk, back, sit,' she ordered when they reached the front door.

Lighting the candle beside it, she took another steadying breath, and finally opened the door, praying her deductions were correct.

'My lady,' she breathed, utterly bewildered as she spotted the figure on the doorstep, arm raised as if to pound the door again. She looked incredible, if mildly startled, and…

*Is that fear in her eyes?*

'Are you well, my lady? Freddie isn't here, he—'

'Came to meet me at the theatre,' Lady Mary said with a brisk nod, tightness invading her features. 'Only he never appeared. It is most unlike him, and I was concerned. I think, now, I had cause to be.'

Dread lurched in Mena's stomach as she distractedly nodded and stepped back from the door so the other woman could enter, which she did.

There was no doubt in Mena's mind. Freddie's past had indeed returned with a vengeance; only not here. It had come back to haunt him; his uncle had come back for him. And Freddie, *idiotic noble dolt* that he was, wouldn't have fought. No, after last night, all he'd revealed… He would have this end another way. Far away from where anyone else could get hurt.

*Breathe.*

Mena sucked in a stilted breath, leaning back against the steady wall of the corridor.

*Another.*

*Breathe.*

She vaguely felt gloved hands take the candle from her, and rub her arms, only she had to pull herself together or she wouldn't be able to help Freddie.

*Help Freddie. Yes.*

*Breathe.*

Her heart didn't calm, her hands didn't stop shaking, but slowly, she was able to think again. Raising her eyes, she met those of the woman she'd envied for so long, and swallowed, hard.

*Think. Sussex. Go.*

'Something terrible has happened, hasn't it,' the lady said, more than asked.

'Yes… I have to… I have to get to Sussex, now, without delay,' Mena stuttered out, pushing herself from the wall. 'I apologise, my lady, I cannot stay, I have to…'

*Do what? Men. Outside.*

'There are men, out there, guards,' she said, going to the door again.

Glancing out onto the street, all she spied were the usual few passers-by, a carriage, and a figure further down.

*Where were they? Not here.*

They would've surely appeared at the lady's knocking. Wherever they were, whatever happened, Mena knew she didn't have time to waste figuring it out. Turning back, she shook her head.

*You're alone in this. Now I need money. A hack?*

*No.*

*A carriage?*

*Perhaps.*

*Where did one hire a carriage quick enough, at this time of the evening?*

*A horse?*

'He's in danger, isn't he?' Mena nodded distractedly, heading for the stairs, uncaring of her behaviour towards the gentlewoman. Later, she could apologise properly, but right now, she needed to go. 'And it's to Sussex you must go?'

'Like the wind,' Mena choked out.

Already, it might be too late.

What time was it? How long before Lady Mary had come here, noticed Freddie wouldn't come? How long before he and his uncle reached the marshes? Before his uncle got what he wanted and killed him.

*No.*

'Mena,' Lady Mary said severely, not in reprimand, but to catch her attention, as if she'd tried several times already. Mena turned to face her, and before she could say anything else, the lady stepped forth. 'Where in Sussex?'

'The marshes.'

'Then there *is* someone outside I believe can help. Do you ride?' Mena nodded. The lady would help. They had a chance. 'My brother's estate is not far from there. We will drive down, and get horses from the stables. It is our best chance to make good time, I think. That is if the gentleman's boasts about his new equipage have actual merit to them.'

She rolled her eyes, and a half-laugh, half-sob escaped Mena's throat.

The lady had as much at stake as she did, and it wasn't that she herself was helpless, but it was such a boon not to waste time making travel arrangements.

'Thank you.'

'We'll make it,' Lady Mary said gently. 'Now, get a cloak, take care of this little beast,' she smiled wanly, glancing down at Hawk. 'And we shall be off.'

Mena did as ordered, adding proper boots, a woollen hat, the pistol Freddie kept in his desk, and the knife that had seen her through so much to the list.

Then, with a final pat on Hawk's head, and a prayer

to whatever great power might exist, she closed and locked the door, and turned to her helpers.

She wasn't entirely sure what she'd expected, or rather, who she'd expected Lady Mary's gentleman companion to be, only it certainly wasn't who she found standing before the carriage now at the steps with the lady.

Tall, slender, and though nonetheless imposing, the man was, undeniably, not only handsome, but beautiful, and young, dressed in rich, artfully tailored clothes which even she knew to be the height of fashion. Dark, long strands were as if constantly caught in the wind; his features were sharp, fine, and his eyes were arrestingly bright, though of a tenebrous colour she couldn't quite make out. He had a Mediterranean complexion, rich, olive skin; a heritage which was confirmed when the lady introduced him.

'Mena, meet Signor Guaro,' she said politely, as if they were all meeting in a drawing room.

The *signor* even bowed, low, and Mena curtsied.

'You may call me Luca,' he smiled when they both were upstanding again.

'Mena,' she said, not timidly, but not with full conviction either.

'It would be a pleasure in other circumstances,' he said seriously. 'For now, let us to my house, and we shall change conveyances, and be off before you know it. My driver has already gone to see everything prepared, so I shall be taking the reins from here.'

'Thank you, *signor*.'

With a smile, he bowed his head, and opened the door for Lady Mary and herself.

A look passed between the two she couldn't read as he passed the lady up, but before she could even make note of it, they were closed in, Luca was at the reins, and they were tearing off through the dark streets.

Tapping her fingers against her skirts, Mena took another deep breath, and said another silent prayer.

*Please, do not let us be too late.*


'There is no need to keep that pistol trained on me the whole journey, Uncle,' Freddie drawled, raising a brow at the man who had once been kin, but whom now he could barely recognise. The years, whatever his uncle had faced during them, and the festering hatred and bitterness, had twisted and distorted his features almost beyond recognition.

His uncle had always been hard, his thick brows perpetually scowling, his full lips never distinguishable for how tight his mouth was continuously set, and his eyes black as an abyss, though they were naturally clear grey. Now... All those features remained, though more emphasised, as if his designer had drawn them over and over, charcoal biting deeply into parchment. The eyes had become glittering pools of nervous disturbance; his skin had become sallow, grey, and marked by scars of illness and violence. His once strong, stocky figure had been chipped away until only the wiry frame remained. And his hands... They were twisted, and gnarled, a fiend's claws. Perhaps this was what people meant when they said a person's nature shone out.

For he could see his uncle's now as never before, in all its cruel, vicious glory.

'I gave you my word,' Freddie added, when his uncle made no move to lower the weapon. 'You shall have everything you wish for, with no fight from me.'

'I wish far yar death.'

'And you shall have it,' he said flatly.

Freddie had known as soon as his uncle put that pistol to his back that he would die. In the marshes, as he was supposed to that night. No point fighting it. Perhaps he believed in Providence after all. Or maybe something older, like Fate.

In the end, he'd lived a good life with his second chance, and he'd had Mena. If nothing else, his life was worthy for that fact alone. And his death would put an end to the danger that might've taken her from the world. That knowledge, and the knowledge that she already had a future beyond him, would set him on his final journey with a peaceful, quiet heart, and a smile on his lips.

*It is as it was always meant to be.*

'We must all pay the piper sometime, Uncle. So I shall tonight.'

His uncle's eyes narrowed, and finally he lowered the pistol to his lap.

Freddie vaguely wished he could stare out the window, see the landscape fly by, enjoy the sight one last time, but instead he'd be forced to stare at his past for the remaining hours of his life.

*Poetic, I suppose.*

'Nodin' t'say to me, boy?'

'Should I?'

He was taunting the man, he knew that.

Knew what his uncle wished for him to say. *Forgive me, I beg you, forgive me my betrayal.* But that was not something Freddie could give him. He couldn't, for he needed ask forgiveness only of his true sins. Not for those actions which would've seen him betray his conscience had he not done them. He was sorry, that his cousin had died, that people he'd known his life through, cared for, bled with, laughed with, had died, but the truth was, he'd neither pronounced the sentence nor executed them. He didn't see himself as any better; he'd done much of what they'd been shot and hanged for, but he'd...

*Been lucky. Tried to make good, before I met the same end.*

So no. He didn't believe his penance redeemed him, but neither had he made the choice the others had. To continue living such a life as they had, when things changed, or at least, when he *saw* what was truly happening. When it became murder, and exploitation, and mindless greed, rather than simply survival, or rising up against unfair laws.

*I stand by my choice, now and for ever.*

It was all he really had, here, at the end of everything.

He let that truth shine in his eyes, and his uncle tightened his grip on the pistol and spat.

'You'll 'ave somedin' t'say befar t'end,' his uncle promised.

'Perhaps. What happened to you?' Freddie asked after a moment. 'All these years, you might've started over. Rebuilt something for yourself. Something good.'

'Like you?' Another round of disgusted spitting. 'Wanna know what I ded after I pulled meeself from de frozen mud you left me in? Watched me son rot in de sun. Lived like a storvin' animal, kep livin' 'cause I didn't know what else t'do and t'eatred far what you'd done wouldn't lit me die. Made new friends. Worked t'parts twixt 'ere and Dev'n till livin' weren't so easy.'

'And then you came to London,' Freddie finished. It wasn't hard to complete the picture; his uncle had done what he'd always done —*stolen, killed, smuggled*— only from the sound of it he hadn't been leading much since his assumed demise. The thought spurred in his gut, as he thought of all those who had suffered this man's deeds over the years. The desire to make it right, *somehow*, was almost enough to make Freddie want to change his fate. 'How did you find me?'

'Were comin' out o'inn night you came back,' his uncle smiled, pure malice and twisted satisfaction. 'Dought me eyes were paintin' fancies. Fallered you, back t'yar shop, den next day t'be sure. Couldn't believe me luck. T'were God 'emself geevin' me what t'wanted most. Vengeance, far me son.'

Freddie nodded—not in agreement, in acceptance.

Of whatever had brought them together again for whatever purpose.

'Did you ever care for me at all, Uncle?' he asked quietly after a long while.

He wasn't sure why it mattered, if indeed it did, but somehow, that desire, that need, to belong, to be *loved*, had informed his life more than he'd ever cared to admit.

*Until it was too late.*

'You were ken. Me broder's blood.'

'And I did good work for you.'

'Aye.'

'Aye.'

Swallowing the unexpected lump in his throat, Freddie nodded again.

He'd always known as much, but as a child, he'd thought that if he did what was asked of him, if he made his uncle happy enough, proud enough, he could be loved as Malcolm had been. If it was even love his uncle felt for his son; if it were even possible for a man like him to have any true love in his heart.

So yes, Freddie had yearned for his uncle's love, *love*, full stop. Now, the knowledge that he never would have got it, in its true form, was freeing. For in the end, he *had* touched it. Felt it, clutched it tightly to his breast, and been bolstered by it. And so, he had been very lucky indeed. Though Mena's love for him was wrong, he was a selfish man, and a selfish man he would remain. To-night, he would keep her love, all for himself.

To see him through this final trial.

## Chapter Twenty-Three

The journey across London to Signor Guaro's house, subsequent change of vehicle, and departure from the city, slow and arduous, though not nearly as much as it might've been in the full light of day, had all been performed with ruthless efficiency, and in tense silence.

The dim lights of the city, reassuring scoring of noise, amplified by the sounds of the eve's revelry, had long since faded, replaced with the thundering of the team's hooves, whooshing of air, clicking and bouncing of the carriage, and tapping of the curtains against the glass as they sped down the difficult, but passable roads. The gentleman had not in fact been lying about the exquisiteness of his *équipage*, in speed, or comfort. The simply, but expensively, furnished carriage made for surprisingly comfortable travel.

Mena focused on it all, creating a symphony in her head, not that she really had any idea what a true symphony would sound like. It would be one of her greatest regrets, that she'd not been able to experience so much; to take Freddie up on his offers over the years to experience so much *with* him. Except that, even now, her body rebelled, telling her to return home. Her heart pounded—both from fear for Freddie, and from that unnatural anxiety she always felt when she went too far. Her palms sweated, as did the back of her neck, and her chest was a tight band, which barely allowed proper breathing. Her mouth had dried, even as her jaw remained tightly clenched. Thank goodness the curtains were closed, and she couldn't see how far she was from all she knew.

*In. Out.*

*In. Out.*

Closing her eyes, she did so, the raucous symphony surrounding her lulling her back to steadiness, and she tapped her fingers against her skirts in rhythm with it.

*There.*

'All will be well, Mena,' Lady Mary said kindly, breaking the silence. 'We will find them.' Mena met her reassuring gaze, and did feel better for it. 'You do have some idea how to find them, I presume?' she asked a moment later, frowning as if she'd only just realised that was rather an important question. 'The marshes are significant in size.'

'I have an idea of where to begin,' Mena nodded. 'And thank you, for your reassurances, my lady. Though I feel as if I should be offering them to you.'

'Mary, please. Unlike my brother, I have always despised the Lady Mary nonsense. Makes me out to be something I am not. Indeed, I am made of sterner stuff than I look,' the lady winked, and Mena found herself smiling again. The woman was so easy to like, and that was what would make it all the more difficult, and yet all the easier, when the time came for Freddie to begin his life with her. 'As are you, I think. It is not a weakness,' she added casually, glancing down at Mena's still thrumming hands. 'Some things will always be difficult to face, and our bodies react in various ways. What you are doing tonight, well, do not think I don't know what it costs you. You have great courage, Mena. Though I already knew that.'

Taken slightly—*very*—aback by the lady's candour and words, Mena simply stared for a long moment. She dared a glance at Signor Guaro, who remained steadfastly invested in his examination of the purple paisley curtains, though she could have sworn she saw the whisper of a smile.

Lady Mary—*Mary*—seemed to sense her discomfort, and continued.

In truth, it was helping, giving Mena more to think on rather than simply stew in her own nerves and discomfort.

'In time, I suspect, I *hope*, we shall become good friends. Perhaps, when this is over, you might give me a tour of your new enterprise,' she smiled, and Mena nodded, stunned. It wasn't by the lady's —*Mary's*— spirit, she'd already known of it, but rather the woman's truthful interest in her. 'Reid's wife—you must know of Reid,' Mary laughed. 'Considering that rather odd visit Freddie and my brother had there some years ago, really, dreadful Spencer was, but in any case, I think you will like both of them. Rebecca especially; I have a feeling you two will get along rather nicely.'

'From what I've heard, she does sound incredible,' Mena agreed, her voice returning, her mind cleared by the disconcertingly startling certainty of Mary's claims. 'Only I don't think I shall ever have occasion to meet her.'

'Whyever not,' Mary frowned, equally as confused. 'I mean, I understand why Freddie was reluctant to bring you along to meet everyone, but surely once this is all resolved, there will no longer be a need for denial, if that is in fact what Freddie was about.' Mary made a little sound in the back of her throat, then shrugged, and forged on. 'Besides, Reid and Rebecca are down often enough nowadays that you would not need venture far should you not be up for it. The same will be true for my family. Elizabeth is really rather fond of Freddie, but then he is always spoiling her.'

'You would wish me to meet your family?' Mena asked incredulously.

She knew the Spencers, and the Reids for that matter, were quite scandalous in their own ways, through their marriages particularly, but still, she'd never imagined the sister of a marquess wouldn't mind her husband parading his once mistress among them all.

*Nor that a marquess wouldn't mind for that matter.*

'Why on earth shouldn't I?'

'I wouldn't have thought… That is, when you marry… I wouldn't think it proper…'

'Marry? Oh…' Mary said, understanding dawning before she began to laugh, quite brightly, which was extremely jarring.

Both given the situation, and the conversation.

Even Signor Guaro glanced over, frowning, as if he too were confused by it all.

'Oh! You thought… Freddie and I?' Mena nodded, and Mary laughed harder. Mena might've felt as if the woman were mocking her had the laughter not been so visibly natural, without malice. 'We are only friends, Mena. Much to my despair, such friendships are often regarded as something more, but you must believe me. Freddie has been a very dear friend to me, and my family. That is all.' The woman truly seemed to wish for Mena to believe this, and, well, she did. After years of believing *Mary* would follow Freddie through the rest of their lives, Mena felt as if her entire world had been tossed asunder. Weakly, she smiled, and Mary looked relieved. 'I did ask him to marry me once,' she added, turning to the window, examining the curtains much as Signor Guaro was, though she toyed with the tassels too. 'That Christmas.' She turned back to Mena, and shrugged. 'I thought we would make a good match. I with my fortune, he with his business... I thought we could help each other. He turned me down very graciously. Said that I deserved better than to settle for what little he could offer. I didn't quite understand at the time,' she continued, and Mena truly wondered where all this was coming from. 'But now... I do. I think he meant I deserved someone whose heart and life, and soul, really, didn't already belong to someone else.'

There was a measure of sadness in Mary's voice of regret, but also of acknowledgement, and gratitude.

'I don't—that is to say— Freddie, he doesn't...'

*No.*

To start believing that again... It would destroy her. Though he might not have chosen Mary, that didn't mean he loved *Mena*. She knew he cared for her, that he'd been drawn in enough to share her bed, but as for love, and souls, and hearts...

*No.*

'He looks at you the same way my brother looks at his Genevieve,' Mary said simply. 'And Reid at Rebecca. In all the years I've known Freddie, other than to speak of me, or trivial things, the only thing he has ever spoken of, has been you. Which is why I permit myself to use your Christian name so freely. Not because of my station, but because I rather feel I know you. In fact, of late, you've been all we've spoken of,' Mary chuckled. 'He kept coming to me for advice, and was quite open about the fact he had fallen in love with you. Well, I forced him to admit it, actually. He thought you would feel only gratitude, and accept him only to repay a debt. And he was terrified, of what he felt. Thought it would prevent you from becoming all you could, if he admitted it.'

'Idiot,' Mena muttered.

'Quite. We shall both be certain to tell him so when we've saved him,' Mary grinned, turning back to the view-less window again.

Signor Guaro glanced over at Mary, studying her for a moment, then returned to his own thoughts. Meanwhile, Mena remained there, shocked to the core, her entire world, her entire belief system, completely overturned.

*Freddie loves me.*

All this time… Believing it was a dream so far out of reach not even an angel could make it come true. Yet it was. She'd grasped it, *felt* it, even as she'd told herself not to believe it.

*But what now?*

What if they did not arrive in time? What if they did? What future would there be beyond that? She'd thought she had it all pictured, squared away and set, with no, or very little, at least, room for surprises. Now…

*It is nought but unknowns. My least favourite thing.*

*Just get through the night.*

Yes. That was exactly right. As with all things, she simply needed a new plan, a new map.

*Get through the night. The morning will bring with it the next steps.*

*Quite so.*

## Chapter Twenty-Four

'**O**w much farder?' his uncle groaned, after stepping into a shallow boggy patch for perhaps the twentieth time since they'd set off. Apparently neither of them were quite as sure-footed as they'd once been, though Freddie still knew every path. They, particularly this path, had been etched into his soul. 'Bisted wanderin' arend dis swank.'

'Not far now,' Freddie said calmly.

The old man was reaching the end of his tether; he could feel the desperation wafting off him.

But then, the journey down had been far more trying than his uncle had likely expected. The first horses had barely made it out of London, they'd had to wait an hour for a change, and those had lasted about ten miles themselves. At that point, they'd had to abandon his uncle's driver cum accomplice along with the carriage as only two horses could be found. Those horses had lasted a little longer, though not long enough. The night was as harsh as one could dream, the roads passable, but barely. Even in the full light of the summer sun, they were hard, tricky roads, especially further south—the closer to the marsh they came.

His uncle was desperate, determined in his vengeance, but he was not, nor had ever been, stupid. He knew that if he wanted to get to his box of treasure—which Freddie doubted he truly wanted for anything more than, yes, the riches potentially therein, but mainly, the satisfaction of having got it, having won—he needed to get Freddie to the marsh alive. So they'd had to travel with more caution and less speed, until they were both frozen, stiff, and slow themselves. Still, their journey wasn't over; though the night was nearing its end, there were miles over marsh to cover, on foot.

Freddie, sore and frozen as he was, still held that peace in his heart, and so, he rather enjoyed the time Fate seemed to be granting him. And there was no doubt she had a hand in this night; so like the last one he'd spent here twenty-nine years ago.

Quiet, still, the reeds and grasses barely moving, though he could smell them, and the brine of the water. Patches of iced-over mud; patches of hardened ground. Mists so thick and cloying, you couldn't see more than a few feet ahead; a cold so enveloping, it was as if you belonged to it. Only the moon was different, barely there, a sliver somewhere above, lighting their way just enough.

So that they could make it here.

The ghostlike skeleton of a tree rose from the mists like some demonic omen, but Freddie smiled as he glimpsed it, saying a silent greeting to his old friend.

'Here,' he said, stopping a little before it.

'Should've known,' his uncle laughed mirthlessly. 'Get deggin' den, boy.'

Though he needn't not, his uncle shoved him towards the tree, and Freddie stumbled before righting himself.

He glanced back at the old man, the grim reaper himself, and nodded. Casting his eyes to the ground, he searched for a hardy stick or rock to aid him, and finding a piece of flint that would do the job, he circled the tree, his uncle dogging every move, but mindful to keep distance, and the pistol between them. Finally, Freddie knelt before the ancient tree, and began his work.

That night, he hadn't realised how hard the ground had been, even here in the midst of the marsh, so frenzied he'd been. He'd only noticed his bloody fingers and broken nails the morning after; even then they hadn't hurt. He noticed the unwillingness of the earth to be disturbed tonight, however. Every stroke screamed at him to stop, to fight, and to prevent his uncle from ever hurting anyone again.

*I will try, I promise*, he silently told it, as he beat the flint into it, chipping away at layer after layer. *I will try to take him with me when I have a good chance*, he swore, having made that decision during the journey.

He couldn't risk someone, *anyone*, getting hurt, but neither could he allow his uncle to simply take his treasure and walk away to hurt others. Only, he had to be smart, and do it when he had a good chance of overpowering the man; and not getting shot in the process. He was ready to die—he could feel Death calling him, its breath on his neck as it reminded him the reprieve was over—but he would not be alone.

*My last act of penance.*

The dig warmed him, as did oddly his uncle's grumbling. The man was getting impatient, and they were both exhausted, though Freddie felt wide awake now. The exertion of this dig was warming him, and soon, he would have the upper hand on his uncle. Perhaps this could even end in something other than death, for them both.

*That is the hope talking. You know how this ends.*

His strokes became wilder as he widened his search in the dirt; apparently, though his memory was good, his accuracy was not. Then finally, he heard it.

*Clink.*

Changing hands with the flint, he let his fingers feel around the bottom of the rather excessively large hole.

*Metal.*

Finding the edges clumsily, his fingers burning with the cold, he managed to outline it in the dirt, then set about chipping away more at the earth surrounding it, until finally, it was free.

Clutching it tightly in both hands, he rose slowly, and turned to face his uncle.

'On yar knees,' he ordered, pistol high and aimed at Freddie's heart. 'Now!' he screamed, and Freddie began to obey, measuring his options, hoping his uncle might come just a bit closer, when another voice sounded in the night, carrying on the mists, and sending chills up both their spines; though for very different reasons.

'I warned you once—you're not to touch him!'

Both men turned, and there, beside the tree, in all her own ghostlike glory, was a woman in white. Freddie might've believed as his uncle did—that it was the same who had saved him, had he not recognised her voice.

*Mena.*

*Move*, Mena urged Freddie silently, though he seemed content to just stand there and gape at her. *Move*, she screamed.

This distraction, this trick, it wouldn't last long. Soon, his uncle would recognise her, and they would both be in trouble. She'd known it wouldn't last long, this far-fetched idea—if it worked at all—but it was all she'd been able to think of when she'd finally found them.

It wasn't as if she could set upon his uncle with her own pistol or knife; there were too many chances she or Freddie could get hurt, and even if her aim had been good enough she could've shot him, she'd had to resign herself that she wasn't quite ready for potentially killing a man.

Though she might kill Freddie if he didn't *move*.

Honestly, the man would be the death of her. All her fear had morphed into frustration after her conversation with Mary, until it had grown into the force propelling her now.

They'd done as Mary said, reached her brother's estate and taken horses to finish the journey. At the nearest village, they'd parted, Mary and Luca setting off to find the law after some arguing, whilst Mena went after Freddie.

*And somehow I found him.*

It had taken all her strength, and frustration too, to get her this far. To get her to St Symeon's, then here, considering she'd only been able to catch glimpses of the moon to show her the right direction.

*'I kept running, deeper, and deeper, into the marsh, thinking I could outrun the moon...'*

The words had repeated themselves endlessly, reassuring in their constancy though every step had been cautious, and filled with dread, that she might fall and tumble into icy depths as Freddie's uncle had all those years ago. Still, she'd marched on, until she heard a voice echoing on the mists, and she'd followed that, and finally, she'd found them. Keeping hidden, she'd remembered his uncle's reaction to the ghost that night, and now here she was, standing in her chemise, probably blue from the cold considering how numb she was, and still, the man she loved refused to *bloody move*!

Finally, *finally*, she saw the astonishment in Freddie's face transform into an angry scowl, and that was good, because it meant his reason was back.

*Somewhat.*

'Wait… I know you,' his uncle said, and that is when Freddie moved at last.

He dived for her as a shot rang out, thundering against the walls of frosty smoke surrounding them. His arms were around her, warm and welcome, but before she could even breathe a sigh of relief, they were running. After a few yards, Freddie dropped his hold, only to grab her hand, and then they were going faster, and deeper into the night, his uncle screaming after them.

Mena followed Freddie blindly; he knew the ways here, she trusted that. Trusted he would keep her safe; and that, hopefully, he would keep himself safe. As long as she was with him, she knew she could at least force him to do so.

The sounds of his uncle receded into nothingness, and all that was left was the sound of their own ragged breaths, tiny clouds escaping them to match nature's. Out of nowhere, the thick, stout Norman spire of the church rose from the ground, and then they were stumbling into the yard. Freddie led them around the back, where they'd all decided to leave their horses, and together they collapsed against the damp but welcome walls of the edifice.

Shivering, Mena felt her teeth begin to chatter, and then Freddie's coats were around her shoulders in an instant, and he was rubbing her arms and holding her close to her chest.

*Where I belong.*

'What the Devil were you thinking?' he whispered harshly. 'What are you doing here? How? In God's name,

Mena, you might've been killed. You still might be! You need to take one of those horses,' he instructed, turning her towards the poor frozen beasts who'd hunkered together near the church's walls. 'Get out of here, now! Devil only knows what you were playing at—'

'Playing at?' she repeated incredulously, turning back on him. '*Playing at?* I was *playing at* saving your life, Freddie!' she hissed reproachfully, aware his uncle could be nearby. 'You—you…feather-brained lackwit,' she continued, poking his chest as he made to take hold of her again, unleashing all the frustration within her. 'You were going to let him kill you! And don't you *dare* deny it,' she warned when he opened his mouth to do just that. 'You were. But let me tell you this, Freddie Walton,' she croaked, her relief now taking over her heart, even though it wasn't all over yet. 'You are not dying tonight. No one is. I won't let you,' she finished on half a sob, poking his arm, her eyes so full of tears she couldn't see any more.

Freddie groaned in pain, and her heart stilled as she blinked away tears, and saw his white shirt had turned red.

There was red on her fingers too.

'You've been shot!'

'Grazed,' he growled back. 'It's nothing.' *Nothing.* She *really* wished to poke him again for that—but refrained. 'We need a plan. I can't leave without finishing this, and since you won't listen and *leave*, we need to be ready.'

'The law should be here soon,' she said, ignoring the pang in her heart at his lack of gratitude or even joy that she might be here. But then, after everything he'd done to keep her at arm's length, going so far as to break her heart this very morning—*was it only this morning?*—was it truly such a surprise? *No.* 'Mary has gone to fetch them. I'm not sure how long ago that was, but at least a couple hours, I think.'

'You brought Mary?' he asked incredulously, shaking his head as if she had entirely lost her wits. 'Spencer will *murder* me if we survive this, you know that?'

'She saved your life,' Mena countered. 'She's the one who—'

Freddie hand was over her mouth, and she was in his arms again in a flash.

His head tilted as he listened intently—and then she heard it too. The barest whisper of sound—along with the nervous huffs of the horses. They stilled, as Freddie gathered them both closer to the wall, and Mena tried to slide her hand down so she could grab the knife tucked in her boot. It took her a moment to manage it—for Freddie to understand she wasn't fighting him or doing something reckless, and release her from his unyielding grasp. Rising again once she had it, she placed the knife in his hand, and gazed up at him.

Unable to speak for fear of making a sound, she stared into those sea-coloured eyes she knew so well, and willed him to hear her again.

*No one dies here tonight.*

Though he could feel her, smell her, see her, Freddie still couldn't believe Mena was truly here, with him, in this, what was meant to be, his final hour of reckoning. It wasn't that he believed her incapable—but really, her finding him here, in the nick of time, it was rather *incredible*. Her wanting to, after all he'd said, and done…

It was unbelievable.

And in truth, he didn't want to believe it. He didn't want to believe that she'd risked her own life, that of others, for his sorry hide. He didn't want to believe she did it out of love—nor even as debt. He didn't want to believe it, because this wasn't how it was supposed to go. Still, he had to accept that she *was* here, or it would end badly. He had to find a way to bring his uncle down, without her getting hurt.

*And hopefully without killing him.*

He could see it in her eyes, that plea, that he do everything in his power to ensure no one else died in this forsaken land tonight.

*I have never been able to resist those eyes,* he thought, looking into the eryngo depths, and nodding, the promise made. Sliding them both down to a crouch, he listened for a moment, trying to determine the direction his uncle was coming from.

*Behind me. Good.*

He gestured to Mena to go towards the horses, and she resisted until he followed her. Ever so quietly, they crept along the wall, the lack of moonlight, and the mists, aiding them in remaining hidden. When they'd reached the corner of the church where the horses were, they slid into the doorway, and after a quick, but blistering kiss, Freddie left Mena there.

She would've protested had she been able to, but luckily he sensed her remain, crouching and quiet, as he continued his own way, her blade comforting in his hand. On he went, until he'd circumvented the building, hoping to come up behind his uncle.

Some moments remained in your heart for ever—and Freddie knew this would be one of them. A moment, when choices were made, which would define and shape who you were for ever.

Stepping out from the shelter of the stone walls, he made enough noise to attract his uncle's attention. The dark form that had been creeping along the same path he and Mena had rose and whirled around, the mists swirling and parting like smoke.

'There y'are, boy,' his uncle smiled menacingly, raising the pistol yet again to finish the job. 'Tald you you'd die tonight.'

'Not tonight after all, Uncle,' Freddie said calmly, a smile on his face.

*Mena won't have it.*

Before his uncle could even process what he'd said, Freddie had raised his own arm, and thrown Mena's knife with the swiftness and accuracy drilled into him by one of his early captains. The knife met its target, and his uncle groaned and screamed, tearing at it. But Freddie was upon him before he could pull it from his shoulder, and after ensuring the pistol was tossed far enough away, he punched the old man unconscious.

*I faced my past tonight—so shall you.*

'Mena!' he called, still astride the man who'd once been kin. 'Mena, all is well!' In the darkness ahead, he saw a figure emerge, and he could feel her watching, asking the question which would seal both their fates. 'He's alive,' he told her, and he swore he could feel her heart embracing his then. 'Take the reins of one of the horses, we'll tie him up and wait for the others.'

They did so, and Freddie wondered if it might be best to get on those horses, and ride to the nearest village, to get them out of this cold, but instead he trussed up his uncle, secured him to the horse post, picked up the box of treasure from where he'd abandoned it before putting his coats over Mena, and then settled with her in the shelter of the church's doorway. They found an extra horse blanket in one of the saddlebags, and wrapped it around themselves, standing nearly nose to nose.

Not that he minded, only he did, because whatever

had happened, nothing in this respect had changed. Forcing himself to look out onto the parcel of fields just beyond the road he could see, Freddie reminded himself of that.

*She deserves better.*

He was about to remind *her* of that, when she spoke.

'Mary told me something interesting,' she said casually, as if nothing at all was extraordinary about this night, and she was merely discussing the weather. 'She said that you loved me. And that you had this ridiculous notion I could only be grateful to you, never truly love you, or something just as idiotic.'

'Mena—'

'Freddie, I spent the entire night travelling to save you, so you will listen to me, and not say a word until you've properly *listened*,' she retorted, efficiently shutting him up. 'She also said you believed I couldn't live the kind of life I deserved until I was free of you, which again, is just plain *stupid*. I am a grown woman, Freddie. Despite some difficulties, some limitations, I am grown enough to make my own decisions, and know my own heart. I spent a long time examining my feelings for you when they emerged. Asking myself that very same question. If I loved you because I was grateful. And the truth is, in a way, I do. I don't love you because of it, but I do love you because you are the kind of man who would do such a thing for someone you didn't know.'

Freddie clenched his jaw tight, willing himself not to give in, to be strong, no matter how her words soothed his heart, and lit it again from the darkness it had plunged itself into when he'd left her.

*She deserves better.*

'And as for the kind of life you think I deserve,' she continued, a mind-reader apparently. 'What would that include? Would it include a purpose of my own? A fulfilling dream to realise? Would it include love, I wonder? The kind which makes your world turn upside down, and makes you value the other over yourself? Because all that, I have already,' she whispered, and he heard the same emotion clogging his throat in her voice. 'For a long time, I let myself believe you could never see me, as I saw you. Love me, as I loved you. That I could never be the kind of woman *you* deserved. Look where that has got us, Freddie. How much time have we wasted, thinking, and making decisions for the other? If you don't want me, I will accept that. But if you could consider us having a life together, as more than friends, then don't let this chance pass us by.'

'Mena, I—'

His response was swallowed by the chaos which followed.

Armed customs and excise men pounded down the road, and swarmed before them.

Raising his hands, looking back at Mena one last time, he went forth to meet them.

# Chapter Twenty-Five

Hushed voices buzzed, and cut through her exhausted, fog-filled mind, dragging her back to the present. Groaning a little, Mena stretched and straightened in the armchair where she'd fallen asleep, and blinked furiously, letting her eyes adjust to the sights.

*Nothing new.*

They were still in the private dining room of an inn, waiting for resolution. A plate of food and some ale had been set before her, and Mary and Luca were standing by the door, bickering like hens. Glancing to her right, Mena saw a bright shining sun streaming in, not that it meant anything; it had been dawn when they'd arrived here. She hadn't meant to fall asleep, she'd wanted to wait for Freddie's return, but the heat of the fire, warm clothes, and exhaustion after the night's events had overridden her will.

After pouring her heart out to Freddie on the church steps, knowing she wouldn't get another chance, that he'd try to leave her again if she didn't speak then and there, the law had come, Mary and Luca with them. It had been utter chaos, men shouting, people taking Freddie's uncle, as they ordered the two of them to mount up and move.

They'd taken them here, where a magistrate waited, and everyone had been ordered to detail the night's events so that some sense could be made of it all, even though Mary and Luca had already explained. The magistrate and excise and customs men had taken them each one by one, and that had been the last time she'd seen Freddie, when it had been his turn. Mary had tried to exercise her position to ease everything—but no one was having it. Though, to be fair, her title and family were likely the only reason Mena and Freddie hadn't been shot on sight.

Not that she didn't still fear for his life. She knew what Freddie would do—*tell them everything*—not that she didn't understand, but it did mean there was a chance his life would be on the line. Smuggling had taken so many lives here, particularly those of the lawmen who didn't line their pockets, so those who remained had long memories.

*Please don't let his past condemn him—extinguish the future we might have*, Mena prayed silently, wishing she could just know *something*, as she leaned forward to grab a morsel of food.

Not that she felt hungry, only she consciously knew that she was, and that whatever came, she would need strength to face it.

Mary and Luca noticed her then, jumping apart as if struck by lightning, and Mena smiled—at them, and to herself.

'Good morning,' she said, her voice a bit scratchy. She'd be lucky if she didn't catch a cold after wandering about in her chemise.

*A more than fair price for a life. Two lives.*

'What time is it?'

'A little past ten,' Mary told her, as she and Luca both

joined Mena by the fire. Mary, across from her, Luca, leaning on the mantel like a brooding dandy. 'You've not been asleep long,' she smiled reassuringly.

'Any news?'

'Not yet,' Luca said grimly. Mary shot him a glare, and he shrugged. 'Soon, I am sure,' he added after a longer glare.

'I want to thank you both—'

The door opened, and they all turned.

*Freddie. Thank God.*

He looked terrible. Worn out, sleep-deprived, with a thick bandage on his arm, circles under his eyes, his older injuries darker, and an air of complete defeat. He blinked before his eyes passed over them all, stalling on Mena, and then they filled with something else entirely.

*Love*, she thought, smiling up at him.

'Freddie,' Mary said, rising. 'Sit, eat, here, Luca will fetch you another plate.'

'Don't,' Freddie countered, waving them all back. 'I thank you, but I am sure Mena will share,' he added, with a crooked grin that was so out of place, yet so familiar, Mena found herself without words. So she nodded, and he took the seat Mary had vacated whilst Luca fetched her another and dragged it to the circle, which he himself did not join. 'And thank you all, for coming to my aid,' Freddie said seriously, when he'd taken a sip of ale, his eyes meeting Mary's and Luca's in turn. 'You risked so much you shouldn't have, and that is a debt I shall never be able to repay.'

'There is no debt, Freddie,' Mary retorted. 'Don't be ridiculous. Actually, there is a debt, and it requires you tell us what is happening before the suspense kills us.'

'That I can do,' he nodded, with a grateful smile to the lady. 'My uncle will be tried, and either transported, or hanged, depending on how many others he gives up. He mentioned working from here to Devon over the years, so if he proves himself useful, they might spare him the noose.' Freddie grimaced, and Mena couldn't stop herself, not that she would've if she could, and placed her hand on his. His eyes closed for the briefest moment, before he met her gaze this time, the dark blue of solemnity in his. 'I told them everything of myself, all I'd done. But I am to go free. They have better to do than find punishment for my old sins, particularly since I gave up my fellows all those years ago.'

He was, and would likely always be, conflicted by that; in time, however, perhaps he would learn to live with his ghosts again.

Heal, a little more than he already had.

'That is good news,' Mary said, with enough joviality to ensure it was an order they *all* consider it so. 'I am relieved I won't have to send someone to fetch Spencer, to knock sense into either you, or the magistrate. Freddie, I…' Everyone looked to her, and she hesitated a moment before continuing. 'You two need to talk, I think, and, well, there is someone you need to meet, Freddie.' Both he and Mena frowned, and she nodded. 'I shall go fetch them, Luca will assist, and we shall return shortly.'

Mary made to exit, Luca at her heels, before she turned back, and leaned down to whisper something in Freddie's ear.

He startled, looking at her as if she'd perhaps grown snakes for hair, but she merely raised a brow, and left. Mena was alone with Freddie again, and something inside her told her whatever followed, would set the course for the rest of their lives.

*Please do not let him leave me now.*

\* \* \*

*'I thought you had more mettle.'*

Mary's words echoed tormentingly in his mind; not only because of their cutting and spurring nature, but because, once, they'd been his own. He didn't know why her brother had related what he'd said, when he'd been trying to push his friend out of grim resignation at losing the woman he loved; but that didn't really matter. She knew, and she'd turned his own words against him, as if she'd known already what he intended to do.

Mena's words last night… He wanted them to change everything. He wanted them to change who he was, his heart, what he had to offer. He wanted desperately to cling to them, to build something out of them which would last them a lifetime. The problem was, they *didn't* change anything. They didn't change who he was. What he'd done.

*Nothing ever could.*

No one seemed to believe him; not even the law when he confessed his crimes, ready to be carted off with his uncle. It would've been no more than he deserved. Yet neither did they seem to care, seem to believe there was any punishment to be meted out.

*'You were a young man, and you set things right then. You've done right since,'* the magistrate had said with a shrug. *'No good'll come of me arresting you when you'll be of more to use to the world living free in it.'*

Perhaps, Freddie could admit, there was truth to that. He could do some good, as he'd always tried to do. However, as for Mena…

He finally met her gaze again, and the hope in her eyes felled him. If he could just make her understand…

'I believe your love is true,' he said quietly, his eyes

falling to their entwined hands, which he couldn't untangle. If this was all he would have at the end, it would be enough.

*A little of her love to tide me through.*

'I do. And I have no words to express how lucky, and grateful, and exceptional, that makes me feel, knowing, that you love me. It is the greatest thing I have ever known, and will ever know. But I can't… I cannot give you what you deserve,' he told her, risking a glance at her face. He shouldn't have; the trust, the acceptance, and the love, still in her eyes, the determination, it pierced his heart. 'I can't love you well, Mena. Look at what I've done, how I've hurt you. I don't know how to love, let alone well, and you deserve better than that.'

Mena nodded, and turned to the fire.

Still, Freddie clutched her hand. He was glad—he *had* to be, he *told* himself to be—that she was finally understanding. That this was best, for her. But her turning from him, it did feel as though he was being cast into the lowest rungs of Hell, and so he kept hold of her, for as long as he could.

After a long moment, she turned back to him—and why was all he'd seen before still in her eyes?

'When I couldn't leave the house for fear of, well, everything,' she said seriously. 'You told me, that fear is not conquered in a day. Not a week, nor a month. Even now, coming here, it took all I had, Freddie,' she whispered, tears clouding her eyes. 'Years, I have battled that fear, beaten it back a little more each day, and still it lives within me. I wonder if it will ever go away, and that is fine,' she shrugged. 'It doesn't have to. You told me that too. There is no book on how to love, let alone how to do it well. I know you are afraid of hurting me, because yes, you already have. I won't deny that. Do you believe anyone who loves, truly, has not done that, nor will ever again? Do you believe even your friends, with their happy marriages, to be without conflict?' Mena paused, letting him think about that for a moment, and the truth was, no, he didn't. Or perhaps he had, but now that he thought about it, that was a mere illusion, an ideal no one could live up to. 'If the only thing stopping you from being with me, truly, is your fear that you cannot love well, your notion that you don't deserve me, then I say: not good enough. Neither of us are perfect, Freddie. And I know, it will take time for you to believe you deserve anything good. But you have already loved me well. For years, in your own way. And together, I do believe we can be happy. Have something extraordinary. I for one am willing to spend a lifetime learning how to love well, with you, if you are.'

Freddie was speechless, and staring again, unable to break the connection with those pale blue eyes so full of certainty, understanding, and love.

Her words, they were like an axe to the hull of a ship, slowly chopping holes into it, into all his excuses, his fear, until it sank to the depths of his soul. Not gone, but somewhat, conquered. Enough for him to finally see that she was, as always, right.

Love wasn't magic, or perfect, and it wouldn't fix the broken things inside either of them. Giving in to love, accepting it, accepting to travel the path together, however, that would make them stronger, and better than they ever could be alone.

And perhaps that is what it meant to love well.

Merely, to accept it; to be open to its gifts, and willing to share them.

Unable still to speak, he nodded, and Mena's eyes widened with joy, tears dripping from them. He leaned over the table and took her mouth with a kiss that he hoped would tell her all his heart felt. That would make her feel the love he carried, the joy, the hope, the pain of healing, even the fear, and regret for all he'd done. Including attempting to take the choice to love away from her.

*Idiot, indeed*, he thought, grinning against her lips.

He felt her rise, and was about to pull her into his lap when a knock sounded on the door.

'I hope all is settled now,' Mary said from the other side. 'For we are coming in.'

They did, and Freddie pulled Mena into his lap nonetheless, not that Mary, Signor Guaro, whom he made a note to properly get to know later, as well as what his business was with Mary, or even the two older women following, who looked strangely familiar, seemed to either care or notice his lack of manners.

Freddie frowned, staring at Mary questioningly, whilst Mena wiped her tears away, and Guaro brought in more chairs.

'Freddie, meet Claire Laurent,' she said, indicating the first woman, greyed by early middle age, beautiful nonetheless. 'And Marie Cornet,' she continued, indicating the second, a little older. '*Mesdames*, this, is Freddie Walton. And Mena Nichols.'

Freddie and Mena awkwardly half stood, bowing their heads in greeting whilst the women did the same before settling into the chairs Guaro provided. Mary too joined them, whilst Guaro held back.

*Why do these women seem familiar?*

'Luca and I chanced to meet Madame Cornet on our way to find a magistrate,' Mary explained. 'When we explained our situation, it came to light that you and she had met before.'

'You were my ghost,' Freddie breathed, tears pricking his eyes now as he finally recognised her. 'And you, Madame Laurent, you are the owner of the box,' he said, turning his attention to the other. Mena wrapped a hand around his, holding it tight as both women nodded. 'You saved my life that night,' he told Madame Cornet, hoping she could see how grateful he was.

'And you saved mine, young man,' Madame Laurent said gently. Swallowing the past guilt, Freddie looked to her, unsure of what to say. The woman had lost her husband that night, and that was on his soul. 'It wasn't your fault,' she continued. 'I was angry, for a very long time, for what happened to my husband. However, I lived, and I lived a good life,' she smiled. 'As he would have wished. I married again, a wonderful man who took me in that night. We have three children, and seven grandchildren. Despite my grief, and my loss, I have been happy. So do not dwell in the past; believe me when I say it does nothing for you.'

Freddie nodded, that conspicuously large lump in his throat preventing him from speaking.

'How were you in the marshes that night, Madame Cornet?' Mena asked after a moment.

'I was an émigré like Claire,' she explained. 'I had come over a few months before, not through the same people, but in a similar fashion. I found myself working at St Symeon's, keeping it, in return for a place to sleep in the sacristy. I heard noises, shouts, and when I went to see what was happening, I saw you running, young man, and your uncle in pursuit. I followed, even though I don't really know what I was thinking, other than I had to help you. The rest, you know.'

'Thank you,' Freddie whispered.

'I am glad to know what little I did succeeded,' she smiled. 'And that you have done so well with your life.'

A pointed look at Mena, and Freddie felt himself blushing.

'Your box,' he said, turning back to Madame Laurent. 'I gave it to the authorities—'

'And they gave it to me,' Guaro said, coming around, the now cleaned box in his hands. 'Madame,' he smiled, handing it to her.

They all watched silently, captivated, as she ran her hands over it, tears brimming in her eyes.

'All we had left was in this box,' she breathed, in wonder, before pulling a chain from her neck, and setting the key on it into the lock. 'Much of it is memories,' she smiled, looking up at Freddie, as if she needed him to know that, and God knew, he did.

They all glanced into the mouldy, red silk-lined box as she began sifting through its contents.

Miniatures, which she took from velvet pouches. Some papers, more or less intact because of their time in the earth, some ribbons, and charms. Treasure; but not the kind his uncle had been after, apart from one diamond bracelet, and a small pouch of coins.

The knowledge somehow seemed fitting; not irony, but poetic.

'I am glad you have them again, Madame,' Freddie said, and she smiled.

'I am glad we could meet again.'

They all remained there, talking, and eventually, having a meal together.

They spoke of their lives, of the years which had passed, and all that had filled them. They spoke of the country, of the weather, even made plans to meet again someday. When the afternoon turned into evening, Guaro and Mary escorted the women back to their homes, promising to return and make plans for the journey back to London.

In the end, Freddie left a note with the innkeeper after taking lodgings for them all. He found that he couldn't quite wait any longer to begin this new lifetime with Mena, and so he took her upstairs, and began the work of loving her well.

*A lifetime of learning to love.*

*I think that is a purpose you would be proud of, Mr Walton.*

*For it is the best purpose I have ever known.*

# *Epilogue*

*January 5th, 1832*

'**D**oes this look right to you?' Mary asked, scrunching up her nose as she examined the kings cake she'd just taken from the range. One of about twenty they'd made so far for tomorrow's celebrations at Nichols House, this one was wholly Mary's, apparently her first attempt at baking on her own. 'It looks a little…crooked,' she said, tilting her head as she held it up to the light.

Mena and Susie both laughed, glancing over at the lady as they mixed up more filling, and kneaded more dough.

'You pressed the dough too hard on that side,' Susie said, making a show of properly investigating. As long as it was edible, no one really cared what they looked like. 'That's all. Now set it to cool, my lady.'

Mary had told her to call her by her name, however, Susie couldn't quite do it; even if Mary looked nothing like the lady she was tonight, having opted for plainer, less conspicuous clothes, not only so she could cook, but also, Mena thought, so she could truly be part of this evening. Which she had been. Susie's reluctance to use the lady's name didn't stop them all from having a fun, and relaxed, evening together, and that was what mattered.

Mary did as she was told, and set the cake to cool, still eyeing it critically.

'This filling is ready, and Susie is nearly finished with the dough,' Mena smiled. 'That is, if you should like to try another.'

'That, I would,' Mary grinned back. 'I shall be giving Genevieve a run for her money, so to speak, the next time we have anything to celebrate.'

The other women laughed, as Mary joined them again.

Whatever her motives—even competing with her sister-in-law—having Mary here was a welcome thing.

The lady seemed determined to live up to her promise to make Mena part of the circle of friends Freddie had been a part of. They'd left Sussex the morning after Freddie had met the women from his past, then spent the night loving her, the woman of his future. Mary and Luca had made all the arrangements, and got them back to London, and in the short time since, Mary had been a regular visitor at both Holly Street and Nichols House, where she'd met, and befriended, Susie in an instant. Mary had also managed the feat of dragging Father Bartholomew inside Nichols House to witness the good being done; he was not a convert yet, but Mena doubted there would be further streetside sermons of hate.

They'd not seen Luca again, though Freddie had sent a note, asking to meet, and Mary seemed unwilling to discuss anything about him, but Mena had a feeling they would all meet again.

*All in its right time.*

The past few days, since their return home, had been strange, and yet, oddly comforting in their familiarity.

When Freddie had rounded the men searching for his uncle, and guarding the house, to dismiss them and pay them, he'd discovered that the guards had been lured away by a decoy, who'd been arrested, along with his uncle's driving companion. After tying up those final loose ends, Mena and Freddie had both taken a day to rest, and settle back into life together, finding their way to being…a couple. Yesterday, Freddie had gone back to the wharf, and though Susie had been keeping the shop with the others, Mena had tried to make herself somewhat useful—if only in updating Susie on the last few days' events. She herself had gone to Nichols House to check the progress of it all today, and there was no doubt all would be ready for their official opening in less than a fortnight. She'd received a note of good tidings from Mr Greer—along with the promise that one of his writers would be present for the occasion.

Everything, *everything*, she'd ever wished for, was coming true. Her heart was fuller than she might've believed was possible, and she had to keep forcing herself to breathe, and think, lest she float away on the cloud of joy she'd made her home.

The sound of barrelling footsteps and the clicking of Hawk's nails pulled her from her daze, and the ladies all looked to the door as Freddie and Hawk came tearing down.

'The first ones are here!' he shouted triumphantly, and the ladies set down what they were doing, wiping their hands, and heading upstairs.

Though wassailers had become fewer in the city, those who still upheld the old traditions knew to come to Holly Street, where gifts and a warm welcome always awaited.

But then, perhaps Holly Street called anyone in need to it.

Freddie grabbed Mena about the waist as she made to pass him, stealing a kiss before allowing her passage. For a moment, she let herself be held, and get lost in the depths of his eyes, now always, for her at least, bright oceans of love.

Grinning, she gave him a kiss of her own, and breathed in deeply of him.

'Are you coming or what?' Susie shouted, tearing them from their moment. 'We can't ask them to stand here and wait to sing all night!'

Mena chuckled and shook her head.

'We should get up there before she comes to drag us.'

She made to move, but Freddie held her back, a very serious look in his eyes now. She frowned questioningly, and he sighed.

'I wanted to do this later, properly,' he said, hesitancy in his eyes that confused her even more, as his fingers found the necklace always around her neck, and began toying with it. 'But this feels right. You, me, in this kitchen, as we were in the beginning. Simply, the two of us… You will, you will marry me, won't you, Mena?' he asked, and it was a good thing he was holding her tight, because otherwise the dizziness that came over her might've toppled her.

They'd talked of shared lives, but not yet marriage.

Freddie had much healing to do—they both did—and she hadn't wanted to rush him into anything he wasn't ready for, not when what they already had was beautiful, and perfect.

'Of course I will,' she breathed, and he relaxed, as if he'd feared she'd not want to seal the vows she'd already made with others. 'If that is what you wish for, I should like that.'

'And children? Would you like those?'

He was doing this *now*?

*Well, better now than later.*

'Yes, I should like children with you, in time, Freddie,' she said gently. 'When we feel ready to be parents. If we do. If not, I can be happy as we are too. We have a strong family as it is.'

'Yes… That is good, I think,' he whispered, leaning in for another kiss.

'That's it, I'm telling them to sing!' Susie yelled.

Hawk barked as if to agree, and Freddie and Mena laughed, shaking their heads.

They took each other's hands before running up to the parlour, where Mary, Susie, and a group of wassailers waited by the fire. Mena and Freddie drank from the proffered bowl, and Mena noted that either Susie or Mary had already seen fit to give one of the prepared parcels.

Smiling, her hand in Freddie's, with two friends and a loving pup beside her, Mena had never felt happier, more fulfilled, more hopeful, than she did then.

*"'Come fill it up unto the brim; Come fill it up, so that we may all see,"'* the wassailers sang.

*All may see how full of love I am.*

*Quite so.*

\* \* \* \* \*

# Get 4 FREE REWARDS!

**We'll send you 2 FREE Books plus 2 FREE Mystery Gifts.**

FREE
Value Over
$20

Both the **Harlequin® Historical** and **Harlequin® Romance** series feature compelling novels filled with emotion and simmering romance.

# HARLEQUIN
## PLUS

Announcing a **BRAND-NEW** multimedia subscription service for romance fans like you!

---

## **Read, Watch and Play.**

Experience the easiest way to get the romance content you crave.

Start your **FREE 7 DAY TRIAL** at <u>www.harlequinplus.com/freetrial</u>.